GONE BUT NOT FORGOTTEN

Also by C. Michele Dorsey

Sabrina Slater mysteries

NO VIRGIN ISLAND
PERMANENT SUNSET
TROPICAL DEPRESSION
SALT WATER WOUNDS

Danny and Nora O'Brien mysteries

OH DANNY GIRL

GONE BUT NOT FORGOTTEN

C. Michele Dorsey

SEVERN
HOUSE

First world edition published in Great Britain and the USA in 2023
by Severn House, an imprint of Canongate Books Ltd,
14 High Street, Edinburgh EH1 1TE.

Trade paperback edition first published in Great Britain and the USA in 2024
by Severn House, an imprint of Canongate Books Ltd.

severnhouse.com

British Library Cataloguing-in-Publication Data
A CIP catalogue record for this title is available from the British Library.

ISBN-13: 978-1-4483-1078-4 (cased)
ISBN-13: 978-1-4483-1173-6 (trade paper)
ISBN-13: 978-1-4483-1079-1 (e-book)

Typeset by Palimpsest Book Production Ltd.,
Falkirk, Stirlingshire, Scotland.

Praise for C. Michele Dorsey

"A full-fledged mystery that grabbed my attention and quickly became a page-turner . . . [A] wonderfully terrific series"
Dru's Book Musings on *Permanent Sunset*

"Mighty good page-turning fun"
Publishers Weekly Starred Review of *Permanent Sunset*

"Dorsey's plot has the requisite twists, turns, and everything else"
Kirkus Reviews on *Permanent Sunset*

"A divine locale and a quick-thinking amateur sleuth make this a great bet"
Booklist on *Permanent Sunset*

"Fast-paced and action-packed . . . I had to know what happens next, and boy did I enjoy what follows"
Dru's Book Musings on *No Virgin Island*

"The cast of characters is appealing . . . The plot is intricate with quite a few red herrings"
Library Journal on *No Virgin Island*

"Fun . . . Readers will look forward to Sabrina's future adventures"
Publishers Weekly on *No Virgin Island*

"Fast-paced, gripping, terrific"
Carolyn Hart, *New York Times* bestselling author, on *No Virgin Island*

About the author

C. Michele Dorsey is the author of the Sabrina Salter series, the Danny and Nora O'Brien series, and the standalone thriller *Gone But Not Forgotten*. Michele is a lawyer, mediator, former adjunct law professor, and nurse who didn't know she could be a writer when she grew up. Now that she does, Michele writes constantly, whether on St John, outer Cape Cod, or anywhere within a mile of the ocean.

cmicheledorsey.com

For SWD
. . . a bushel and a peck
CMD

ACKNOWLEDGMENTS

While writing a book may be a solitary endeavor, bringing it to the eyes of readers takes more than a village. I am grateful to all who have helped me launch Gone But Not Forgotten, including my agent, Paula Munier, who never lost faith in the story of Olivia Rose, and to Gina Panettieri, founder of Talcott Notch Literary Services.

Thank you to my trusted circle of beta readers, especially to my husband, Steve, who listens tirelessly and with enthusiasm to my pages at the end of each day, and to my daughter, Julie Grant, who encourages while not sparing me.

A special shout out to the law students who took the last mediation course I taught at New England Law (once known as Portia Law, where Olivia attends) for their suggestions about what would make a romantic interlude in Boston.

ONE

Sheila Fairclough? Who the hell was Sheila Fairclough? I looked at the graceful signature on the document and then into the vacant eyes of the woman who had just executed it. She was seated on a wingback chair, dressed in a straight navy-blue skirt and crisp white cotton blouse, as if she were about to leave for her job as chief faculty administrator at UVM Medical School, which she had done for more than twenty years. Her penmanship was elegant. I had often wondered if nuns with rulers in their hands had taught her cursive. The feminine script perfectly suited the dignified woman of a certain age who had written it. My mother. Claire Taylor. Not Sheila Fairclough.

For the past four months, my mother has resided at Thompson House, a memory-loss center in Boston close to where I lived. I had snagged a suite in the front parlor of the original Victorian mansion that had been converted into Thompson House when she was admitted. The original oak floors and doors and bay window made it feel less institutional and had assuaged my guilt that she could no longer live with me.

Losing my mother to Alzheimer's disease had proven to be as exasperating as living with her secrets had been when she was lucid. The document on which my mother had signed Sheila Fairclough's name was the title to her Prius. My closest friend and classmate expected to purchase the car tonight.

The name Sheila Fairclough couldn't have just dropped out of the sky. I knew it could be the name of another patient, a doctor, or someone on a television show Mom watched. But it also could be my mother's real name. I was determined to find out, yet understood pushing her now could be counterproductive. She panicked whenever she sensed pressure or urgency to remember even a tiny insignificant detail.

I noticed a small new jade plant sitting on the windowsill. The bay window in her small suite was overflowing with plants and flowers designed to make Mom feel at home.

'Where did you get the little jade?' I asked.

'Dr Alexander. She knew how much I miss the one I gave to you, Liv.' Mom beamed, looking over at the new addition to her indoor garden.

'Who's Dr Alexander?' I asked, sure I was feeling more confused than my mother was.

'You know, that young one who comes at night after doing research all day. She's looking for the cure. I told you that, didn't I?'

'Are you talking about Dr Nightmare?' Mom had previously complained about a doctor she called Dr Nightmare waking her up in the middle of the night to take vital signs.

'Who's that? What a strange name for a doctor,' Mom said.

I steered her back to the topic I wanted to quiz her about. I was certain there was a logical explanation about why Mom had signed the name 'Sheila Fairclough' instead of her own on a legal document. She was reduced to nearly constant confusion after declining for several years. But it wasn't that simple. Here, on a typical misty day in October, my mother had just dropped what may have been the first and only clue to the true identity of my family in twenty-five years. Just as I was heading out to attend evening classes at the law school I'd been attending for three years. Just as I did every weekday after visiting Mom. Just like that.

I held my breath. I had prayed for an opening where I would finally get information before Mom's memory was totally obliterated. I was nearly thirty years old and knew almost nothing about my father and our family history. I had to ask, not knowing if freed by the wings of Alzheimer's, unshackled from years of lying, my mother might actually tell me what I desperately wanted to know. Deserved to know.

'Mom, who's Sheila Fairclough?' I asked, picking up my back-pack bulging with law books. I tried to seem casual, hoping she couldn't hear the palpitations thundering in my chest.

I watched her frown as she often did when she was trying to capture a word or recall a name. I hated waiting, witnessing her agony, sometimes bordering on terror, while she struggled to hold on.

'I have no idea,' she said. She folded her hands on her lap, her longstanding signal that a discussion was over.

I could bear no more of the Jabberwocky.

I prepared to leave quickly, afraid I would lash out at her in anger. I knew it was irrational, that she was technically mentally incompetent. But keeping the family history from your own daughter was illogical. Mom's fears about our safety may have been valid when she fled with me to Vermont to escape my father whom she said intended to kill us both. But twenty-five years later, I considered them groundless.

I gave Mom a peck on her forehead before heading to school, closing my eyes. She still smelled like my mom. She still looked like my mom. But she no longer sounded like my mom.

I trudged over rotting wet leaves that covered the ground along Glendale Road, the busy street in front of Thompson House. I couldn't tell where the sidewalk ended and the curb began as I headed toward the parking lot. Even in sturdy L.L. Bean rubber mocs and with an excellent sense of balance acquired during the years I spent figure skating, it was slippery going. Glendale Road was a major short cut for commuters heading to work in Boston, but even in off hours there was still steady traffic. I kept my head down, concentrating on where I was stepping. I vowed to tell the staff they needed to rake ASAP before someone got seriously hurt falling on the sidewalk, or worse on to the street. The shriek of a woman interrupted the scathing lecture to the administration I was practicing in my head.

'Look out. No. Oh my God!'

She was talking to me.

I lifted my gaze ahead but saw nothing. I turned my head to look behind me and through the drizzle I saw a small light-blue sedan speeding toward me, swerving off the road toward the curb where I had unknowingly veered over the wet leaves. The nondescript economy car was coming directly toward me.

'Mother of Christ. Jesus, Mary, and Joseph.' Those words out of the mouth of my would-be rescuer told me I was in huge trouble. I prayed my mother was taking the afternoon nap she usually had after our visit and wasn't peering through the plants on her windowsill, which was the perfect spot to witness the demise of her daughter.

I leapt to the right, past where I expected the sidewalk lay buried beneath the clump of leaves saturated by yesterday's rainfall, then instinctively swayed to the left to avoid catapulting into a cluster of creeping junipers. At some level, I knew that was crazy and my risk assessment skills had faltered. I felt myself losing balance. I extended both of my arms out to the side like a surfer trying to ride a huge wave, thinking I could catch myself from falling. As the light-blue car drew closer, I could see that the driver was wearing a baseball cap and sunglasses. I was determined not to fall, knowing that if the car struck me while I was lying down, I would be crushed to death.

The seconds that had passed since I first heard the woman's scream felt like hours to me. Just as the car was within yards of me, I lost any sense of balance that remained. Now I was sure I would die outside the window of my mother's room while she watched. Down I went, landing on my hands and knees and forehead, spared pain and injury by the rotting leaves that had cushioned the impact. Let it be quick, I implored, and may the answers I have been demanding from my mother come from the Divine.

But as quickly as the car had careened toward me, it returned to the road. I sprang up in somewhat of a reverse downward dog, while my books tumbled out of my bag that had slipped forward on to my shoulder. No one would ever guess I had been a fairly graceful figure skater in high school. Once erect, I could see the car rush off into traffic.

'Are you all right, dear?' An older woman in a beige belted raincoat wearing thick glasses with round tortoiseshell frames approached me. She was carrying a canvas Costco shopping bag. She bent down to pick up my Domestic Relations textbook.

'I'm fine,' I said, pretty sure that I was, but not certain what had just happened. Even if I couldn't see where the sidewalk ended and the curb began, surely the driver must have known he or she was veering off the street. The mist, easier to feel than see, was unlike the frequent downpours that make Boston a soggy city. The fine spray was almost invisible, having no impact on visibility.

'Do you want me to call the police?' she asked, pulling out a Jitterbug smart phone designed for seniors and flipping it open. I recognized the phone because I had bought one for Mom when we first moved from Vermont to Boston.

'No, but thank you,' I said. Her thick glasses and her phone suggested her eyesight was poor. I doubted my rescuer had seen much other than a car racing toward me.

'He was probably texting. They say more than half the accidents these days are because people are texting while driving. I don't understand. Would you read a book while driving? Write a letter? I just don't get it. And what are they all talking about anyway?' She was beginning to wheeze. I worried the situation could worsen.

'Thanks for your help. I'm fine,' I said. I turned toward the Thompson House parking lot, then stopped. I wondered if my Good Samaritan might be able to do one more good deed.

'You said "he." Was it a man? And by any chance, did you get a license plate?' I knew I would be lucky for an answer to the first question and hit the lottery if I got one to the second. It was worth a try to learn more about the driver who had nearly taken me out. I would report him to the police.

'I'm pretty sure it was a man. He had a baseball cap on. And sunglasses on a day like today. I didn't get the plate, but I know it wasn't a Massachusetts license plate. Or it might have been one of those vanity plates. I'm not sure. Sorry.'

I didn't want to get into a discussion about assumptions and how lots of women wear baseball caps, especially on a bad hair day. I realized the woman was much older than my mother and had probably been traumatized by my near miss.

'Are you OK? I'd be happy to give you a lift somewhere,' I said, even though it was the last thing I felt like doing. But she declined my offer and we parted ways without ever introducing each other.

By the time I reached the parking lot, my knees and the palms of my hands were beginning to burn. My textbook and notebooks were dirty and my jeans soggy from the knees down. I started the car, relieved to be heading to school where I could escape into the world of crimes and misdemeanors.

TWO

L eaving Thompson House behind me, I approached the rotary, which is near my home in the Moss Hill section of Jamaica Plain. I considered skipping school, but I knew it was better to stick to routine and not let a little incident like almost being killed get to me. I was about to enter the Centre Street rotary I used every day on the way to Thompson House to visit Mom and later again when I drove into Boston where Portia Law School is located. I know this rotary intimately.

I entered where Centre Street spilled into the circle, prepared to go one hundred and eighty degrees and then exit on to the Arborway. Someone in the outer ring of the circle kept going around directly next to me so that I couldn't exit. He was driving door handle to door handle. They don't call people who live in Massachusetts 'Massholes' for nothing.

I went around a second time, but the same car remained to my right and wouldn't yield. The palms of my bruised hands began to sweat. By the third rotation, I was convinced I was going to go around in circles for the rest of my life. I would never get answers, never be allowed to exit. I was born to terminally rotate. And to sweat, because now I could feel the hair sitting on the back of my neck, heavy and wet. I would be memorialized like poor old Charlie in the song about the MTA my mother used to sing to me.

What I could now identify as a pale-blue Honda Civic circled the rotary next to me like we were planets in the same constellation. I couldn't see the driver through the darkened windows but I guessed I had encountered a second fanatical text messager in a single day. It occurred to me it might be the same car I had encountered in front of Thompson House, but I was more focused on getting away from it. Rather than go around a fourth time, I reeled myself in and implemented a proven Massachusetts driving strategy. I leaned on my horn. Finally, the little bugger got out of my way. But not before rattling me.

I felt giddy from my second escape in twenty minutes. A silly memory about what the inspector at the registry of motor vehicles told me about rotaries when I first registered my car after moving from Vermont popped into my head.

'There's a question on the Mass. Drivers' test you may not be familiar with. Who has the right of way in a rotary in Massachusetts, Miss?' he asked, his tone stern and serious. He was right. I was stymied.

I was honest and told him I didn't know the answer. He paused for a moment and then said, 'The answer is "who cares?"' He laughed and laughed until I joined him. I was never afraid of a rotary after that. Until today.

By the time I pulled into the six-story parking garage next to the law school, I had another dilemma to face. Erin Rivera was thrilled to be buying her first car, having secured a car loan she never thought she'd qualify for. But the title to the car that my mother had signed as Sheila Fairclough was useless.

I had extra blank copies of the transfer documents the registry required with me. I knew what I had to do. It was less risky to commit a misdemeanor than to try to get my mother to sign her own signature on the title to her car. I spent an extra minute in the creepy parking garage committing forgery. I did my best to imitate Claire M. Taylor's signature, sad that it didn't matter if it looked anything like it. No one would question its authenticity. At least Erin wouldn't be disappointed.

I scurried to the elevator after locking the car doors. There had been several assaults in the garage during recent years, after which garish new lighting had been installed. Law students were cautioned not to use the stairs alone. No one had to tell a girl who grew up in Vermont this twice. I'd taken a self-defense course in college but had never needed to test my skills.

I rushed into the law school lobby and opted to climb the five flights of stairs to my classroom. The pokey elevator would ensure I would be late for class. I entered the classroom panting, vowing to join a gym, only to find that Professor Cohen hadn't arrived yet. Although we didn't have assigned seats, my classmates and I all returned to the same spot every night. It was as if the chairs had been sprayed with a territorial scent. Erin sat at the back of the room, her spiral black curls more frizzy than usual in the October humidity, even though the air-conditioning was on full blast. A white envelope sat on the desk in front of my empty seat next to her. I knew it must be the bank check for the car.

Erin frowned down at her fuchsia iPhone as her fingers pranced over the screen. She seemed oblivious to the laughter from other students waiting for class to begin.

'Hey there,' I said.

'Where have you been?' Erin sounded a little like my mother to me. I remembered how frantic Mom would get if I was a few minutes late coming home when I was a child.

'Visiting my mother. Why? What's up?' I hadn't expected Erin to be this uptight about the car. She has a great sense of humor, but is not someone I would want as my enemy. When one of our classmates asked her one day how a Puerto Rican got a first name like Erin, she told him that this was America and mothers got to name their kids what they want. Then she called him a dickhead.

'Security came in looking for you a few minutes ago. They say they have a message for you,' Erin said, holding out her phone to me. 'I tried calling and texting you.' I could see how frustrated she was with me.

'I'm sorry. I forgot to charge my phone in the car after I left my mother. I'll go see what they want.' I had been too rattled to remember to do anything after almost being hit by a car. But I didn't want to go into it with Erin. I was too exhausted. I started back out of the classroom with Erin in tow.

'I'm going with you. I don't want to alarm you, Liv, but they seemed worried.'

My mother. It had to be my mother. It was always my mother these days. I might as well have a baby, which happened to be the current topic for debate between my husband, Daniel, and me.

'You need to call Terry Walsh at your mother's nursing home,' said the security officer who looked too young to have a driver's license, handing me a Post-it Note with Terry's name and a phone number on it.

I wanted to scream, 'It's not a nursing home. It's a top-rated memory care facility!' But I recognized my reaction was rooted in the fear about what Terry, my favorite nurse, had to say to me. Images of my mother wandering off again or falling ill flashed before me.

Reading my mind, Erin put her hand on my shoulder.

'It's probably nothing. Just make the call,' Erin said, handing me her phone.

'She had ten pizzas delivered here about a half an hour ago. Said she was sick of eating institutional food and so were her friends,' Terry said. 'Then she bitched that Beneventos in the North End wasn't nearly as good as Leonardo's in Burlington.'

I laughed. Not so bad and so my mother. Under her always-play-it-safe, take-no-risks armor hid the heart of a rebel. I loved it when the rebel came out to play.

'Of course, none of them are supposed to eat it, but I'd need every cop in District E-13 to tear it away from them. That's not the least of the problems.' I detected a mixture of amusement and irritation in Terry's voice. I needed her as an ally to keep the Thompson House administration at bay until after the holidays. I had been pressured to either produce the durable power of attorney my mother had executed, giving me authority to act on her behalf, or to go to court and be appointed her guardian. But I was not prepared to give up on Mom yet. I would let both of us cling to the illusion of her competence until we reached the arbitrary milestone of my thirtieth birthday.

'What's the worst and how can I fix it?' I watched as Erin rolled her eyes at the conversation.

'Reimburse me for the $234.87 I had to pay when your mother tried giving them a bad check. They don't pay well here and I live paycheck to paycheck,' Terry said.

My mother would never write a bad check. Mom's small personal checking account had enough money in it to cover small expenses and give her the impression that she was still in charge of her own life.

'Terry, she's got enough in her account to cover that,' I said.

'Maybe so, honey, but not when she signs the check with someone else's name. Who's Sheila Fairclough?'

THREE

Who was Sheila Fairclough?
That was all I could think about during class, although Professor Cohen was giving a very entertaining lecture about the history of Alienation of Affection in Massachusetts. I had done a lot of research about memory loss, but didn't know if using someone else's name was common or if patients borrowed a name from the past or invented an entirely new one. Trying to understand my mother and her illness confounded and depleted me, which was one reason I had not just one, but two therapists.

I considered texting my husband and asking. Daniel is a third-year psychiatric resident in Boston, currently on rotation at McLean Hospital ten miles outside Boston in Belmont. He might know or could maybe steer me toward the answer.

Even if Sheila Fairclough wasn't my mother's former name, maybe she was a real person from my mother's past. She might still be around and have information about what had happened when I was only four and my mother and I had to flee to Vermont.

I normally paid close attention during class, believing I was paying good money for my education and that it was disrespectful to meander online while a professor was lecturing. Portia was the law school of last resort for most students who came from working-class families that typically didn't breed lawyers. This was especially true of those enrolled with me in the evening division, which took four years to complete instead of three. I had chosen Portia over more prestigious law schools in Boston because it offered the most flexible class schedule, which meant I could also take care of Mom.

I had been surprised to find most of my classmates slugged away during the day at jobs as wait staff, cab drivers, and retail clerks. I delighted at their colorful backgrounds after growing up in a homogenous community. One had been in the circus. Another was a sixty-year-old butcher. There was a special program for police officers who wanted to become lawyers. They were all overworked, ambitious and industrious, and would make good lawyers. I appreciated why they had to multi-task online during class, paying bills and catching up on email. Having lived a sheltered life growing up in Vermont where my mother provided for me financially, I hadn't realized that being a student and not having to work at the same time was a privilege. I was glad I hadn't succumbed to pressure from my husband to attend one of the five other law schools in Boston with elite student populations, even though I could well afford to with the funds my mother had provided to me for my education.

Tonight, I juggled the same balls along with my classmates. Time was running out. Mom's deterioration was accelerating. She was no longer losing her memory one brain cell at a time. I googled 'Sheila Fairclough.'

There weren't many Sheila Faircloughs. Most of them were dead, in Australia or England, and none seemed near my mother's age. There was one fake Facebook profile with a photo of a woman in a military uniform with no friends. I was going to have to dig deeper than Google and reach into the toolbox I had used in my former career as a reference librarian. I remembered the excitement I would experience back then when I found the answer to a query. It had been satisfying, but not enough to quash my desire to burst out of the quiet life I had been relegated to and to join the adventures of women breaking professional barriers. I had secretly dreamed of becoming a lawyer ever since writing a paper about Ruth Bader Ginsburg in high school.

After class, I handed Erin the keys to her new car that she would have to drive me home in.

'Take me to a bar. Any bar. But first, can we swing by Thompson House so I can pay Terry back for the pizza?'

'Of course. I just need to find Andrew. He's coming with us. We have to set up a schedule for the study group. He's bringing another guy who wants to join us. That's OK with you, isn't it?' Erin asked, loading her notebook into her black leather satchel.

I had forgotten that tonight was the organizational meeting for the study group Erin had invited me to join to prepare for the Massachusetts Professional Responsibility Exam, otherwise known as the MPRE. I wasn't thrilled the study group was getting larger, but I wasn't going to tell Erin that. Ryan and I had apparently attended the same part-time program at Portia without ever having taken the same class together. I was uneasy about having someone I didn't know in the group, although I knew I had to get over being shy, given the profession I had chosen to switch to.

My mother had always cautioned me about groups and crowds. When I was very young, she warned me not to let go of her hand and instructed what to do if we became separated while out in public. I had our address and telephone number memorized before I could read. The thought of something happening where I couldn't find my mother had terrified me. As an adult, I still avoided groups, unable to overcome my fear of crowds. I had more than enough issues to keep two therapists busy.

Erin hooted when she caught sight of the blue Prius perched on the parking-lot roof, giving me a high-five. I got in the passenger seat, happy to let her drive us to meet Andrew who had texted to say he was already at Brendan Behan's Pub in Jamaica Plain with his friend. I was weary and almost asked her to take me home, but then I remembered I had to stop at Thompson House.

'We're running a little late. Can we stop at your mom's to drop off the check after drinks?' Erin asked as we headed down Huntington Ave. I loved that she said 'your mom's' as if we were dropping by a two-bedroom cape in West Roxbury, not a memory-loss facility.

'Sure.' I went to check my text messages but my phone was still dead. I had forgotten to plug it in when I returned to class after checking in with security earlier. Daniel usually sends me a text message during his dinner break. I didn't bother plugging the phone into the car. I could charge it when I got home and read his messages when I knew I would be feeling lonely.

Occasionally when he had the time, Daniel would write long, affectionate messages about how our lives would be once his residency was over. I would read them again and again. Once I tried to calculate how much time we had actually spent together during the three years we had been married. I longed for emotional intimacy in our relationship. With his crazy work schedule, we were lucky to find time to share a pizza.

Erin and I entered Behan's in Jamaica Plain, which she likes to describe as an intentional dive. It was crowded as always, Irish fiddlers playing away while customers knocked down beers like bowling pins. No food here, cash only, Behan's had Poetry Night on Thursdays. My kind of bar.

Andrew sat in a corner with a man about the same age as he. But that's where the similarity ended. Andrew had shaved his head rather than endure the insult of hair loss, plugs, implants, and weaves. It looked good on him, accentuating his hairless face, bright blue eyes, and toothy grin.

The thirty-something young man wearing a brown leather bomber jacket sitting across from him had a full head of thick black hair and enough of a five o'clock shadow to suggest it was from five o'clock the day before. Below bushy eyebrows, his wide-set eyes were even bluer than Andrew's, but with a hint of green. When he stood to greet us, I realized he was built like a lanky basketball player, towering over Erin. He was the guy everyone wanted to date in high school, which was the second reason I disliked him.

'This is Ryan,' Andrew said, pushing over in the booth to make room for Erin to slide next to him, gesturing for Ryan to do the same for me. Erin extended a beefy hand to Ryan.

'We've already met,' I said, which was the first reason.

He narrowed his eyes, looking at me, clearly not knowing who I was.

'Sorry, have we been in a class together?' he asked.

'No. You escorted my elderly mother home in her pajamas a while ago,' I said, ordering a neat whiskey from our waiter.

The others added their orders. I noticed car ownership had at least momentarily made a teetotaler out of Erin, who ordered a Diet Coke. Ryan wore a silent frown. I guessed I had him wondering what I was talking about. Andrew expounded on the beauty of a Black and Tan, filling the awkwardness my reminder to Ryan had created.

'Wait, the woman walking around Jamaica Pond in her bathrobe and slippers. Trying to find her way to Southie when she lived in a gorgeous house in Moss Hill,' Ryan said, triumphantly looking at me. 'Of course. How is she?'

'In a memory-loss center,' I said, glaring at him. I was too tired to hold back.

I'd left her in the conservatory to tend to her plants on a warm June morning before six while I went to fetch us coffee from the kitchen. Mom loved those early mornings playing in the dirt. We'd bought this house because of the conservatory. I had wanted to lessen the pain of leaving her garden in Vermont. I never expected her to wander out the door, through the herb garden, down Moss Hill on to the Arborway and over to Jamaica Pond, but she had. An early commuter noticed her and called the police, who had found her circling Jamaica Pond. Two uniformed cops flanking Mom had arrived at my door, just as I realized she was missing.

'Dear, can you get my two friends some coffee?'

Daniel had landed downstairs in time for the debacle.

'You need to keep better tabs on her, Ma'am. She's trying to find her way to Southie. My partner and I are just trying to find our way out,' the other cop had said light-heartedly. Clearly he was the good cop cracking a joke about living in South Boston.

Bad cop loomed over me, leaning in so Mom couldn't hear.

'Seriously, we could report this to Elderly Protective Service. There's no lost and found department for seniors in Boston. She could have been hit by a car on the Arborway and God knows what might have happened at the pond. You need to keep better tabs on her,' Ryan had said. He had written a brief incident report and had me sign it acknowledging return of my mother and receipt of a copy of the report.

Daniel pounced on the opportunity to reinforce his opinion. 'Do you know what would happen to my career if Claire was harmed while on my watch? "Psychiatric resident fails to provide supervision for mother-in-law who suffers from dementia." My reputation and my license would be in ruins.' A week later, Mom was admitted to Thompson House.

Erin jumped in, changing the subject to the study group's schedule and where we could meet.

'Well, three of us live on this side of Boston, so it should be around here, especially now that you have that hot car,' Andrew said, winking at Erin. She groaned since she lived in Somerville, next to Cambridge, across the Charles River. In Boston commuter time, this could mean twenty minutes or two hours, depending on the traffic.

'You're right in the middle, Liv. How about we meet at your house?' Erin asked.

No. That will not work. We can't do that. Daniel would not like it. Daniel valued his privacy. I struggled to find a diplomatic way to decline.

'My husband is a medical resident and works crazy hours, which means he often sleeps during the day. Sorry,' I said.

'Really? A resident can afford a house like that in Moss Hill? I should have gone to Harvard Medical School, not Portia Law,' Ryan said, shaking his head with mocked regret.

'Actually, what you should have done is enroll in the Fletcher School of Diplomacy and learned some tact,' I said, wanting to add 'asshole' at the end. I was beginning to doubt whether I wanted to belong to a study group with a guy who had such talent for irritating me.

'Well, my place is just too tiny to hold all four of us,' Andrew said, ignoring the barb.

'Easy. We meet at school in an empty classroom,' Erin said. She handed each of us a paper that included email addresses, telephone numbers, and a portion of the text to outline for our first meeting.

'You really ripped Ryan a new one, Liv. What's with that? You're usually so mellow,' Erin said on the ride to Thompson House.

'He's the reason my mother didn't get to stay in her own home. The reason we were disconnected earlier than need be. He was so damn officious. Ryan's reprimand was all Daniel needed to hear. He's just a pompous jerk in uniform,' I said. I felt better sharing my frustration with Erin after holding it in for so long.

The second whiskey had taken the edge off, so when I rang the night bell at Thompson House by the ambulance entrance while Erin waited for me in the parking lot, I wasn't feeling as annoyed as I had earlier about having to stop by to reimburse Terry. I left a check with a nurse I didn't know who had apparently relieved Terry and worked the third shift. She told me Mom was sleeping soundly. I decided not to peek in on her and risk waking her up. Since she had been admitted to Thompson House, my mother often wandered in the middle of the night when she couldn't sleep.

I walked back toward the Prius, noticing a familiar small car turning from Glendale Road on to Centre Street at the corner. It looked just like Daniel's Fiat 500, but I had to be mistaken. He was working ten miles away in Belmont. Too bad. I dreaded going home to an empty house.

FOUR

punched in the code to the security alarm while Erin waited in her new car and watched me get inside safely. I stepped into the silence of the dark, over-sized Tudor and poured myself a nightcap since I now felt more wired than tired from my outburst with Ryan. Even I could tell I was becoming increasingly unhinged as my mother deteriorated and slipped into a world where I wasn't included. We had never been apart until now. I took the tumbler with me into the room that was the reason my mother bought this house for me and where I could sense her presence.

A conservatory. A real honest-to-goodness conservatory with glass walls, a pebble floor with flagstones, and at least a hundred plants, minus those I had taken to Thompson House to put in my mother's suite to make it feel like home to her. I collapsed into one of the two white wicker chairs with plush floral Sunbrella cushions, placing my Courvoisier on its arm. The empty chair next to it had been my mother's. I breathed in the silence and the scent of green plants with the hint of fragrance from a few flowers still in bloom. This room was the only reason I had been able to persuade Mom to move away from her beloved Green Mountain Vermont and her huge overflowing garden to Boston where Daniel was starting his residency. She didn't seem concerned or even aware about where she was moving, only that she was leaving the home and garden she loved. Mom couldn't live alone, but telling her that only agitated her. When I told her we wanted to buy a house that had a large conservatory I planned to fill with plants that I would never be able to manage without her, she graciously agreed to move with Daniel and me. But neither of us was fooled. She had no choice. We both knew what would eventually happen.

'I don't suppose it matters where I live now,' Mom had finally said as I fought off tears.

I looked at the oldest plant we owned, a jade Mom had carried with her when we fled for safety. It was the only item from our past. I was grateful it had survived along with us. I felt the full smooth shiny leaves, rubbing them like worry stones. The jade, sometimes called the Money Tree, had been the genesis of Mom's passion for indoor and outdoor gardening. As she slipped away from me, I grew to appreciate how it must have helped her fill the great loneliness when she left everything and everyone but me behind.

I thought about the new tiny jade and wondered where had it come from. I had never heard of Dr Alexander before and doubted she existed. She was more likely a colleague of the imaginary Dr Nightmare. Daniel had explained to me very gently how the darkness and quiet of night can increase confusion in elderly, especially already-disoriented patients. Maybe Mom was recasting the night staff of nurses and aides as doctors who were researching the cure. Mom had often speculated about whether they would ever find a cure for 'this hideous disease.'

I took my glass to the kitchen and put the evidence into the dishwasher out of habit. I had learned a valuable lesson about conflict long before I entered law school. It was far easier to avoid than resolve. Daniel didn't appreciate that having a cocktail was a pleasant ritual to end the day and relax, a practice I had joined my mother in when I came of age. Although he indulged in an occasional glass of wine, he was disdainful of mixed drinks. I enjoyed the elegance of a martini or the vulgarity of a painkiller. Daniel could flatten the bubbles in my Prosecco with one frown.

The large empty rooms I passed on my way to bed saddened me. All I had ever wanted was to be part of a normal family. It was too late for my own childhood, but I dreamed of raising a houseful of kids racing down halls on razor scooters, leaving muddy handprints on my finger towels, and arguing about who got to lick the frosting bowl.

I had assumed Daniel wanted the same, but he wasn't having any of it. I hadn't realized I would have to present a case for babies and negotiate starting a family. I also knew it was easier to have babies while in law school than to accommodate maternity leave once in practice.

Daniel knew the little information I had about my family of origin, which is what Mom had told me. My father was a violent, mentally unstable man who had threatened to murder us. Daniel was adopted and had opted not to search for his biological parents.

He said we would be kinder not to inflict our collective undetermined gene pool on future generations.

I glanced into the formal dining room with its elegant polished mahogany table that sat twelve, where I had pictured serving holiday meals to new friends. We'd bought much of the furniture from the estate that sold us the house. Mom had lasted at home with us long enough to have a few Christmases huddled with Daniel and me at the far end of the table.

The master bedroom was long enough to hold a bowling alley. Daniel loved that it had three bay windows overlooking Moss Hill and Jamaica Pond in the distance. On those rare weekends when he was off, we would sit in two slipper chairs reading the *Sunday Globe* in the morning sunlight while sipping coffee.

The home was perfect for a doctor or a lawyer. The first-floor library with a private bath off it had served as Mom's suite. Within a week of her admission to Thompson House, Daniel had commandeered it as his study. 'You don't mind, do you, Liv? You've got the conservatory after all.'

I fumbled to plug my cell phone into the charger on my nightstand, disappointed not to find a message from Daniel. I set the alarm, not trusting myself to wake up early naturally as I normally do. I stepped out of my jeans, leaving them on the floor right next to the bed because Daniel wasn't there to give me that look I get when I am being sloppy. Daniel is a neat freak, while I am far more casual. I slipped my bra off from under my jersey, deciding to forego one of the silky nighties Daniel likes me to wear. I get a new one each year for my birthday. He loves the way they feel against his body, but they make me feel sweaty. When you grow up in Vermont, you sleep in flannel in the winter and cotton in the summer. I toppled under the covers dizzy with the images of dank rotting leaves, a man in a baseball cap, and the signature of Sheila Fairclough before my closed eyes and then fell into a mercifully alcohol-induced sleep.

Tuesday, October 14th

I woke up from a deep sleep to the sound of Sara Bareilles singing 'Brave' on my cell phone, telling me I had a call. It was from the same nurse at Thompson House with whom I had just left the check for Terry several hours before.

'Your mother collapsed, Olivia. You'd better come,' she said, sounding more irritated than worried.

'Is she—' I started to ask.

'Just come,' she said, hanging up.

I stepped into my jeans and kept on the jersey I had been sleeping in, not bothering with a bra. I slipped into clogs without putting socks on and ran out of the house, not troubling to click the alarm system back on.

In less than five minutes, I pulled my Mini Cooper into a spot in the parking lot where an ambulance with red lights flashing but without a siren blaring was pulling out. I panicked. I figured my mother was in the ambulance, but I wasn't sure. I didn't know if I should follow it or go into Thompson House in case my mother wasn't in the ambulance. It was possible two patients could have emergencies at the same time in a facility for the elderly.

I never know what to do at times like this. The damned if you do, damned if you don't decisions in life overwhelm me. I'm just not wired for making rapid decisions. I need to weigh the pros and cons on a piece of paper with a line dividing it down the middle. I opted to stay at Thompson House.

Inside, I saw the same nurse I had left the check with. Denise M was rubbing her eyes while talking to Caleb, a male aide I had met before. He had been very kind to Mom, taking her feisty attitude in good humor once when she asked if he was related to her good friend, Dr John Miller. Caleb was black and wore scrubs. So was John but he was thirty years older and the dean of UVM Medical School.

'Caleb, what's wrong? What's happened to my mother?'

Denise leaned over the counter as if to share a secret, but surprised me with a scowl.

'They've just taken her to the Brigham in an ambulance.' Her cigarette-scented whisper sounded more like a hiss. I guessed I had shouted to Caleb and she was afraid I might wake other patients up.

'How is she? What happened?' I didn't understand why I had to repeat that question. But I knew not to bother interrogating Denise any more. Obviously, she had been sleeping during her shift and had no idea what happened to Mom.

'I found her on the floor between her bed and the bathroom. The EMTs were working on her while they took her,' Caleb said.

'Why the Brigham and not the Faulkner? It's closer,' I said.
'Because your mother's doctor is at the Brigham and that's
where she's supposed to go,' Denise said.

I started to turn toward the door, but stopped, hearing Mom's
voice in my head.

'Always grab my purse if something happens to me, Liv,' she
had instructed me ever since I was a little girl.

I spun around and rushed to her room where her navy-blue
leather purse sat wedged between her nightstand and bed. I noticed
an empty Dunkin' Donuts strawberry banana Coolatta. Mom had
obviously persuaded someone to fetch it for her. I spotted her favorite
navy cardigan over a chair and snatched it, remembering how cold
hospitals always seem to be. I hoped to see Mom wearing it at the
hospital and that my efforts weren't fruitless.

At the Brigham, I barely remembered to put my car into park
and threw my keys at the parking attendant, grateful hospitals now
had valet service. I ran through the expansive automatic sliding
doors of the emergency room into a bright waiting room filled with
people slouched on chairs. I headed for the desk with the sign
'Concierge' above it. I said who I was and why I was there to the
older man in a red jacket sitting behind it on a stool. He told me
to take a seat while he sorted it out. It was maddening. I wanted to
run past him through another set of sliding doors beyond the desk
and find my mother. I wanted to tell him he wasn't the Great Oz.

But I did as I was told and found a seat next to an older woman
who was snoring. I clutched Mom's purse as if it were a teddy bear
and waited. I speculated about what had happened and kept thinking
my mother must have had a reaction to the sugary drink she had
indulged in. Maybe she was developing diabetes. Many people her
age were diabetics. But then I considered it could be something
more serious, like a stroke or heart attack. Mom's physical health
had remained stable despite her Alzheimer's, so I could only guess.

When I heard my name called out by a young woman in baby-
blue scrubs, I knew from the flickering look in her eyes that my
mother was dead. She led me into a small examining room.

'I'm so very sorry. She was DOA. There was nothing we could
do for her,' Kaitlyn Hathaway, RN said. There was kindness in her
voice. She told me they wouldn't know the cause of death until an
autopsy was performed. I wasn't prepared for the vision of my

mother being hacked up on a cold stainless-steel autopsy table. My knees buckled. I reached for the edge of the counter next to me to prevent myself from sinking to the floor and falling into a fetal position. Kaitlyn reached under my armpit and caught me.

I knew my mother would die someday, but I hadn't expected such an abrupt departure. In my version, I was holding her hand while she slipped away under crisp white sheets and a rose-colored blanket that I had crocheted for her. Her grandchildren were standing around the bed with tears streaming down their cheeks. Mom had been all I had for most of my life. She had saved my life when she rescued me from my father who was intent on killing us both. She left everyone and everything she had ever known behind to create a new life for us where we would be safe. I wasn't ready to give up on Mom in death, any more than I had been when she was alive and slipping into oblivion.

'I need to see her,' I said.

'Of course,' Kaitlyn said. She led me past a series of cubicles with curtains drawn around them into one where my mother lay as if taking a nap. I had expected bruising from the fall on her still-beautiful face, but there was none. The garish fluorescent lights gave her skin an ethereal glow.

I stood immobile, feeling tears coming from the sides of my eyes running down my cheeks, wondering what would I ever do without my mother. My compass, my friend, my savior. Hell, I wouldn't even have a husband if it weren't for her.

Husband. I should call Daniel. But I lingered, not wanting to leave her and punctuate her unexpected departure. I knew once I completed the tasks her death required, she would be lost to me forever. I stood beside her, oblivious to the clamor of activity outside the curtain around us until I knew I had to let her go. I leaned over the bed, kissed Mom's cold forehead for the last time, and turned away. Kaitlyn brought me back to the room where we had first talked so I could have some privacy to make calls. I had only one to make.

When Daniel didn't answer his cell, I texted him. 'Mother dead at the Brigham.'

My phone belted out 'Brave' in seconds.

'I'll be there as soon as I can get someone in to cover. It won't be long, Olivia. Hang in there. Love you,' he said quickly.

But I wasn't going to wait. There was no reason. My mother was dead. I wanted to go home. I wanted to sit in the conservatory.

I started for the door toward the parking valet when a tall young man in a brown leather bomber jacket passed by. He turned back toward me.

'Olivia?'

Ryan from the study group faced me with another man standing behind him. I recognized good cop.

'What are you doing here? Is everything OK?' I guessed he knew everything wasn't OK if I was in the ER in the middle of the night crying, but like Kaitlyn, his voice was gentle and kind.

'My mother died,' I said. I heard those words come out of me as if spoken by someone else. Then reality came crashing down on me like a tree in the middle of a hurricane. I began to bawl.

'Oh, Olivia,' Ryan said, hesitating then sweeping me into his arms in a bear hug the likes of which I had only read about before. I wanted to resist a hug from the man I had lambasted just a few hours before, yet couldn't. I needed to be held right then and it didn't matter who was doing the holding. I buried my face and breathed in the smell of leather while he held me tightly in his long arms. His hands pressed gently into my back. For the moment, I felt safe and protected from the truth about what had just happened.

When I realized I might be getting tears and snot on his nice jacket I stepped away, immediately missing the warmth of his embrace, which had reached me through a layer of leather.

'Thanks,' I said.

'Is anyone here with you?' Ryan asked, looking at good cop, who seemed to sense he should go take care of whatever brought them to the ER. He nodded and walked past us.

'My husband's on his way. I'm going home,' I said.

'Don't you want to wait for him?'

'I can't. I just can't be here.'

'Can I drive you?' Ryan sounded concerned, as if I might not be making sense.

'No, thank you. I don't even know how she died. I just need to be out of here. Really. Now,' I said. I dashed toward the valet station, not looking back at Ryan. I retrieved my car and drove home through vacant streets glaring with garish streetlights to my dark, empty house where I would still feel the presence of my mother among the living greens she so loved.

Once in the stillness of the conservatory, I sat in the shadows on the same wicker chair where I'd sipped a nightcap, just hours before. This time I had a glass on the arm of the chair and the bottle of Courvoisier at my feet. When Daniel eventually walked in, I was justifiably shitfaced.

'Liv, you have to be careful with that and the medication,' he said. He nodded toward the bottle, which was illuminated by the early-morning sunlight beginning to spill into the conservatory. Daniel was referring to the anti-anxiety medicine he knew my therapist, his colleague Kayla Vincent, had prescribed for me. What he didn't know was that I wasn't taking it. I hate taking pills.

'Is that all you can say?' While I relied on Daniel's rationality during most catastrophes, I had hoped for a more visceral response to my obvious grief. I almost told him I wasn't taking the medication.

'Of course not. I am so sorry about Claire and that I couldn't get to the hospital sooner. I had trouble reaching Kayla so she could cover.' Daniel knelt before me, placing the Courvoisier bottle to the side out of my reach, putting a hand on each of my knees.

I resented Kayla's name entering my ears while I was so raw. I also resented being treated by a woman who spent more time with my husband than I did. Daniel and Kayla had quickly become friends after meeting at orientation for the residency program at Mass General. 'Thick as thieves, those two. Watch out,' my mother had said after Kayla and her social worker husband, Josh, came for dinner while Mom was still living at home. Kayla, with her shiny straight brown hair, painted pouty lips complete with a natural beauty mark perched above them, and tennis-player figure, made me feel like an invisible washed-out strawberry blonde straight from the farm.

'Couldn't someone else cover?'

'She had borrowed my car. Josh is in the Berkshires hiking. He had theirs,' he said in what I recognized as his very intentional therapeutic voice. Josh was my ally when we socialized as couples and the conversation turned into psychiatric soup. He knew how to spin all of the downtime that comes with being married to a resident into gold. I wanted to be hiking with Josh and erase the past twenty-four hours.

'Daniel, I don't know why she died. She was fine yesterday. She even ordered pizza for her entire floor. What could have happened?' I was crying again.

'I'm not sure, but they'll do an autopsy and be able to tell. Maybe it was merciful, Liv. Things weren't going to get better for Claire. She had a good run.'

I knew he was trying to console me, but I wanted to throw his hands off my knees and knock him over on to his ass. His bedside manner was atrocious. Condolences should never sound condescending.

He knew nothing about Claire having a 'good run.' He never appreciated how she struggled to create a normal life for us. He couldn't possibly comprehend what it was like to intentionally live in obscurity. To fear recognition. To avoid excellence. Even to downplay beauty. Adoption had made Daniel a champion. Flight had made me a freak.

'Come with me,' he said. He took my hands and pulled me up from the chair. 'I know how to make you feel better.' I knew what he was saying. Sex always made him feel better, but it was the last thing on my mind.

'I don't think I can, Daniel,' I said for once.

'At least come get some sleep and let me hold you. After all, it's just you and me now,' he said.

Exactly, I thought, as we walked up the elegant stairway that led to our bedroom. I began to undress and felt something in my jean pocket. I pulled out the paper Erin had given me with the contact information and assignment for the study group and placed it on my nightstand. I knew that although Mom had died, I still would be taking the MPRE. Life would go on. I glanced at the names and numbers and was startled to see ryanmfairclough@gmail.com. Fairclough. I knew it was a bizarre coincidence, but it would have to wait. I had reached my limit.

FIVE

By mid-morning, I was fully awake, showered and dressed, ready to make the few calls necessary to share the news about Mom. There were no arrangements to make. My mother had already seen to that. Her directive had been for cremation and a memorial service to be held at UVM, whenever convenient. There was no need for a death notice in the *Boston Globe*. My mother didn't know anyone here. The obituary she had written herself when she was first diagnosed would be placed in the *Burlington Free Press*.

Daniel remained sleeping, as I knew he would. He often sleeps twelve hours straight after working twenty-four. I didn't need him underfoot. I had things that needed to be done.

I put my glass from the night before into the dishwasher, the Courvoisier bottle back in the pantry, while my K-cup brewed. When it was ready, I perched at my spot at the eight-by-four-foot granite kitchen island where I conduct my daily business as family CEO each morning. I took a long sip of the smooth French Roast brew I drink black to fortify myself.

I was startled when there was a knock on the back door. I looked out the window before entering the mudroom that led from the kitchen to the door. A delivery truck from Winston's was parked in my driveway. I never get flowers so I thought it was probably a mistake, but then I remembered people send flowers when there has been a death.

The delivery man stood in the relentless mist holding a huge white triple moth orchid. My mother would have loved the broad white winged petals that looked more like butterflies than moths. I took the plant from him and carried it to the conservatory where I placed it on the glass-topped wicker table next to the enormous ancient jade plant. A small white envelope had been tucked into a clear fork-like plastic stick. Inside, I found a card signed Erin, Andrew, and Ryan written in Erin's handwriting. Ryan must have shared the news with the study group. Word was out.

I checked my phone. There were three text messages. The first was from Erin, telling me she was so sorry about Mom and to please call her. Andrew asked if there was anything he could do and told me he was thinking about me. Ryan's message said, 'I'm really sorry about your mother.' I still couldn't fathom his last name was Fairclough. I wondered if it wasn't a coincidence. Perhaps my mother absorbed it into her muddled brain when he had retrieved her from Jamaica Pond long ago. But that didn't explain where she got the name *Sheila* Fairclough. I would have plenty of time to contemplate the possibilities, but today wasn't the day.

I texted Andrew and Ryan, thanking them for their messages and the orchid. I called Erin, who answered on the first ring.

'Oh my God, Olivia. I am so sorry. You were just there. What can I do?'

I replied that there was nothing that could be done, but thanked her anyway and told her how beautiful the moth orchid was. I explained I was heading to Thompson House to pack up Mom's suite.

'Will Daniel help you?' Erin asked. I explained how he needed to sleep after working twenty-four hours straight.

My next call was more difficult. UVM Dean John Miller sounded just as he had when my mother and I said goodbye to him right before we moved to Boston. He still had the subtle hint of a southern accent after years in New England. He was Mom's dearest friend and had been a father figure to me.

'We've lost her,' I said. I couldn't bring myself to use the word 'died' yet.

He said nothing for a few seconds.

'Ah, but we lost her a while ago, didn't we, Liv?' he said softly. We chose a date for the small memorial service at UVM that Mom had insisted on being her only requiem. 'We'll have time together to talk when you come up for the service. And I have something she wanted me to give you when she passed.'

Hope surged through me as I pictured an envelope with my name on it written in her classic cursive. Inside I would find an explanation about all Mom couldn't tell me when she was alive, with a sketch of our family tree and photos. I indulged in the fantasy of finally having answers. But I wasn't counting on it.

My last call was to Dr Charles Evans, a psychiatrist who

specializes in Ambiguous Loss, which is what you experience when you suffer the loss of a person you love without there being visible signs of their absence. For some, it meant the loss of a loved one in combat when the body isn't recovered and there can be no closure. For people like me, it meant I could sit across the table from my mother sipping her black coffee and chewing on her usual morning fare of raisin toast with orange marmalade. Some mornings, she wouldn't recognize me or didn't understand why we wouldn't be going to church for Sunday Mass when we hadn't been inside anything other than a Unitarian church during my entire life.

I left a long, rambling message for Dr Evans, telling him that my mother had died and asking whether he still wanted to see me. Dr Evans has been the only secret I've kept from Daniel since we were married. I considered it more of a nondisclosure than a lie. Having Dr Evans as an alternative therapist was one of many secrets I've kept from Kayla Vincent. It tickled me to think that I was doing something uncharacteristically naughty. I was cheating on my therapist.

I had tried to explain my frustration with Kayla to Daniel one night when we had escaped for a rare break to an inn on Martha's Vineyard to celebrate our anniversary. He wanted to know how therapy was going and I wanted him to know it wasn't.

'She doesn't listen to me, Daniel. She dismisses my concerns,' I told him. I hoped I could persuade him a new therapist was a good idea.

'Olivia, Kayla's the perfect therapist for you. She's a contemporary, female, and brilliant. She graduated from Emory and Johns Hopkins, for God's sake. Not to mention, she's free with the professional courtesy she extends me,' Daniel said.

'She's non-responsive and lacks empathy. When I confided in her that Mom was complaining about being treated in the middle of the night by Dr Nightmare, she scoffed at me. "Paranoia isn't one of the things you want to inherit from your mother, Olivia."' I had imitated Kayla's condescending tone. Daniel grimaced.

'Pettiness doesn't flatter you, Liv. I would think you'd be grateful to Kayla,' Daniel said.

I didn't feel grateful. I resented sharing my personal feelings with someone who knew Daniel so well. I especially didn't like how well she knew him. I wondered why neither of them realized it was a conflict of interest for her to be treating me, something I had learned a lot about in law school.

I liked Dr Evans so much better than Kayla Vincent. He was earnest, gentle, probing when necessary and, most of all, practical. He had tips about how to handle Mom and my misgivings about feeling manipulative when I did. Best of all, Dr Evans didn't ridicule me when I wondered if my mother's reports of being treated in the middle of the night were true. I hated the thought that I might lose him too now that my loss was no longer ambiguous.

The prospect of clearing out my mother's room filled me with a void I had never experienced before. Even when I had emptied our home in Burlington, I had hope for a future with her in Boston. I choked up when I walked past the vacant spot in the driveway where Mom's Prius had sat unused for so long. The sight of my beloved British racing stripe green Mini brought a downpour of tears. My mother had encouraged me to work retail at the Church Street Marketplace in Burlington while in high school so I could buy my first car. I deposited my checks at the local credit union until I had enough to buy a used pick-up truck, which I drove all through college. The Mini was a surprise college graduation present from her, but the real gift had been a lesson in how to balance frugality with generosity.

I waited patiently at the foot of the driveway for the tears to stop as I watched neighbors pass by in their cars about to start their ordinary days. My day was one I had dreaded all my life. I finally backed out and followed a silver Honda to the end of our road. I remembered the joker who wouldn't let me off the rotary the day before had driven one like it. Yesterday felt so long ago.

When I entered Mom's room at Thompson House, I was surprised to see Erin sitting in Mom's wingback chair with three empty cardboard boxes at her feet. She rose and came to give me a hug, something she'd never done before.

'I hope it's OK that I'm here,' she said. I saw tears in her eyes and was touched she cared enough to cry for me. One of the things we had in common was the ability to keep our emotions in check.

'Of course,' I said, looking around at the room where the bed had been made with institutional linens, the nightstand cleared, and the trash emptied as if Mom had never existed.

'What are you keeping?' she asked.

I told her I was taking the plants home and perhaps a few pieces of jewelry, although my mother had already given me her better pieces. I was donating her clothes to Rosie's Place for homeless women. We decided I would tackle the closet and Erin would take the bureau. I began removing clothes from hangers, placing them into a box. I was grateful Erin had thought to bring them.

'They won't take undies,' Erin said, placing undergarments in a wastebasket. 'I know these things.'

'How? Have you donated to Rosie's before?' I asked. I was relieved to be having a normal conversation.

'No, my mom and I were recipients. We lived at a shelter for a while when I was a kid,' Erin said.

'Do you want to tell me about it?' I was moved she would confide in me. I wasn't the only person in the world with a painful childhood. Erin was consoling me in a way that prayers or flowers could never accomplish.

'We were evicted. My father had taken off and there was no money for rent. We had no real family here. Everyone was back in Puerto Rico. My mother had enough money for a one-way plane ticket to Boston and the name of a cousin who lived in Mattapan when she arrived. Within months, she was pregnant with me. She thought by naming me Erin I'd fit right in with all of the Irish Americans. Right. Erin Rivera. I ended up being a freak who didn't fit in with Puerto Ricans or Irish Bostonians. She tried, but she was just eighteen and a little crazy,' Erin said, opening another drawer.

'Aren't we all a little crazy at that age?' I asked. I remembered how painful adolescence had been for me. I couldn't picture what it would be like for a teenager in a new city with a newborn.

'No really. It turned out she was more than a little crazy. Actually, the months we lived in the family shelter with other moms and their kids were a relief from the chaos my mother created. At the shelter, there was structure. Meal time, homework time, bedtime. Clean clothes every morning. You were never left alone at night. I was sorry to leave in a way,' Erin said, holding up a white full slip with lace trim. 'Did she really wear this?'

I laughed at the sight of Erin unapologetically ample in purple yoga pants, a tight hot-pink long-sleeve jersey, and a pair of lime-green Nike Air Max sneakers staring at my mother's slip as if it were an artifact.

'She sure did. Did you ever see the movie *On the Waterfront* with Marlon Brando and Eva Marie Saint?'

'No, is it on HBO?'

I shook my head. 'It's a classic. There's a famous scene in it with Eva Marie Saint wearing a white slip. Mom said men found that sexier than if she were stark naked. You need to see it to understand. We'll do a girls' night and watch it sometime,' I said, thinking I would invite Erin over to watch movies with me while Daniel was working. I needed friends in my life.

'So, where's your mom now?' I asked. I didn't want to pry, but I did want Erin to know I was interested and cared.

'Dead. After she had my little brothers, she got mixed up with drugs and ODed.' Erin's back was to me, so I couldn't see her expression.

'I'm so sorry . . .'

We were interrupted when Terry Walsh wandered into the room, having come on duty.

'I can't believe she's gone. I would have pictured her hopping on a plane at Logan Airport for Dublin before I expected this. Only yesterday she was ordering pizza for the entire floor,' Terry said, giving me my third hug in less than twelve hours, a lifetime record. She took her glasses off and wiped her eyes with a tissue. I asked if she would like anything of Mom's.

'Just to have her back, honey,' she said, turning to leave the room.

'Do you know who gave this plant to my mother, Terry? I'd like to say thanks and see if he or she wants it back. She kept mentioning a midnight doctor.' The small jade was still sitting in a plastic container, something my mother would never tolerate. She must have been given it recently.

'She told me that one too. Even called her Dr Alexander the Great. I have no clue what she was talking about. It never happened on my shift. Maybe you should ask Denise, the overnight nurse.' Terry backed out of the room, clearly uncomfortable with the shift in conversation.

'What about these, Olivia? They're lovely,' Erin said, holding up a gray cashmere glove. I had given Mom the gloves and a matching scarf when she moved into Thompson House so she would be warm during our daily long walks. The exercise seemed to soothe her and reduced her proclivity for wandering off on her own. We would circle Jamaica Pond until she had worn us both out on days when her energy surged.

'I'll keep them and the matching scarf,' I said. Erin handed me the glove she was holding and reached for the other still in the drawer.

'Hey, Liv. There's something in this one,' she said. She handed me the glove, which was bulging where a finger went. I wasn't surprised that Mom might stash things hidden out of sight. She had complained about the staff at Thompson House handling her stuff, so I did her laundry at home.

'I think they should be more respectful with people's personal property, don't you?' she had asked me on more than one occasion. She was more irritated by the night staff, it seemed. My guess was that she had placed a piece of jewelry in the glove, even though she had already given me her better pieces.

I grabbed the glove from the top and looked inside. It was filled with pills. Hundreds of tiny white pills. Oval pills. I didn't say anything, but I tilted the glove so that Erin could see them. She nodded silently.

I held one of the pills up to the light from the bay window. There were a few numbers and letters that would let me identify them in the PDR, the Physicians' Desk Reference. Daniel, like all doctors, had one handy on his desk. I'd bet money they were Xanax.

'She hated taking pills,' I said softly to Erin.

'I guess so,' she said.

'I don't want to get the nurses in trouble for her not taking her medication,' I said, twisting the top of the glove so the pills didn't pour out when I placed it in a box.

Erin passed the matching glove, which was empty, to me along with the scarf. Mom hadn't needed to wear them yet this year. We would never take another walk around Jamaica Pond. I was on the verge of losing it again.

'You must have her sense of humor,' Erin said.

'Why do you say that?' I asked.

Erin held up the glove again. I noticed only the middle finger had been stuffed.

SIX

Erin lugged my mother's plants to my car while I handed a philodendron to Terry on my way out. I assured her she couldn't kill it and if she did, my mother would come find her. We laughed a little and hugged again. I was glad to leave on a lighter note.

I said goodbye to Erin in the parking lot and gave her one of Mom's African violets. She promised to take extra-good notes in class that night. While there wasn't anything more I could do for my newly departed mother, I was too ragged to contemplate going to school. It felt disrespectful to even consider it. I wished I had something constructive to do. The rituals that accompany death really exist for the survivors. Picking out a casket, selecting flowers, choosing verses and hymns offer the surviving family a sense that they are doing something helpful for their lost loved one.

I knew my mother would be cremated after the autopsy. Then I would transport her ashes to Vermont for a memorial service in a garden she created at UVM that was named in her honor. But I didn't know what I was supposed to do in the meantime.

I wondered if Daniel had woken up so I checked my phone to see if he had texted me. I saw I had a voice message I must have missed while loading the car.

'Olivia, I'm so sorry to learn about your mother. Of course I'll continue as your therapist. In fact, you have your weekly appointment later this afternoon, which I fully understand you may not want to keep. But I'll be here, in any event. If you want to reschedule let me know.' Dr Evans' voice was just the tonic I needed.

I started the car and popped on to the Jamaicaway, a narrow roadway designed with horse-drawn carriages in mind. I hoped I would beat early commuters on their way home. I saw Dr Evans late every Tuesday afternoon before I headed over to school. I knew the short cuts, the roads to avoid, and where the potholes were.

Dr Evans was in his sixties and had a headful of wild white hair that refused to lay flat. His office was in his home on a quiet narrow street in Cambridge lined with towering Victorian houses. We met in his study, which was filled with more books than I had seen in some libraries. His furniture was mismatched cracked leather, which I imagined he collected at the edge of driveways waiting for trash pick-up.

I arrived with five minutes to spare. The rule was you waited outside until two minutes before your appointment in order to make certain the patient before you had left. Dr Evans' study was the former parlor in the house. There was no waiting room, only a long entry hall. The three minutes felt like three hours. My mission felt urgent. I wanted to run to Dr Evans and ask what I should be doing, what I should be feeling.

He looked no different today than he ever did, but he spoke a little more softly when he told me how sorry he was to hear about my mother.

'We both know that she was ill, but did something happen to speed up the end, Olivia?' he asked, his Santa Claus eyebrows arching.

I explained what little I knew and that there would be an autopsy, which might provide some answers.

'I'm sorry. If I'd known she was this close to the end, I would have tried to prepare you better. But I wasn't hearing anything that suggested her brain function was in enough decline to interfere with vital bodily functions,' Dr Evans said, taking off his wire-rimmed glasses and placing them on a pile of journals.

'What do you mean?' I asked. I was surprised to hear a doctor agree with me that my mother's death seemed unexplained.

'Just that in our conversations, you never mentioned your mother having difficulty swallowing or with her mobility. Those are hallmarks of a decline beyond memory loss.'

'She seemed fine, at least physically, when I saw her yesterday afternoon. Although, something was off,' I said, remembering Mom had signed legal documents with someone else's name twice in the same day.

'Why do you say that?' Dr Evans asked with one of those psychiatric prompts that sounded innocuous coming from him, but incendiary when Daniel spouts them.

I hesitated. I didn't know if I should tell him about Sheila Fairclough. It didn't have anything to do with Mom's death. It might not have any significance. But I was emotionally raw and had no filter. I plunged ahead and told him about the signatures.

'What do you make of it?' Dr Evans asked. He leaned forward, giving me full consideration.

'I don't know, I mean . . . I think I need to know if you'll still be my therapist before we get into some stuff,' I said.

'If you'd like me to, and think I can be helpful to you, Olivia.'

'I do. Up until now, we've talked mostly about my mother and how her illness was affecting her and what I could do to help her,' I said.

'That's been our focus. Where would you like to see our work directed now?' he asked, leaning back in the sagging chair that coughed under the strain of his weight.

'I need to know more about me.' It sounded hollow, even selfish to me, but it was the truth.

'What are you looking to learn about?' Dr Evans asked.

'I told you my mother fled from my father, convinced he was going to kill both of us. She was terrified he'd find us, which is why she changed our names. She died never telling me what our real names are. What my father's name is,' I said. I was surprised to find my hands forming fists.

Dr Evans shifted in his chair. 'I can see how that might be disturbing. Do you know where she fled from?'

'No. I know nothing. I know she was trying to protect us, but Jesus, don't I have the right to know who I am? Who my father is? Before I decide whether Daniel is right or wrong about us not having children.' A sob escaped from the back of my throat.

'And you want to have children?'

'Yes, more than anything. But Daniel says it wouldn't be fair for us to pass defective genes on to them. I don't know if my family was genetically screwed up or if my father was just a bad person.' I reached reluctantly for a tissue out of the Seventh Generation box Dr Evans stocked. They may be planet-friendly, but they were scratchy as hell.

'You're wondering if it's nature versus nurture? Do you worry about that same concern for yourself?' Dr Evans asked.

I did, although I hadn't realized it until this moment. I'd always couched the query under the guise of concern for my unborn children.

'Yes, I guess I do. If my father was so terrible, and I am a part of him, do I have the potential to become evil? I need to know this stuff.' By now, I was sobbing openly.

'Of course you do. It's only natural for you to want to know who your people are, Olivia. Shakespeare knew what he was saying when he wrote "What's past is prologue,"' Dr Evans said.

'Exactly. How can I have a future if I don't have a past? My mother refused my pleas to tell me anything about my father, even his frigging blood type. Now she's gone. How am I supposed to figure it out without her?' Now I was shedding tears of anger directed at my own recently deceased mother.

'Well, you might want to start with the name Sheila Fairclough,' Dr Evans said, an innocent smile on his leathery face. This was where he distinguished himself. Dr Evans knew when it was time to quit 'processing feelings' and to start fixing things.

'I will. I started on Google without much luck. I need to dig deeper. And it turns out one of my more obnoxious classmates has the same last name. I'll see if he can help,' I said with more resolve than I had felt before.

'Olivia, it sounds to me like you've had your own ambiguous loss. You've lost your father and any family you had before you and your mother fled. We can work on that.'

I was comforted by the sound of Dr Evans' pledge, yet something else was gnawing at me.

'Wait a minute. I almost forgot to ask you a question. If my mother wasn't taking her meds, could it kill her?'

'It would depend on what the medication was. I don't think we've ever discussed that specifically. What was being prescribed for her?'

'She hated taking pills and would get angry when the nurses tried to give them to her. Since she was so healthy, I convinced the medical staff when she was admitted that all she needed was the Razadyne for the Alzheimer's, which she took in syrup form, and Xanax in pills for anxiety. That was it. She didn't even need medication for high blood pressure or any of the other ailments common in people her age,' I said. I pictured the glove full of pills sitting in my car.

'So the only pills she was prescribed were the Xanax? Not taking Xanax wouldn't kill your mother,' Dr Evans said. 'Was she hoarding the pills?'

I nodded. I hadn't told Terry I found the pills. I didn't want the nursing staff to get in trouble. At some level my mother's noncompliance made me inexplicably ashamed.

'Well, you needn't worry about that any longer. Not taking the Xanax would only increase her anxiety. It wouldn't cause her death, Olivia.'

I glanced at the small digital clock sitting on top of a pile of journals next to Dr Evans' glasses, which he now placed back on his eyes. I understood that he was signaling me that 'our time,' which he never called 'our session,' was over. I stood to leave and then plopped back down.

'I know my time is up, but I need to tell you something else,' I said. I saw him look out of the corner of his eyes at the teeny clock. We both knew about the ten-minute intervals therapists schedule between patients.

'Go on,' he said, nodding at me, but letting me know I'd better spit it out quick as he turned his head toward the clock.

'I've been seeing another therapist, one of Daniel's colleagues. Daniel made me. He thinks I need medication. I don't and I haven't been taking it and I won't ever see her again,' I said, now determined to fire Kayla. While lying to her had tickled my inner rogue, not being candid with Dr Evans had weighed on my good-girl side.

'You understand, we'll need to talk more about this during our next conversation, don't you? Olivia, do you feel safe?' Dr Evans asked.

I knew it was a standard question therapists are urged to ask patients if there is any suggestion to the contrary, but it startled me. I considered his question and wondered what Dr Evans was concerned about. I hadn't even told him about my experiences in the rotary or at Thompson House. I couldn't go there.

'Yes,' I said, letting him decide which question I was responding to.

'You also must terminate your other therapist if we are to continue working together. There are ethical rules about these things.' I had never heard Dr Evans sound so somber.

'I know. I'm studying ethics. I'm taking the ethics bar soon. She's history. I promise,' I said. I sprung out of my chair, nearly running out of the room into the entry hall and out the door before Dr Evans had a chance to reconsider keeping me as a client.

I raced down the rickety wooden porch steps on to the brick walkway moist with fallen leaves and a final crop of summer weeds. Turning on to the sidewalk, I almost slammed into what I supposed was Dr Evans' next patient, embarrassed I had taken the extra time that protected our respective anonymity. The slim man in a baseball cap turned away just in time to let me by without colliding into him.

SEVEN

was so exhausted when I pulled into our driveway, I was tempted to leave the plants in the car, but I couldn't. The temperature had dropped and several were tropical. Although my mother often said the garden was forgiving, she also reminded me more than once not to press my luck. I started carrying plants toward the back door where Daniel greeted me. He stood in the muted light of the onion lamps, looking rested and boyishly handsome in his tee shirt, jeans, and socks without shoes.

'Let me come help you,' he offered, taking the first box from me.

'There are only two others,' I said. 'I'll hand them to you.' I pushed the box with the scarf and gloves under the passenger seat on the floor. There was no need to bring them in and risk Daniel's discovery of Mom's stash of little white pills. I would verify they were Xanax in his PDR when he wasn't around.

Inside the kitchen, I could see Daniel had been busy prepping for chicken salad. He had culled the meat from the roast chicken I had made on Sunday. Chopped celery and fresh tarragon waited in small pinch bowls for me to combine. This was the extent of Daniel's culinary skills. But since I enjoyed cooking, having my own sous chef worked. I was touched that he knew to maintain some semblance of routine amid tragedy.

He must have seen me glancing toward the glass of white wine sitting next to the ingredients.

'Can I pour you one?' he asked.

'Please,' I said, washing the dirt that had fallen out of the planters from my hands.

'How are you doing, Olivia?' Daniel sounded more clinical than Dr Evans ever had. I wondered how that boded for his future as a psychiatrist. He might do better in research or academia. But at the same time, I appreciated his effort at tenderness.

'I'm OK, a little tired, but I'm good.'

'I want you to see Kayla tomorrow. She's got some time early in the afternoon before you have to be at school, if you're planning to go to school. Even though we both knew Claire wasn't well, I don't think either of us expected her to go so quickly or so soon. You may need your meds tweaked.' Daniel took a tiny piece of celery and popped it in his mouth.

I took a sip of the Sauvignon Blanc he had poured me before responding. Before telling him, I would see her gladly because I was firing Dr Steel Heart.

'Oh, and Josh called. He wants us to come for dinner next Sunday night. Kayla's rotation at McLean will be over and I'm off.'

'Sunday? I don't know, Daniel. It's so soon. I could make us roast chicken or grill some steaks, if you'd prefer. If you're off, I'd like to stay home. Just the two of us,' I said. I've been making roast chicken on most Sundays ever since I was a teenager and discovered I was a better cook than my mother. I was newer to the grill, but not bad at it. I found cooking therapeutic.

'It's a special meal for you. He wants you to call him so you can select the menu,' Daniel said.

'I'm not feeling up to that right now,' I said. I felt ready to scream or walk out. I was spent. As sweet as it was for Josh to offer to make dinner for me, for us all, tonight was not the night to be choosing a menu.

'Of course, I understand. I'll have him text you.'

I suppressed a groan and chugged down the rest of my wine. I handed Daniel my empty glass and assembled chicken tarragon salad on a bed of arugula surrounded by avocado slices. We sat at the kitchen island where I lit a single pillar candle.

I hadn't taken my second bite before Daniel picked up his phone and read a message from Josh saying that he had texted me, but I could reply at my leisure. I chewed and nodded, saying nothing. Daniel reached for my phone and handed it to me.

I put it down next to my wine glass and speared an avocado slice on to my fork.

'Aren't you going to answer him?'

I almost said, 'Are you kidding me?' but I couldn't find the energy.

I looked at the screen. Josh was sorry about my mother. Could he cook me my favorite comfort meal on Sunday? He was so sweet, I couldn't help but respond, which meant I didn't have to listen to

Daniel. *Chicken or meatloaf?* Meatloaf. *With gravy or draped in bacon?* Bacon. *Mashed or baked potatoes?* Baked. *Sour cream and chives or butter?* All of the above.

When dinner was done, I loaded the dishwasher and turned it on. 'I'm going to bed,' I said.

'OK, I'll turn off the lights down here and be on my way,' Daniel said. He moved toward the switch to the indirect lights above the counter.

'Be on your way? Where are you going?' I asked.

'Back to Belmont.'

'Aren't you on the seventy-two-hour bereavement leave you told me they give you when there's a death in the family?' I asked. We had several discussions about 'what if' and 'when something happens' when Mom went to Thompson House.

'No, I saved it for when we go to Vermont for the memorial service, so I'll have some time to catch up with my old colleagues.'

'Seriously?' I asked, wondering if I had inherited my father's murderous tendencies. 'You're going to leave me alone the night after my mother dies so you can use bereavement time to be with your buddies? Nice.' I rarely challenged Daniel, but I had never been this raw before.

'Wait a minute, are you complaining about me spending a few hours with some friends? Me, the guy who has no time off? You, the girl who goes out with her drinking buddies every night after class?' Daniel raised his voice for the first time since our argument about whether my mother was no longer safe living outside of an institution. He didn't get this exercised when we debated about having children.

I refilled my wine glass to the top and took a long sip.

'You don't know what you're talking about. You're going to abandon me tonight so you can see a couple of guys you have barely talked to during the past three years. They're what you call acquaintances, Daniel, not friends,' I said. I was glad the windows were closed because I was screaming louder than I had during the debate about Mom entering Thompson House.

Daniel looked at me with disdain. He set his wine glass in the sink.

'How would you know what real friends are, Olivia? You've lived your whole life in a petri dish in your mother's lab.'

'You bastard,' I said, flinging the wine from my glass into his face. I could see he was shocked. So was I.

'Daniel, they are not my "law school drinking buddies." They are my friends from law school, members of my study group. And they care about me. This morning they sent a beautiful triple moth orchid from Winston's. Come see,' I said, choking on sobs. I walked toward the glass door that opened into the conservatory. Daniel stayed planted by the kitchen sink, wiping his face on a fresh dishtowel.

'Come, Daniel. I want you to see how lovely it is. I happen to know how much they cost. This is a gift dear friends would send, not "casual drinking buddies."' My sobs turned to hiccups.

Daniel followed me into the conservatory, which was dimly lit with grow lights scattered to illuminate plants in need of constant light. I hit the dimmer to light the room, ready to proudly point out the magnificent orchid.

It was gone.

The giant jade we'd had for decades was still on the table by the wicker chairs. But the triple moth orchid I had placed next to it was nowhere to be seen.

'Where is it?' I demanded out loud. I walked around the center of the room where the wicker furniture sat. I looked between the chairs, under the table, and then reconnoitered the entire room. Daniel stood still, barely inside the conservatory, observing me.

'It was here. It was here, Daniel. Did you move it?' I didn't try to hide the accusatory tone in my voice. I had lost control of the volume button.

'Liv, you can't be serious. Listen to yourself,' Daniel said, fully in charge of his own remote control. The more reasoned he sounded, the more hysterical I became.

'Well, you've been home all day. What became of it?'

'You didn't tuck it in a bathtub of water to soak it, did you?' he asked. More than once he'd had to ask me to remove dry, dying plants from the shower where I had tried to revive them.

'Of course not. It arrived right before I had to leave to pack up Mom's room. It was in perfect condition. Winston's would never deliver anything but,' I said, no longer crying as my eyes swept the conservatory jammed with plants of all kind. But few had white flowers and none were the moth gypsy.

'Liv, did you take your meds today? Maybe I should call Kayla and see if she wants me to give you something stronger. You're unraveling.' Daniel moved closer to me.

'No, I don't need more. Of course I took my medication,' I said, sinking into the wicker chair. I had witnessed Daniel's zero tolerance when a family member unraveled before. Mom had been sentenced to Thompson House without a second chance after her morning jaunt. I knew I had to get a grip or my future would include Kayla and medication I didn't want and didn't need.

'Maybe you dreamed you got the plant. You've had a huge shock, losing your mother. People have strange dreams when they're under stress.' Daniel took both of my hands in his and gently pulled me up from the chair into his arms.

'No. I didn't dream it,' I mumbled into his tee shirt wet with the wine I'd thrown. He felt warm as he rubbed my back, soothing me. He smelled like shea butter soap and tea tree shampoo all at once, reminding me of endless embraces we shared as I clung to him when my mother first began her mental descent. I closed my eyes, taking in the scent of him and steeling myself to do what I knew I must.

Lie.

'Go to work, Daniel. What I need is sleep. I didn't sleep at all last night and I'm afraid the fatigue has gotten to me.'

I stepped back and looked into his frowning brown eyes. 'I just need sleep. I'm going to bed. I'll be fine. I'll call you in the morning,' I said, moving toward the light switch, waiting for him to follow me to the kitchen.

'I didn't mean to raise my voice,' Daniel said. He stepped back into the coliseum that had once been our kitchen.

'I know you didn't,' I said. I handed him his backpack from the kitchen island. 'I didn't either. These are tough times.'

Daniel reached for a fresh tee shirt out of the backpack. I took the wet one from him as he put on the dry one. He reached for his backpack, then placed it on the counter, before sweeping me into his arms again.

'You know how much I love you, Liv, don't you?' His whispered words tickled my ears.

'Yes, Daniel, I do.' And I did. He was all that I had left.

EIGHT

Wednesday, October 15th

I was awake but my eyes remained glued shut with the goo that comes from a full day of crying. When I opened them, I was shocked to see I had slept until 10:30, something I had not done since I was in college. I leaped out of bed, concerned I wouldn't have time to visit Mom and read my assignments before class when I remembered.

My mother was dead.

I collapsed back on to the bed and turned over to view Daniel's empty side, still perfectly made. I never roll over on to his territory unless he is there.

No Daniel. No Mom. I considered having what Mom and I called a 'pajama day,' when you lounge around in jammies, binging on snacks, marathon movies, and trashy novels. Then I remembered Daniel had made an appointment with Kayla for me, which I needed to keep.

I indulged in a long, hot shower, smelling the lavender soap and at the end letting cold water pelt against my eyes and sinuses. I hadn't dared to look in the mirror but I could feel my face was swollen. I wanted to look good when I met Kayla, which I hoped would boost my confidence. I remembered Mom's advice to always dress for the role.

Jeans were out of the question, dirty after my fall on to the leaves and not serious enough. I was a young professional woman meeting another. I chose gray slacks, a crisp white blouse, and black jacket, but I couldn't face wearing heels after my tumble on the sidewalk. Black leather ballet flats would have to do.

My unruly hair would have to be tamed for my mission. I pulled the hair blower out from a drawer in the bathroom vanity where it had been sitting unused for the entire summer. Most days, I can't be bothered with the tedium of standing, straining my hair over a round brush, waiting for the blower to create a sleek, smooth look.

Today was different. I might no longer have a mother to guide and bolster me, but I knew to heed her advice to look confident even if I felt insecure. I was determined to learn about my family. That meant firing Kayla so I could continue to see Dr Evans and talk to Ryan Fairclough.

I did my best with my face, applying a little concealer and blush, which is more than I often use. Mascara brightened my blue eyes. High-gloss berry lipstick was the finishing touch. I was about to go downstairs when I remembered I had no jewelry on. I grabbed Mom's prized pearls out of my jewelry box and put them on. As an afterthought, I added dangling silver hoop earrings for a playful touch and set off for the kitchen.

Daniel had sent me a text during the night, reminding me my appointment was at 12:30. I had time for a cup of coffee and some toast. I made a K-cup and found the end of the loaf of ciabatta that Daniel and I had bought over the weekend. It had already gone stale and moldy. I had no appetite anyway.

I transferred my Constitutional Law textbook from my battered backpack into a buttery British tan leather tote Daniel had given me last year for Christmas. I suspected Kayla had helped him choose it because she had the same bag in black. Both were from Levenger. I had been saving it for my first days in a courtroom, but reconsidered. Today was the day for its debut.

I looked professional and was committed to my mission, yet I vacillated about my decision to fire Kayla. While I hadn't skinned my knees when I fell, they were swollen and sore. My head throbbed and my eyes stung. My stomach churned but I was hungry. I had just lost my mother. Maybe it wasn't a good day to confront Kayla. I considered postponing my appointment with her for a day when I was more on my game, but I knew delaying firing her would only make it harder.

I cut myself a little slack and chose to drive to Kayla's office on Longwood Ave via Huntington Ave, which was a shorter distance but one with more traffic. There would be less chance of encountering crazy drivers on a congested route where the cars are bumper to bumper. My anxiety about firing Kayla mounted as the time for my appointment drew nearer. I didn't need to encounter another wacky Massachusetts driver on my way.

I practiced what I would say as I drove next to the trolley tracks, passing people walking on sidewalks under umbrellas as the mist turned to a downpour. 'Kayla, I've considered this very carefully and I believe it's best if we terminate our professional relationship.' No, that sounded overly formal. I was invited to this woman's home on Sunday for a dinner her husband had planned just for me. My dress rehearsal was interrupted by the music from my phone. John Miller's voice crooned through my Bluetooth. 'Good morning, Olivia. How are you doing, dear?' he asked. He sounded like he would really like to know, but I spared him the details.

'When we set the date for your mother's memorial, I totally forgot it was homecoming weekend. We can move it up to this weekend if you'd like. I'm sure you'd like the service sooner rather than later. I called Sam Turner, a former colleague, who's Chief Medical Examiner in Massachusetts, to see if he could expedite Claire's release. He's happy to help,' John said.

'Oh yes, please. Let's move it up and not wait. I'm having trouble believing Mom is gone. The memorial should help,' I said. As soon as I hung up, I left a voicemail for Daniel with the new date, hoping he could get the time off. I experienced an odd sense of relief knowing Mom's service was this weekend and that I would soon be rid of Kayla as my therapist.

The parking garage where I always parked was almost full. I had to park on the level next to the top and nowhere near the elevator. Ever since the assaults on the women in the garage next to the law school, I made it my practice to get a space as close to the elevator as I could. I dashed from my car to the elevator without seeing anyone. I was happy to see the elevator empty and rode straight to the ground level. I rushed through a steady rainfall down the sidewalk past the world-renowned Children's Hospital toward the medical building where Kayla and Daniel and other burgeoning therapists rented space as they began their individual practices. I had forgotten to transfer my umbrella from my backpack to the leather tote that was now spotted with raindrops.

I headed directly for Kayla's office, not bothering to see what had happened to my previously smooth hairdo. Curls were already coiling around my face. I knew it didn't really matter what my hair looked like.

I had to wait for fifteen minutes, which made me angry. My time was just as important as Kayla's. I never waited for Dr Evans. I made a mental note to remember when I practiced law how disrespectful it felt to have a professional make you sit and wait.

Kayla looked her usual gorgeous self when she greeted me wearing a cream-colored pencil skirt with a thin black leather belt and a black boatneck sweater with three-quarter-length sleeves. She was so effortlessly chic, I wanted to topple her off her three-inch almond-toe black heels. Kayla towered over me in my frumpy wet flats that squished as she led me down a hall to a small antiseptic room with two chairs, a pole lamp, and a limp ficus tree. We took our usual seats.

'I am very sorry about Claire,' Kayla began.

'Thank you. It was so sudden,' I said.

'But not totally unexpected,' she said, crossing one leg over the other.

'Well, it was for me. She had been physically healthy.' If she told me my mother 'had a good run' next I wasn't sure what I would do.

'I suppose you'll find yourself with a lot of time on your hands now,' Kayla said.

'Law school keeps me pretty busy,' I said.

'And I'm sure you'll have a lot of things to do, winding down your mother's affairs. Did she leave everything in trust or will you have to contend with probate?'

'My mother was very thorough about her personal business,' I said. Kayla's inquiries were odd for a shrink. I thought she was supposed to be asking me how I felt.

'Well that's good. But if the title to your home is still in her name, that might get complicated, couldn't it?'

I wondered how Kayla knew my mother was on the title of the house with me and not Daniel. He must have confided in her. I tried to keep my cool by concentrating on the small beauty mark right above her lip, wondering how it would feel to peel it off.

'Look, the title to the house was in both of our names, but since we held it in joint tenancy, the title is automatically vested in me upon my mother's death,' I said. I sounded like my law professor in Property. I didn't appreciate Kayla's line of questions.

'And I'm sure she had life insurance,' Kayla said, prodding for more information. That was enough.

'What's this all about?' I said, sounding irritated even to my own ears.

She paused, doing that shrink 'sitting with the silence' thing. It's supposed to make the client uncomfortable enough to break it with a revelation. I know about it. I'm married to a shrink. I was insulted Kayla underestimated my intelligence.

'Olivia, I just want to be sure you're prepared for the challenges you may face after losing your mother. It's not just grief you will have to contend with. I'm only trying to ground and guide you.' She leaned forward to emphasize her concern. I wanted to puke.

'I just lost my mother, Kayla. I can't get past that yet and I don't think I should. I'm just beginning to grieve,' I said.

'Of course, and how are you doing with that? Do you have any support beyond Daniel?' Kayla asked.

The bitch. She knew my mother was my only living relative and that my circle of friends had been limited by her illness.

'I have terrific friends at school.' I described Erin coming to help clear out Mom's room and the gorgeous orchid that had arrived from Winston's.

'And has Daniel been able to comfort you?' she asked, almost as a casual afterthought.

'Oh, yes. Daniel has been so wonderful and, of course, he can comfort me in a way no one else can,' I said. I waited to see how she would react. I wanted her to at least flinch at the suggestion of any intimacy I shared with Daniel. But Kayla has a shrink's poker face and moved on.

'I think we should up your medication dose for a while, Olivia. Until some of the strain from your loss has dissipated.'

Bingo. My opening.

'Actually, Kayla, I've given a lot of thought to my treatment with you and I think it's best if we terminate therapy,' I said. I sounded more firm and confident than I felt.

She winced – ever so slightly, but she winced.

'Oh, Olivia, this is not the time to quit therapy—'

'Maybe not, but I'm concerned about the questionable ethical implications of being treated by my husband's professional colleague. Have you considered how it might appear? I wouldn't want to engage in a physician/patient relationship that might compromise anyone's professional standards. I'm just about to take the Ethics bar myself,' I said with just a hint of a smile on my mouth. She was clearly ambushed and anguished by my decision.

'Well, I've only treated you at Daniel's request as a professional courtesy,' she said, tugging her skirt toward her knees.

'Of course, and I appreciate it. We'll continue to see each other socially, right? Josh is making dinner for us Sunday. He is so sweet. You're a very lucky woman,' I said, rising, bringing our session to a close far before the fifty-minute allocation was reached.

Kayla stood, pursing her lips, but saying nothing more.

When I got to the door, I remembered one more thing I needed to confide with Kayla.

'Kayla, I know we share a patient/physician privilege, and you would never tell Daniel anything I said in our sessions, but I want to be certain you understand. I'm sure you know the HIPAA laws better than I do. Nothing I've said to you today about why I am terminating our professional relationship can be shared with Daniel, right? The next time he tries to set up an appointment for me or wants to talk about my medication, you can just tell him you can't discuss privileged information with him. You know, client confidentiality, HIPAA, and all. Got it?' I smiled.

She nodded and sat back down on her chair as she glared at me with contempt.

NINE

Once I left Kayla's office suite, I made a bee-line to the elevator. I felt a little unnerved by what I had done. Not only had I fired Kayla, but I also sent a message to Daniel that I was establishing some new boundaries in our relationship. Up until now, I had been so afraid of losing him, I let him control our lives rather than risk displeasing him. And it was a bit of a test. I had wondered how much Daniel and Kayla discussed my treatment. I had hoped they were respectful of my privacy, but I had my doubts.

I would have expected my mother's death to make me more insecure, but in an unanticipated way, it had liberated me. There was no longer anyone to warn me that our very lives were at stake if I asked too many questions or attracted too much attention. I wouldn't hear why I should never hike alone in the woods or enter a contest in case I might win. We had lived in the shadow of fear since we fled to Vermont. I was tired of the fear. I was tired of the unknown. And I was tired of not knowing who I really was.

I believed Daniel loved me, but I worried he might stop if I didn't need the nurturing and direction he provided. I sensed he enjoyed my dependency on him. Sitting across from Kayla in that tiny room had allowed me to admit for the first time another fear I had denied until now. I worried that Daniel was in love with Kayla and suspected they might be having an affair. I hoped his puppy-dog devotion was simply a professional crush, but even my mother had misgivings about their relationship and she had been the queen of hyper-vigilance.

I entered the elevator and rode down the eleven floors, wondering if Kayla had already called Daniel to report that I had terminated therapy with her. My guess was that she hadn't, but it was out of my hands. I would head off to school, do my reading, and find my study group to say thank you.

The rain had lightened to a drizzle by the time I reached the parking garage elevator. I got in, relieved to have the elevator to myself again, and hit the button. No one appeared to be on the floor where I had parked when I got off, but still I stepped up my pace and strode toward my car.

I knew immediately something was wrong. My Mini is close enough to the ground under normal circumstances, but with four flat tires, it looked more like a child's pedal car. I stopped and took the sight in. I couldn't imagine who could have done this or why. I was being punished. I shouldn't have been so brash with Kayla. It had been a mistake to challenge Daniel through her. I was hopeless without my mother. Anybody could just slash my tires and stop me in my tracks. Things like this didn't happen to other people. I was pathetic.

I took a deep breath into my lungs, sending it further into my abdomen like I had learned in a yoga class. I kept thinking, 'Breathe, Olivia, breathe,' and I did, restoring my equanimity. I reached for my cell phone, but thought better of it. I had been parked for less than an hour. I shouldn't hang around when my tires were recently slashed. The culprit who had done this could still be nearby.

This time I sprinted to the elevator, which was fortunately still at my level. I pushed G for ground and hoped it went straight down. I held my breath until the doors opened and hurried over to the booth where you pay as you exit.

'Excuse me,' I said, banging on the window of the booth. I startled the woman, who scowled at me looking up from the screen on her phone. I could see she was playing some kind of game.

'What?'

'Someone's slashed my tires on the top floor,' I said, sure I'd get her attention.

'You got Triple A?' she asked, sounding bored.

'What about the police?' I asked.

'What about them?'

'Shouldn't you call them? I mean, it's vandalism. It happened on your property. Aren't you concerned?' I was getting as angry with this woman as I was with the person who had vandalized my car. She leaned forward in her seat and pointed to the right and upward with her index finger, which sported long black fingernails. Nice.

I looked up in the direction where she gestured. 'We are not responsible for any property damage which may occur in this facility. Park at your own risk.'

I walked back into the lobby where the elevator was located and called Triple A. The response time would be two hours and even then, the person on the telephone couldn't assure me how quickly the tires could be repaired, or if they could be repaired. She asked if I wanted them just to tow the car to my local garage. You bet I did.

TEN

I took a cab to law school, totally spent. I was famished and ready to eat something, but felt nauseated at the thought of food. I bought some cheese and peanut butter crackers out of a vending machine and treated myself to a real Coke. I tucked both into my bag to sneak into the law library where food and drink are verboten. Once at my favorite table in the back corner of the library, I put my head on my arms on the table and closed my eyes.

'Olivia?'

I looked up to see Erin standing in front of me.

'I didn't expect you to come to school tonight,' she said.

'I had to do something. I'm having trouble realizing she's gone,' I said.

'I'm sure. It takes a while to sink in. We're meeting after class at Behan's to divvy up the MPRE assignments. I thought we'd each take a part of yours. Do you feel up to coming?' Erin asked. She was wearing a gray sweatshirt that said 'Portia Proud' on the front, which referred to the fact that our lower tier law school claimed at least one notable distinction. Portia was the first law school in the country established exclusively for women in 1908. It was one of the reasons I had chosen it over others. Men were not admitted until 1938.

'Yes, but I'll need a ride. My car is in the garage.' I didn't have the energy to explain why.

At Behan's with a Guinness in front of me, I explained to the group that my car had been vandalized. The garage had called while my phone was off during class and left a message that the tires could not be repaired because the sidewalls had been punctured, not slashed. All four tires had to be replaced. I ranted about the parking lot attendant's indifference to my plight.

'That's really shitty. The bastard didn't mean to just inconvenience you. He wanted you to have to buy new tires. Parking garages are supposed to call us when stuff like that happens. You should have called me. You have my number, don't you?' Ryan asked.

'Yes, but forgive me, you weren't exactly helpful the last time you were summoned to my door,' I said. I wasn't sure why I was calling him to task again, especially after he had been so kind to me at the emergency room. Maybe I didn't want him to think that one bear hug could undo the irreversible harm he had caused my mother. Or perhaps I was uncomfortable at the memory of how safe it felt to be held by him. I couldn't erase the memory of the scent of his leather jacket.

'Does someone have a beef with you?' Ryan asked, ignoring my barb. It hadn't occurred to me that the vandalism might be directed toward me for a motive. I had assumed I was a random target.

'No, I don't think so. At least, not that I know of.'

'Well, you should still be careful.' I appreciated his concern but my life was so antiseptic, it was hard to get too worried. I didn't have any old lovers or cranky neighbors who might enjoy slicing up my little car.

'Liv, you should consider signing up for one of the legal clinics now that you've got the time. There's an opening in the family law clinic Professor Cohen mentioned in class the other night when you were absent,' Erin said, leaning across the table and raising her voice over the sound of 'The Black Velvet Band' being sung by an Irish crooner. I knew she was trying to direct me to more positive thoughts.

Clinics offer law students the opportunity for practical experience in courts, government agencies, and private law firms as part of their curriculum. I hadn't signed up for a clinic even though I hungered to taste what it was like to be in a courtroom. Clinics were scheduled during the day when I had to take care of my mother. Part of me had resented the limitation on my legal education, the other half had been grateful for the excuse. I wasn't sure after a lifetime of being programmed to avoid attention I was ready to be front and center in a courtroom.

'Unless you've got all of that estate stuff to do with your sibs, like empty your mother's house and look for life insurance policies. My dad died without a will. My brothers and sister and I couldn't agree on anything. Two of them wanted to buy his house. It held things up for two years,' Andrew said, chugging the last sip of his Black and Tan.

I shook my head.

'I'm an only child. Do you all come from big families?' I asked. Large clans had fascinated me since I was a child living alone with my mother. I was curious about what it was like to have brothers and sisters to play with, to fight with. I dreamed about how it felt to share a huge Thanksgiving meal with aunts and uncles and cousins. I pictured Christmas morning wild and crazy with giftwrap and ribbons flying everywhere while kids tore open presents as their exhausted parents watched on.

'I have three older sisters, who all like to boss me around. A lot of good that did. None of them were able to talk me out of marrying the woman who just divorced me. I mean, just because we broke up on a monthly basis right up until the wedding, how was I to know?' Ryan said with a cryptic laugh.

'I'm sorry,' I said and I was. I knew I had judged him more harshly than he deserved and that my anger was misplaced. It was just that I had tried desperately to delay residential placement for my mother. I had known it would be the beginning of the end for her.

'I've got three little brothers, all back in Puerto Rico where my grandmother is trying to raise them. Thank God, she's a pistol and has four sons ready to get in their faces if necessary,' Erin said.

And there I was. The orphan. The family law clinic was beginning to sound good. I would have time on my hands without my mother to fill the hours before I was due at class. I no longer had an excuse to avoid immersing myself in the new profession I had chosen even though Daniel had disapproved of it.

'Liv, you love being a librarian. You were made for the job,' he'd said the night I told him I had decided not to pursue an advanced degree in library science at Simmons University only ten minutes from our house, as Daniel had expected.

My decision had been influenced in part by what he said to me the day he met me, when I was summoned to the UVM medical school after my mother had one of her early 'spells.' She had experienced something like a panic attack while searching for documents in a file room. Disoriented and terrified, Mom had become agitated when the staff tried to calm her down. A professor, who was also a medical doctor, had telephoned to summon me.

When I arrived, I found my mother sitting talking to an earnest-looking young man wearing a lab coat and the most absurd red bow tie with polka dots. I have a weakness for polka dots. He introduced himself as a third-year medical student and offered to walk us to my car. I wasn't as surprised as I pretended to be about my mother's confusion and her insistence that Daniel was a cab driver. I had been trying to ignore small but growing signs that her cognitive functioning was impaired.

I accepted Daniel's offer to play cab driver and drive us home. Once Mom had settled down for a nap, I brewed coffee for Daniel and me. I listened to him talk about his experiences at medical school and how he was looking forward to his psychiatric residency, which he hoped would be in Boston. He probed gently about Mom's condition, but offered no diagnosis. Instead, he turned the questioning to me and asked what I did for a living.

'I'm a reference librarian at the college,' I said.

'Of course you are,' he said, making me wish I had been able to say I was a tattoo artist or cyber spy. Anything that didn't make me sound ancient, boring, and predictable. I was too shy to tell him I had always dreamed of being a lawyer. Not a patent attorney or a bank lawyer, but a litigator, who spent her days in the open fray of a courtroom.

He had surprised me by asking if he could see me again. Six months later, he proposed. Now he thought I was as loony as my mother had been, fantasizing about plants that didn't exist. I knew the moth orchid existed, I just didn't know where had it gone. I didn't remember placing it somewhere. Maybe I should be taking the medication Kayla had prescribed for me after all.

'Do you think I should really sign up for a clinic?' I asked Erin as she wove around the dark streets of Jamaica Plain taking me home.

'It's a great practical experience, Liv, and you've got the time now. Plus, well, you need to get out a little more,' Erin said, keeping her eyes on the road, not looking at me.

'Erin, do you think I'm unstable?' I hadn't known I was going to ask her that until it slipped off my tongue.

'No, of course not,' she said. 'Why would you even ask that?'

'Come inside,' I said as she pulled into the empty driveway. 'I'll make you a drink while I try to explain.'

I went to turn off the alarm when I realized the lights weren't on. I had forgotten to set it once again, which drives Daniel crazy.

Erin followed me through the door, into the back hall and then into the oversized kitchen. I had spent copious amounts of time and money modernizing it while struggling to retain the original Victorian flavor. Erin gasped.

'You do know that people would kill for this kitchen,' she said as I walked into the pantry to fetch a bottle of Grey Goose, Erin's favorite. I had stocked it months before, thinking I should invite her over. But this was her first visit to my home. Way overdue.

'My kitchen is smaller than your pantry,' she said, as her eyes continued along the counters, over to the antique desk I had placed in the corner where I studied. I would have loved to reclaim the library off the living room, which had been my mother's suite before she moved to Thompson House, but Daniel had seized it before I had a chance.

Erin took the bottle from me, competent bartender that she is. I handed her glasses and ice and a lemon.

'Do you happen to have any fresh basil in this fancy-ass kitchen?'

I reached into the Sub-Zero refrigerator which I knew contained basil and tarragon and handed a bunch of basil to Erin. The financial gulf that separated our lives made me feel awkward about asking, but I had to.

'Erin, you guys did send me a plant from Winston's, right?' I took a sip of the slippery vodka she handed me. I was amazed how a little lemon and a few herbal leaves could make it taste so much like lemonade.

'Of course we did. You already thanked me. No need to say more,' she said, sliding on to a stool next to me.

'But I can't find it. Daniel thinks I'm crazy. Come. See if you find it anywhere,' I said, taking her pudgy hand still cold from handling the ice.

I steered her toward the conservatory, flipping on the switch.

'Sweet Jesus, Liv,' Erin said. She stepped into the room with hesitation, her eyes bulging at the sight of the plants I saw every day and took for granted. I tugged her toward me and walked her in front of the wicker chairs and the table with the ancient jade plant where I had added the baby jade from my mother's room. I explained what had happened, expecting her to roll her eyes and tell me I was crazy.

Instead, Erin began a slow, deliberate tour of the room, stopping every few steps, tilting her head, taking it all in. I noticed her inhaling the fragrance when she sauntered past the few flowering plants left. On her second round, she stopped in front of a large calming peace lily with showy white blossoms, which was overgrown and should have been transplanted months ago. With Mom gone, I would now have the time to tend properly to the plants. The irony would make her chuckle.

Erin bent over and began moving the drooping branches of the lily. She pulled at something that made a scraping sound on the gravel. She stood up, holding the moth orchid in front of her like a joyful bride about to walk down the aisle.

I gasped.

'It was tucked in and under that other big guy,' Erin said, wearing a big grin like she'd won a scavenger hunt. 'Someone hid it. It didn't just get there by itself, Liv.'

She handed me the moth orchid, one of its leaves limping, but the white flowers were intact. I took it from her and placed it on the table between the two jades.

'You don't think I'm crazy?' I asked, afraid Erin would change her mind.

'No. I think someone's screwing with your head. Moving a plant around isn't exactly threatening, but it sure is strange. You need to be careful, Liv.'

ELEVEN

Before she left, Erin insisted on checking the entire house to be sure I was safe. Between her oohs and ahs over the grandeur of the house, she assured me again that the moth orchid had been cleverly placed under the lily, so that its white flowers were hidden. If she hadn't been looking for the orchid, Erin insisted she never would have spotted it.

I put the alarm on as soon as the door closed behind her and went to see if Daniel had texted me. I missed him most late at night. When he was home with me I didn't worry about being alone, something I had feared since I was a child. Being an only child is one thing, but when you have only one parent and no extended family, you become acutely aware that parent is your lifeline. The umbilical cord is never severed. Just reading next to Daniel in bed, the warmth of his thigh against mine, was comforting. I knew I didn't show my appreciation for him enough and was beginning to blame him for everything. I was becoming a cliché.

Above the text I found from Daniel was one marked 'URGENT.' What could possibly be more urgent than the sudden death of your mother, I wondered, thinking some liberal ultra-left organization wanted more money from me. Daniel jokes that my Vermont upbringing made me overly vulnerable to pleas to save the environment and democracy. But my mother instilled a deep commitment in me to support the causes I believed in.

But it wasn't from any organization. It was from John Miller, telling me to call him regardless of the hour. I tapped 'call now.'

He picked up on the first ring.

'I'm not saying this is true, Olivia, but I wanted you to hear it from me,' John said, his voice tender but stern.

'Go on,' I said. I couldn't imagine what he was going to say.

'I talked with Sam Turner a while ago. He's the Massachusetts Chief Medical Examiner I told you about earlier; he's a colleague of mine. He called to tell me the autopsy report on your mother says Claire's death was suspicious and that the toxicology report would confirm the presence of alcohol and medication. Liv, "suspicious" in this instance is code for suicide.'

'Suicide? My mother? Suicide? That's ridiculous. John, you know she would never, ever take her own life.' I realized I was screaming at him, the blood rushing through to my head, which was throbbing.

'I know, Liv, I know. But I wanted you to hear it from me. Your mother is the last person I would expect to kill herself. But I have to ask you, since I haven't talked to her since she left Vermont, how much did the Alzheimer's change her? Could she have become desperate about the deterioration of her mind or in a moment of lucidity decide it was better this way?' John asked.

I pictured tears coming down his face. He had loved my mother as much as I did, which hadn't been easy for either of them. While Vermont may be tolerant, the relationship between a tenured African American, married professor and dean with a feisty, single white woman with a child had tested some friends and faculty. Mom had been defiant in her devotion to John, whose wife had left Vermont long ago to teach at Dartmouth.

'No one will ever tell me again who I can love,' I'd heard her say to a friend during a telephone conversation that ended with Mom slamming the phone down. I had been in my teens, already rabid with curiosity about the family history.

'Who tried to tell you who to love before, Mom?' I asked. But she went silent on me.

'John, my mother would never commit suicide. She still had hope for a cure. She talked to people at Thompson about research being done. And you know how she felt about suicide. She viewed it as cowardly,' I said. An urgency to defend my mother surged within me.

'I know. I remember her reaction when we would hear about a celebrity suicide. She would be angry about the way it affected loved ones, especially the children. I'd try to persuade her it wasn't a matter of choice for some people, but this is where that joke about her seeing things as black or white began.' He chuckled softly.

'No, your mother didn't commit suicide. I know that. But was she drinking and taking meds? It sounds like she had a lot of both in her according to Sam. He spoke directly to the pathologist who performed the autopsy.'

I hesitated. I trusted John Miller as much as I trusted any human being on earth. I just wasn't sure if sharing information about finding the medication my mother hadn't taken or even that I'd found a Dunkin' Donuts drink container in her room the night she died was a good idea. I needed time to absorb and distill so much information.

We ended the conversation by agreeing to talk again on Friday. For now, we would deal with plans for Mom's service. Her body had been released to a local funeral home that would transport her on the long ride home to Vermont. Except it wasn't home. Only my mother knew where that was.

TWELVE

I woke up angry. Angry that my mother was dead. Angry that her death was being labeled a suicide. And furious there was nothing I could do about either.

I hated feeling helpless. I swung my legs over the side of the bed and stood up, looking out the window at the gardens below. When we bought the house, they were in a state of neglect, although my mother knew at first sight they once had been grand. We worked side-by-side pulling weeds, trimming shrubs, and adding nutrients to the soil for months. We planted bulbs and perennials, herbs and succulents. Occasionally I had to remind Mom about what she was supposed to be doing, but in the garden she retained more of who she had been than in any other setting.

I showered, jumped into jeans and a sweater, and headed to Thompson House where I knew I had an ally. Terry Walsh had taken to my mother. She had the same tenacity and candor that had been Mom's hallmark. While I cursed and resented my mother's refusal to share information about my father and extended family, I admired that she didn't make up some saccharine story about him being a dead war hero. Although that might have been easier for us both.

Terry was another woman who didn't bullshit you. Her frankness could feel a little brutal, just as Mom's had, which is probably why they hit it off. Terry would tell me like it was. The only way I could reconcile my mother killing herself was by accepting her disease had distorted her nature. Otherwise, she had been a victim, which meant someone had orchestrated her death.

I sat waiting in the central sunroom, which connected the new wing from the original part of the house where my mother lived, while Terry dispensed her morning round of medications to patients. The room had hardwood floors with oriental rugs strategically scattered and glued down so they wouldn't catch a walker or wheelchair. The reproductions hanging on the wall were all classics.

You might be fooled into thinking you were at the Isabella Stewart Gardner Museum just a few miles down the road if it weren't for folks wandering around with empty expressions looking lost. Many were elderly, but enough were middle-aged to frighten me about my prospects for inheriting dementia.

Terry beckoned me to follow her. I was surprised when she led me into my mother's room, now unoccupied and sterile.

'I hope you don't mind talking in here. It's the only empty spot in the house at the moment and that will change this afternoon when the new occupant arrives,' Terry said, sitting in a straight-back chair that hadn't been there when Mom occupied the room. I had scouted through the building when she was admitted and scooped furniture I thought looked less institutional. Someone must have done the same. Mom's favorite wingback chair was gone.

'Of course not,' I said, because I wanted to talk to Terry more than I hated sitting in a room where my mother had died on the cold floor in the dark of night. Terry opened a small canvas bag and took out a plastic container, a napkin, and a fork.

'Do you mind if I have lunch while we chat? If I don't eat now, I won't get a chance until three and I'll die of starvation.' She peeked under the lid and took a sniff. 'Tuna. It must be Thursday.'

I looked at this woman who was around Mom's age from what I could see and realized how little I knew about her, other than how she fit into my mother's life.

'Do you make tuna every Thursday?' I asked.

'No, but my son does. Joey makes our lunches every day. He works at Stop and Shop in Hyde Park. His job is to buy the groceries and make the lunch. I do everything else. He has special needs,' Terry said, taking a bite of her sandwich. I could see baby carrots in a section of the container and two chocolate chip cookies in another. Special needs. Joey must be an adult. Terry had her own story to tell.

'I hate bothering you during your break, Terry. I don't know who else I can turn to about what I learned last night. I think you knew my mother better than any other staff member,' I said.

She looked at me over her glasses and laughed.

'That I did. Claire Taylor scared the daylights out of most of the staff. She could do schoolteacher scorn better than a real teacher.

"Do you really expect me to eat *that*?"' Terry's imitation of Mom was on the mark.

I chuckled. I knew that tone. I had lived with it my entire life. '"You aren't going to wear *that*, are you, Olivia?"' I could see Terry appreciated my version of Claire Taylor.

'I just dished it back to her and before you knew it, she considered me her peer. "We're going to have to do something about the third shift staff, Terry."' And she was usually spot-on. The meals she criticized were crap. The staff she found incompetent were slackers. She was a bright woman who just happened to fall prey to a horrible illness. Sad.' Terry shook her head, not looking at me as she remembered the woman who was my mother.

'Terry, they think my mother killed herself. That she overdosed on medication and alcohol. Does that sound like the Claire Taylor you knew?' I tried sounding neutral so I would get an honest response from her, not one designed to comfort a grieving daughter.

'Claire? Kill herself? Intentionally? Commit suicide? Never.' Terry pushed her lunch container away and looked at me. 'Who is saying this?'

'The autopsy showed pills in her stomach. There was alcohol. They need to wait for the toxicology reports to determine exactly what the pills were, but they think it's the Xanax she was prescribed.' I hated making Terry feel guilty, but I couldn't help it.

'Do you think she was stashing her meds, Olivia? That's the only thing I can think of. Although, I thought I had persuaded her to take the one damn pill she had been prescribed. I even watched to make sure she swallowed.' Terry looked up at the ceiling or the heavens and rolled her eyes.

'She was stashing pills, Terry. A lot of them. I found a glove in her drawer filled with them. I haven't had a chance to count them or verify in the PDR that they were Xanax, but I'm pretty sure that's what they were. There were so many pills, I can't help but wonder if she ever took them, which makes me wonder where the pills in her stomach came from. And where did she get alcohol?' Some of my questions were new even to me.

'You don't think I would ever—' Terry wiped her hands on a napkin she began wringing.

'No, of course not,' I said quickly. I didn't want to offend my sole ally. 'But when I went into her room to retrieve her purse to take to the hospital, I noticed a Dunkin' Donuts Coolatta container next to Mom's bed. I wondered where it came from and if it could have had alcohol in it.'

I saw Terry glance at her watch and knew her break must be nearly over.

'I work ten to six, six days a week. I took this job as the medication nurse because the hours let me drive Joey to and from work, even though the pay is shit here and the administrators are pompous assholes. Lisa, the gal who works second shift here, is OK. I don't see her buying booze for the patients. But the third shift, I'm not so sure about. My hours don't overlap with theirs. There have been complaints.' Terry began wiping out the container with her mangled napkin.

'Why would someone give my mother alcohol, knowing she was on a medication that would enhance its effects?' I wondered out loud.

'That's what we need to find out,' Terry said, reaching over for my hand. 'Let me do a little snooping and I'll get back to you, OK?'

I squeezed her hand as I fought back tears. I had been right about Terry.

'Thank you. Be careful, Terry.'

THIRTEEN

I was grateful I had scheduled an additional session with Dr Evans for today. My head was spinning while my heart was shattered. I hated to think someone on the night shift brought my mother alcohol mixed with the sweet drink from Dunkin' Donuts. I doubted Mom would drink it. Mom had been a martini or Manhattan kind of girl. She scoffed at what she called 'sissy drinks.' But she had liked her alcohol and may have missed it enough once she was institutionalized to stoop to vodka in a strawberry Coolatta. I wished I had taken the drink container with me that night. I never guessed it might be of any significance.

I spilled the latest information about Mom to Dr Evans as soon as I sat down, including that I had fired Kayla. I had fifty minutes to cram in all my questions and needed every one of them.

'Could it have been an accident? Might she have been drinking and then decided to be compliant about taking her medication?' I asked. As unlikely as I thought it was that Mom had committed suicide, I believed it even less likely someone would want to kill her. What would be the motive, unless it was someone twisted getting his kicks by murdering an elderly woman with dementia.

'Both you and Dean Miller are skeptical that your mother committed suicide. Do you think it may have been an accident involving someone giving your mother alcohol? Unfortunately those kinds of things happen all of the time in facilities for the elderly. Often underpaid staff members can be persuaded to buy alcohol for patients. People don't realize that the rate of alcoholism in older people is quite high. But the mystifying piece of this is the number of pills Claire would have had to take with the alcohol to result in her death. Your mother's abhorrence for taking pills was well documented. The stash you discovered in her glove would suggest that hadn't changed,' said Dr Evans, rubbing the spot between his eyebrows. I was comforted by his puzzlement but frustrated he didn't have answers for me. I had to accept that shrinks never give you answers.

'That's what I thought, but I find myself doubting everything I think or do since Mom died,' I said.

'Give me an example,' he said, beckoning with the palm of his hand.

'I don't know. I seem accident prone, narrowly escaping crazy Boston drivers I used to be pretty good at avoiding. I lose stuff, including a plant delivered to my house. I keep carping at Daniel instead of being grateful for his concern. I wonder if I am strong enough to deal with all of this. I'm not made of the same stuff Mom was. Maybe I shouldn't have decided to go to law school. Maybe I should just be warehoused safely in a library.' I looked up at the cracked high ceiling, resting my head against the back of the chair.

'Are you worried about falling behind in your studies?' Dr Evans asked.

'Not really. I managed to get good grades even while caring for Mom.'

'Do you think your mother was a lot stronger than you are, Olivia?' he asked, touching his fingertips together to create a tent with his hands. I'd noticed he did this when he was about to embark on a new line of inquiry.

'Yes, she was incredibly strong. Look at what she did. She left behind everyone she knew and cared about to begin a new life where we would be safe from my father. I can't imagine doing that, especially while being terrified someone might kill you and your child.' While my mother never asked for my gratitude, she repeatedly reminded me how important it was not to divulge information that might compromise our safety. I was always guarded when asked questions by teachers or classmates, giving only minimal answers. I could engage in extracurricular activities and sports, but not compete for fear I might excel and find my way into the local newspaper. My social life became non-existent after my mother declined most invitations on my behalf.

'You had to be a pretty tough kid to deal with all of that secrecy,' Dr Evans said, reading my mind, I feared.

'I hated not being able to compete in figure skating,' I said, feeling a lump form in my throat.

'Were you good?' he asked, sitting up in his chair at attention.

'I was very good. I loved it. I could do a Salchow by the time I was 15. My instructor wanted me to compete. She said I had the strength of an athlete and the grace of a dancer. In Burlington, there are a ton of girls who figure skate. Being singled out was a big deal.'

'Do you still skate?'

'Not in years. It was just one of many things I couldn't do because of my father,' I said.

'What else did you miss out on?' I wished he would change the topic, but he was like a dog with a bone.

'I thought it would get better. That Mom would decide that my father would lose interest, stop looking for us. But even when I was selecting a college she was adamant. No urban areas, not even Boston, which was only a few hours away. I wanted to spend my junior year at Trinity College in Ireland. You know, the Book of Kells, the Long Room, not to mention the pubs were calling me. But no, I think my mother thought getting a passport would trigger a disaster. I still don't have one. I spent one semester during my junior year in Washington at the Library of Congress. It was the most she'd give.'

Dr Evans' questions were grueling, an interrogation I hadn't expected, even though I'd asked if we could concentrate on me during our sessions. Now I felt like a target.

'Your father had to be very formidable to frighten a strong woman like Claire that much. You must have many questions about him. What are some of them?'

I sat back for a moment, stunned. No one had ever asked me this before. Certainly not my mother. Nor Daniel. Not even Kayla. I lurched forward in my chair.

'You bet I have questions. I'd like to know what he looked like to start with. I look nothing like my mother, although she was beautiful and I wish I inherited her good looks. I'd like to know about his health. Does diabetes, high blood pressure, or psychosis run on his side of the family? Is he smart? Educated? Did he fight in a war? Is he alive? Where is he now? Do I have siblings? And what the hell did I ever do that was so bad he wanted to kill me?' I was surprised to find myself standing and shouting at poor Dr Evans.

'Those are all good questions to start with, Olivia, but let's talk about that last one first,' he said. 'Do you think you did something to provoke him?'

'I must have. I get that he might want to kill my mother. God knows, I wanted to strangle her more than once myself,' I said, needing to lighten the heaviness trying to escape me. 'But why would he want to kill his four-year-old daughter? What could I have possibly done that was so terrible?' I sat back down. I hid my face and the tears streaming down it from Dr Evans. I am not a pretty sight when I cry. I felt ashamed for yelling at him and for the torrent of emotions I had unleashed.

'Of course, you did nothing to warrant such rejection, Olivia. You were an innocent child. Do you have any memory of him?' he asked very softly after pausing a moment. 'Think. I know it's painful, but try to remember.'

'I don't know if it's a memory or a fantasy, but I remember being on a long empty beach with my mother and a man. I can't remember what he looked like but I recall thinking he was handsome and that he was more interested in my mother than me. It wasn't summer and the beach was empty. I went off to build castles by the edge of the water while they sat on the sand. He had his arm around her. When I said I was cold, he picked me up and put his jacket around me. He must have cared for me a little to do that,' I said.

'Did you like him?' Dr Evans spoke to me softly, as if I were that little girl on the beach.

'Yes. I liked that he cared about my mother and me. It must be a dream about what I wanted as a child rather than a memory. It's so infantile.'

'There's nothing infantile about wanting to have a mother and a father in your life, Olivia. I've spent my entire career listening to people who share that same primitive desire,' Dr Evans said, glancing at the little clock sitting on the pile of books next to him.

'I'm just so pathetic,' I said. Pathetic, needy, flawed, unworthy. I'd spent my entire life feeling as if I didn't deserve what everyone else is born with naturally and without effort. Two loving parents. While I might not be able to recreate my childhood, I had clung to the hope that I could provide my own children with what I had missed. If only Daniel could be convinced.

'We need to discuss this further, Olivia. You are not pathetic. You are a young woman with legitimate questions and entitled to the answers. You have a right to know who you are. You want to have children and care enough about them already to want information they will need and want.'

I felt better hearing Dr Evans defend me.

'What can I do?' I asked because I always feel better if I can at least try to solve a problem. I needed a plan.

'Well, have you thought about talking to that classmate you mentioned about the Fairclough connection? It's not that common of a name. And what about Daniel's family history? Isn't that important to you also? Isn't it part of the reason he's reluctant to start a family?' He was standing. There were only a few grains of sand left in the hourglass.

'Yes, of course,' I said, standing also.

'Olivia, you're a research librarian about to become a lawyer. You don't need me to tell you or give you permission to do what you already know how to do. You know how to dig in, research, and plow through records. If Daniel doesn't want to know who his family of origin is, that's his business. But if you're thinking of bringing children into the world with him, don't you and those children have a right to know?'

I felt wings sprouting. Dr Evans had done more than give me permission to engage in the search for Daniel's and my lineage. He'd shown I didn't need it. I was entitled to our family histories. It was the first step in becoming a loving, caring mother.

'Thank you,' I said, not knowing if I could articulate the gratitude I had for the gift he had just delivered.

'One last question. You dodged my question about safety last session. You have lived in isolation, both with your mother and from what I'm hearing, to some extent with Daniel. Isolation can be the prelude to abuse, be it physical, verbal, or emotional, or a combination. It usually follows a period of adoration of the victim in a relationship. Would you share with me if Daniel were abusive toward you or would you feel the need to protect him? I'm asking because I sense your vulnerability.' While Dr Evans was gentle in his probe, I knew I could not escape answering him a second time.

'Daniel can be insensitive, even indifferent, but he's not abusive,' I said.

'Do you feel safe, Olivia? Are you feeling threatened that someone may want to hurt you, or perhaps are you so preoccupied that you're being less careful, say about cars, than you might be otherwise? You've got so much going on, it would be easy for you to be vulnerable to either,' he said.

Perhaps that was the answer. With all that had been happening in my life, I was being careless about driving and parking. Maybe I had moved the moth orchid near other flowering plants while my brain was wandering. I vowed to be more focused. I rallied and committed to my family research project. I didn't feel the need to ask Dr Evans if he thought I would be OK participating in the family law clinic, which I had intended asking him.

'I'm feeling better after our talk. I promise I'll be more careful. I can't imagine anyone is trying to hurt me. If I managed to escape my own father, I'm not going to let some imaginary villain drive me off the road,' I said.

Besides, I thought as I walked toward the car. My father's probably dead by now.

FOURTEEN

I drove the little red Ford Fusion I had rented carefully to the law school and headed for my spot in the library. I loved my favorite table at the back in a nook where it was quiet and felt private. I took off my jacket, unpacked my backpack, and took out my phone. With just a moment of hesitation, I texted Ryan Fairclough and asked if he would come meet me in the library when he arrived at school. I didn't say why. I wasn't even sure how I would explain it when and if he showed up.

He called within a minute. I told him where I sat so he could find me.

'I know where you sit, Olivia,' he said and hung up.

I shoved aside any feelings of reluctance I had about contacting him and asking for help and clicked on my laptop. I connected to the Internet and looked for Faircloughs in the Boston area, but there was no Sheila listed. I had no reason to believe my family was from Boston, but I had to start somewhere and Ryan's surname was it, even though it was likely a coincidence.

I decided to move on to the Buchanans. I found the search engine I knew would be most helpful to locate Daniel's adoptive parents. I figured I would start with their death records and work back to Daniel's adoption and then move to the more difficult task of locating his birth mother. Adoption records are often sealed but states have become more liberal about opening them so that adopted children can learn about their medical histories or even seek reunification with their birth parents. There was hope.

I settled into my search, comfortably plunging into what I had loved doing as a research librarian. Treat any question like a mystery to be solved, collect information, assimilate facts into theories, and reach a conclusion. I had realized the same skillset applied to lawyers when I decided to get an advanced degree. I liked that lawyers got to take a step further than librarians. Lawyers got to see how it played out. They got to deal with the people who had the problem and help them initiate a resolution. I hungered for that kind of human contact, even though I was terrified by it. That's why I was at Portia Law and not at Simmons getting a master's degree in library science.

I accessed the Washington vital statistics website, wondering how Barbara and Chet Buchanan had died. Daniel had never mentioned the specifics, even though I had shared every intimate detail I knew about my own dismal origins. I hadn't wanted to probe and open his wounds. Losing two sets of parents was unimaginable to me.

I couldn't find Barbara's obituary/death record anywhere and since I didn't know her maiden name, I decided to concentrate on Chet. When nothing showed up under what I assumed was his nickname, I checked out Chester Buchanan and then Charles on a whim: he might not have liked being called Charlie. But both of those were a bust.

Not to be deterred, I forged on to look through the street directories for Seattle and surrounding suburbs. Sure enough, I found both Barbara and Chester Buchanan listed at an address that seemed active. I knew that real estate transactions occasionally go unrecorded for years, especially if property has been deeded to a trust. I checked to see if Barbara or Chester were grantors in any real estate transaction in the past ten years, meaning they had deeded their real estate to others, but no luck. The only record I could find appeared to be the residential address listing both of Daniel's parents. Then it occurred to me that I should check the probate records. Perhaps Barbara and Chet had died while they were still the owners of record 114 Clifton Ave. The estate could still be open. When I took Trusts and Estates, I learned lawyers can be very sloppy when probating estates and frequently do not complete some of the formalities that can later place a cloud on the title to the property. I was about to look for the Washington probate court website when I heard someone clearing his voice.

I looked up over the reading glasses I am forced to wear when I traipse through public records with tiny print to find Ryan Fairclough standing in front of my table. Any animosity I had felt for him previously disappeared.

'You look like you're in another world,' he said.

'I was,' I said, noticing he was wearing the same leather jacket I had blubbered all over in the emergency room. It didn't look any worse for the wear. 'Thanks for meeting me.'

'Look, Olivia, I'm sorry if we got off wrong to start with. I didn't mean to cause you or your mother any harm. I only—'

'Stop. Please. You were only doing your job. I realize that now. She might have been seriously injured or even killed if you didn't bring her home. I'm afraid I blamed you for what was inevitable,' I said, motioning for him to sit down. It had been so convenient to vilify Ryan, even though he had actually rescued Mom. And Daniel, who had simply stated the obvious. My mother had no longer been safe at home.

'Still, I know it had to be tough to put her in a home.' His long legs extended under the library table, almost touching mine. I drew back, not wanting to feel any more awkward than I already did.

'It was, and even there she wasn't safe,' I said.

'What do you mean?' he asked, sitting up at attention.

'Just that she may have taken some medication that contributed to her death,' I added quickly. The last thing I wanted was for Ryan to jump into what Terry was discreetly investigating. We were so not ready for police intervention at this point. I changed the subject.

'You don't happen to know someone named Sheila Fairclough, do you? I know you said you had a large family.' I tried to sound casual, then realized if I didn't let Ryan know how important this was to me he might not take my question seriously.

'I do. The Ryans are a much bigger clan than the Faircloughs on my father's side. Sheila doesn't ring a bell. Why?'

I'd reached a juncture. Either I tell Ryan the truth, at least some of it, or make something up. I couldn't conjure a story. I didn't have it in me. It was taking all of the energy I had to find out what happened to Mom.

'Ryan, my mother had to change her name a long time ago in order to protect us from my abusive father. She died without telling me her real name, or mine for that matter. The day before she died, she signed a check and the title to her car in the name "Sheila Fairclough." When I asked who that was, she drew a blank. I have to think the name meant something to her.' I let him digest what I'd said for a moment. He squinted his eyes as he considered my statement.

'You think she may be Sheila Fairclough?' he asked.

'Maybe,' I said. 'Or maybe Sheila was someone Mom knew. I'm

trying not to get overly excited, but Ryan, I've wanted to know about my family for as long as I can remember. My mother insisted it was unsafe to tell me and went to her grave withholding that information from me. I know it's ridiculous to think she'd be related to your family when I don't even know where she was from. My only thought about it possibly being Boston is that she was so dead set against us ever coming here, and when I suggested I might like to attend college here, she hit the roof and claimed Boston was too urban for me.' It was a little humiliating admitting how much control my mother had had over my life, even with the reason she'd had for doing so.

'Olivia. I'm sorry.' Ryan reached across the table and took one of my hands into his, which were warm and big like the hug he'd given me in the emergency room. He was so naturally affectionate and kind, I couldn't help but begin to like him.

'Thank you,' I said, gracefully removing my hand from his. 'I'm sorry to bother you, but I wondered if you might ask your family if they know who Sheila Fairclough is. I doubt my mother came from Massachusetts, let alone Boston. But it's a place to start.'

'Wait a minute, she did say she was trying to get back to South Boston that day Denny and I found her walking around the pond. I remember him joking with her we were both trying to get out of Southie.'

I'd forgotten about that. Ryan was all at once the Boston detective I'd first met. Sitting up straight, taking a small notebook out of his pocket, he asked how she spelled Fairclough.

'The same as you,' I said.

'It would have been easier if she'd written "Sheila Ryan." They're still a pretty tight family and I think my mother's aunt may have been Sheila. They own Ryan's, the pub/sports bar in Southie. The Faircloughs are a little splintered, but I'll check it out,' he said.

'What's your mom's first name?' I asked, curious about his family, especially since it could turn out to be mine, although I knew chances of that were remote. I was surprised to see him wince.

'Siobhan. Siobhan Ryan Fairclough. She and my twin died when I was born. That's why I'm named Ryan.'

Ouch. Never knowing your mother felt much worse than not meeting your abusive father. I wanted to reciprocate his kindness and take his hand, but I didn't have the natural warmth and spontaneity Ryan had.

'I'm sorry. That had to be unimaginable,' I said. It was the best I could give, for now.

FIFTEEN

I stopped at Professor Cohen's office on my way to class. I enjoyed Family Law, often called Domestic Relations, more than courses that were more business oriented. The Uniform Commercial Code and Corporate Tax bored me, they were so void of human drama.

Professor Cohen greeted me warmly and welcomed my interest in the family law clinic. He invited me to join him at the Suffolk Probate and Family Court on Monday morning to observe so I could be certain I wanted to sign on. I hesitated for a second, knowing I would be returning from Mom's memorial in Vermont during the weekend and wondering what shape I would be in. But I said yes because, whether I was a mess or not, I had to plow ahead.

I sat next to Erin in class, who offered to drive me home.

'No thanks. I got a rental. A hot red Ford Fusion that will make you want to get rid of your sensible Prius,' I said. She rolled her eyes and laughed.

I couldn't concentrate on what Professor Gomez was saying, although she was clearly animated about the new immigration laws being proposed. My mind was clogged with thoughts about Terry Walsh, Dr Evans, and Ryan Fairclough. I had been bolstered by the support each had given me, but I was still my mother's daughter. 'Be cautious about who you trust, Liv.' The words gnawed at me. I began fretting.

I remembered Dr Evans talking about how low-paid staff at facilities for the elderly could be persuaded to purchase alcohol for patients. Terry had admitted and groused about her low wages. I considered if it could be she who bought alcohol for Mom. She might even believe she was doing Mom a favor. I hoped I hadn't showed my hand to the wrong person. More likely, I was despicable questioning the integrity of the woman I had enlisted to help.

And I had almost taken Ryan Fairclough's hand. His mother had died decades ago. He didn't need me consoling him now.

I couldn't even get therapy right. I probably shouldn't have shared my fantasy about being on the beach with my mother and a man I dreamed had been my father. My credibility with Dr Evans must have plummeted after he heard my little fairy tale.

I had been neglecting my husband ever since our skirmish about the moth orchid. The truth was I had been avoiding his scrutiny because I wasn't sure how well I would endure it.

I'd been careless driving, probably invoking the ire of Massholes already prone to road rage, and should have known better than to park on the rooftop of the parking garage near Kayla's office.

The inescapable conclusion was that I was a mess without my mother to guide me, which was what I had long feared I would become once she was gone. I had been dependent on her, even after marrying Daniel.

'Come have a drink with us,' Erin said after class was over.

'No thanks. I'm not myself tonight,' I said, shoving my notebook into my backpack.

'I noticed. You couldn't have written three words in that notebook tonight. How will I study for finals?' She was shaking her head, her curls bouncing, while she pretended to scold me.

I laughed. Erin takes scant notes during class in unintelligible handwriting, while I tended to enter copious methodical comments in outline form. Erin was always borrowing my notes.

'You'll get through,' I said. We were among the few people who took handwritten notes. Our younger classmates used their laptops, but often were more interested in video games than the law.

I headed to the parking garage while Erin left to meet Ryan and Andrew in the lobby. I realized their company might help distract me from the hypercritical voices swirling in my head, but I had to pack for Vermont and I was reluctant to see Ryan Fairclough again today. I'd already shared too much with him.

The kitchen was ablaze with lights when I pulled into the driveway, lifting my spirits. Daniel was home. I could fill him in on what I had learned about the cause of my mother's death and see what he thought. My mother's advice about who to trust be damned. Daniel was my husband.

He swept me into an embrace uncharacteristically romantic for him.

'I've missed you, Liv,' he said, tickling my ear with his words.

He had cheese and grapes on a plate and two wine glasses waiting on the kitchen island. An open bottle of pinot noir sat breathing next to them.

I told him what John had learned from the medical examiner.

'I've been warning you, Liv. Alcohol and prescription medication can be a deadly combo.' He sipped his wine with his pronouncement making me want to giggle at the irony. But Daniel's voice was so ominous, I resisted.

'We don't know where the alcohol came from,' I said, before Daniel waged another warning toward me and took my glass of wine away.

'We? Who is "we"?'

Whoops. Daniel didn't know about Dr Evans and may not even have been aware I had fired Kayla. He had no idea I'd reconnected with Ryan Fairclough or that I'd recruited Terry Walsh to help. That left John Miller.

'John and I. I'm looking forward to talking to him tomorrow,' I said.

'So am I. I'm all packed,' Daniel said, gesturing toward a small gym bag and a suit bag over toward the corner where my desk was located. 'I can put my bags in the car. Which car are we taking?'

'Yours, unless you want to spend four hours in a Ford Fusion,' I said, knowing what was coming.

Ten minutes later, after having to explain the situation about my tires to Daniel and listen to him remind me that Simmons is located in what he considers a better neighborhood than the 'mongrel' school I opted to attend, I ran upstairs to grab a suitcase and throw my things in. When I returned to the kitchen to hand Daniel my bag, he was waiting for me.

'Where did you rent that wreck?' he asked.

'Just because it's an economy car, doesn't mean it's a wreck, Daniel. I was just being frugal,' I said. Daniel would rent the top of the line, which I considered a waste of money just to drive for a few days.

'Sure, but I can't believe they rented you a car that's clearly been keyed. Where did you get it? In Mattapan?' he said.

I ignored his slight on a poorer neighboring section of Boston. The car had been rented here in Jamaica Plain and was perfect when I picked it up. It had been fine when I left Dr Evans. Someone had keyed it while I was in class. I was beginning to think someone didn't like me.

SIXTEEN

Friday, October 17th

The sky was still an inky blue when we left for Burlington before sunrise. Daniel followed me in his car to the car rental agency. I deposited the vandalized red Fusion with the keys and a lengthy note about the damage. Daniel asked me to drive because he was still exhausted from two sleepless nights keeping watch on a psychotic patient intent on killing herself.

This is how it would always be, being married to a doctor, I told myself, as Daniel snored in the passenger seat while I maneuvered through the sleepy streets of Boston. Once on I-93 heading north of the city, I began to relax, sipping on the coffee I'd packed for Daniel and me to share while we chatted about our future.

I had decided having Daniel captive in a car for four hours would provide the perfect opportunity for a much-needed talk. Our lives were so fragmented by our respective schedules that we never seemed to be able to have a discussion that reached a conclusion. I hoped if we had the chance to talk through the issue about having a family, Daniel might relent. In the past, his statements had sounded like edicts. I didn't like that. Having children was important to me and I didn't think the decision should be wrestled from me without a discussion.

But I understood. Sleep deprivation was a way of life for Daniel. I relaxed, putting music on very low. Before I lived in Boston, where driving to endanger is considered a sport, I loved to take long drives through the Vermont countryside, often to think a situation through. Green hills, under towering crisp blue skies, sometimes snow covered, were the canopy for drives while I brooded. I always returned feeling better.

There was little traffic and, even though I was driving to my mother's memorial service, I felt oddly at peace. I knew John would have tended to all of the details. There would be the piano music she loved. Flowers and food in abundance. And most importantly, there would be people. When you come from a tiny family, its very size can cause embarrassment. But I didn't need to fear there would be a dearth of mourners. Although my mother's social circle had been small, she was well known within the medical school community. John would see to it that the chairs would be filled in the Garden of Healing, where the service would take place.

Daniel stirred just as we entered Burlington. John had arranged for us to stay in one of the guest units usually reserved for dignitaries visiting the university. We found our way to our room and unpacked. Daniel left to meet his former classmates and colleagues at the medical center to catch up, while I walked over to John's office to meet him for lunch.

He looked older than he should have after the four years had passed since I left Vermont, but he was still handsome and the closest thing I ever had to a father. He trembled a little when we hugged. I noticed he had lost weight and worried his health was failing, but he was mourning just as I was. I probably looked just as bad to him.

'Olivia, it's so wonderful to see you, dear, even under the circumstances. I've missed you,' he said.

I choked up. I'd forgotten how kind he had been to me, even when I didn't deserve it. I felt a flash of shame about how difficult I'd been as an adolescent. I had caused pain to more than my mother when I acted out. John never judged me.

We walked in the autumn sunlight to his car, a Subaru, because even though he was the dean and could afford a Lexus, he was a sensible Vermonter.

'This will sound silly,' he said, opening the door to the passenger side for me, removing a briefcase from the seat. His brown hooded eyes gleamed with tears I could tell he was trying to hold back.

'You never sound silly,' I said, trying to lighten the conversation.

He walked around and got into the driver's seat, placed the keys into the ignition, and started the car.

'I thought she might get better. I thought she might come back. Even though I'm a doctor. Christ, I'm the dean of a medical school, yet I could never convince myself Claire was gone.' Now tears flowed down over the crevices of his aging face. He grabbed a handkerchief from his pocket and wiped them away as if trying to erase the hopelessness Mom's death had delivered. I placed my hand on his forearm but had no words. I knew he loved her almost as much as I did. His long-distance marriage of convenience to a tenured professor of anthropology at Dartmouth College in New Hampshire made a long-term discreet love affair with Claire possible and for him to be a father figure to me. He had stolen time with both of us and it had run out.

'I'm sorry. I should be consoling you,' he said, putting the car in reverse.

'Aren't we supposed to console each other?' I asked.

He drove to the Farmhouse Tap and Grill, a hip spot that had been my favorite as an adolescent and where I insisted he and my mother take me when we ate out together. I was touched that he remembered.

After we placed our orders and chatted about changes in the Burlington scene for a few minutes, the waiter brought John a glass of Merlot and me a signature hard cider.

'Before we talk about your mother's service and the implications from the post-mortem, Olivia, I want to give you this.' He handed me a small blue envelope with the logo for the New England Federal Credit Union. I took it and felt something hard inside.

'That's it. This is what you told me you needed to give me?' I knew I sounded critical, but I had hoped for a bulging envelope or even a cardboard box filled with memorabilia my mother had preserved for me. I was crestfallen over the size of the envelope.

The waiter placed a steaming bowl of cheddar ale soup before John. I had ordered my old favorite. Bacon and blue cheese sandwich with radicchio and pears. I looked at my plate and then at the tiny envelope and lost my appetite.

'I don't know what you expected. Your mother asked me to give you this when she died. It's the key to a safe deposit box. I never asked what was in it and your mother never told me.' John paused to take a sip of his soup.

'I don't know what I expected either. Nothing. Something. The answers,' I said, still not touching my sandwich, but my glass of cider was empty. John motioned for the waiter to refill it.

'Perhaps they are in the safe deposit box.'

'Why wouldn't she just leave a letter for me with you if she wanted to give me information after she was gone?'

'I can't answer that, Olivia. You may not know that your mother and I had many conversations about her unwillingness to share information with you about your family history. The truth is we argued about it. I told her it was unfair and selfish, especially when you had those problems in high school,' John said, looking at my uneaten sandwich. I picked it up and took a bite. It was magnificent despite my intention to hate it.

'I didn't know,' I said, not wanting to say more, lest John begin to reminisce about those high school problems. I'd spent more than a decade trying to forget them.

'Olivia, Claire was genuinely terrified, whether rightly or not, about you coming to harm if she revealed any of the family history to you. She truly believed there was a significant threat of danger to you both. Only when you graduated from high school and were attending college did her anxiety seem to abate.'

I took a sip of my newly replenished cider.

'Did she tell you why she was afraid, John?' Because if she did, I was going to demand he tell me.

'No, she was almost as adamant about that. You can imagine the issues of trust we had between us. Me, with a wife living a state away, unable to divorce her without my sons disowning me. I chose to live a lie. Claire lived a life under a pseudonym, not daring to share her past with the man she purported to love. She also chose to live a lie.' He looked down at his half-empty bowl and pushed it away.

'She did love you, John. You know that. If you're suggesting the fact she didn't confide in you about her past means she didn't really love you, what does that say about how she felt about me?'

I could see that I had stunned him and I wasn't sorry. In a twisted way, I wanted him to see how wounded I had been by my mother, even though I believed that was why he had advocated on my behalf with her. Here I was, just a day before scattering her ashes, raging at him over what she had done to us both. No wonder I had needed two shrinks at once.

'The only thing I can tell you, Liv, is that she loved you more than life. Whatever her past was, wherever she belonged, she walked away from it all to protect you. I know that in my heart. So do you. Let's get this lunch over with and get over to the credit union before it closes at four. Remember, it's not open on Saturday.' He waved for the check while I took a few more bites of my sandwich.

We rode the short distance in silence to the credit union where my mother had banked and where I had opened my own first bank account. We were both hurting and there was little to be said until I saw what was in the safe deposit box.

John introduced me to the branch manager, who took us into a small conference room that he had to unlock with an electronic code. He excused himself as a teller slid a long metal box to him from behind a heavy vault door over a counter. He placed it in front of me on the cherry conference table where I was seated on a slate-blue leather chair.

I hadn't invited John to join me while I opened the box. The moment felt too intimate. It was between my mother and me. The branch manager excused himself and showed me where to ring a buzzer when I was done.

I took a deep breath and prayed I was about to discover the secrets of my ancestry. So much depended on what might be in this cold metal box.

I turned the small key and pulled up the lid, which easily slid off. There was a strong and unpleasant smell like rotten leaves uncovered in the spring after the heavy blanket of snow from a long Vermont winter had melted.

At first, I couldn't make sense of the sight. Neat piles, stacked on top of one another, next to rows and rows of the same. Dollars wrapped together with green elastics. The kind Mom used to get at the grocery store and saved. Each pile had a small Post-it with the amount written in her handwriting. None was for less than $5,000.

What the hell? Mom had been frugal, but this was ridiculous. I looked closer. The bills weren't singles. They were one-hundred-dollar bills. I started to count the number of piles until I realized there was at least a million dollars in the box, probably closer to two.

The stench of the money nauseated me. So did the thought about where it may have come from. Even though she was a committed penny-pincher, Mom could never have earned this much money. And she had already spent what I thought was most of her cash on the house in Jamaica Plain when she had agreed to move to Boston.

Then it occurred to me. My mother hadn't fled an abusive husband. She had absconded with a fortune that belonged to someone else and created a horrible lie to explain our life of secrecy.

I noticed several yellowed three-by-five index cards tucked into the front of the box. I removed them, terrified to read a confession of sorts. But on a few there were detailed instructions about how to deposit money into a bank account without raising suspicion. The last index card read: 'If you ever feel in danger, you must call Nikolai Wojcik.' There was a telephone number next to his name.

I put the index card in my purse and shoved the lid on the metal box. I pressed the buzzer like I would a fire alarm. I had to get out of this little room before the stink of the money and my mother's memory made me vomit.

SEVENTEEN

Who the hell was Nikolai Wojcik? I speculated whether he had been my mother's partner in crime. Then it occurred to me he might be my father. The name sounded Polish. My Ancestry.com results said I had a smidgen of eastern European in me. I found it unlikely Mom had been involved in some kind of international intrigue, but I also never imagined her having a stash so large.

I didn't know what to say to John. I hated lying to him, so I left it at, 'She left me some money, some cash.'

'Well, I know you were looking for answers, but maybe you can use the cash to help find them,' John said.

He offered to take me for a ride through Burlington and I agreed. We rode by Orchard Grammar School, Tuttle Middle School and South Burlington High, none of which evoked happy memories. Instead, I felt the beginning of a familiar stomachache I had gotten as a child attending those schools with anxiety and dread. Unless it was the sandwich and two ciders.

I felt better when we stopped in front of the three-bedroom ranch where Mom and I had lived for as long as I could remember. Overlooking the Adirondacks and Lake Champlain on nearly two acres, much of which had been cultivated with gardens, Mom had made the 1,500-square-foot house our world. I had never questioned how she came to own it. The quiet and cozy house with its sweeping view to the rear became a sanctuary for my childhood. At least until I hit adolescence.

I could see some of the gardens had been returned to Mother Nature. Keeping up with Mom's horticultural standards would be difficult, even for a professional landscaper. It had been her canvas and her salvation. The anger I had felt in the bank began to seep out of me as I remembered the world we lived in.

We had our routine. She worked. I went to school. Every Saturday we went grocery shopping and then to the South

Burlington Central Library, which I would have loved to visit, but I knew had recently been relocated. Mom never limited the number of books I could take out. She must have known how they would fill the week ahead.

On most Sundays we attended service at the Unitarian Church on Pearl Street, where Daniel and I were eventually married. Mom would take me for breakfast at Henry's Diner where I would feast on silver dollar pancakes, while she enjoyed the Vermonter with her beloved corned beef hash.

Eventually I began taking figure skating lessons several afternoons a week. I made a few friends at school and at lessons, but I was a shy only child, content with my mother's company for the most part until I reached middle school.

'Does it look different?' John interrupted my thoughts as he drove toward the university.

'Yes and no,' I said. Things had changed but Burlington still felt familiar. It was home.

My cell phone rang. It was Erin.

'Hey, Liv, I just wanted you to know we're here in case there was anything we can do to help,' she said.

'You're where?' I asked, confused. No one had told me anyone was coming to Mom's service.

'In Burlington. Me, Andrew, and Ryan. We figured we'd better come up the night before the service, just to be sure we made it,' she said.

'You're coming to Mom's memorial?' I asked, the incredulity making my question sound loud even to me.

'Of course. "That's what friends are for,"' she sang.

I laughed for the first time that day as John pulled into the university guest center.

'You didn't have to do that, Erin,' I said, feeling guilty she and Andrew and Ryan were traveling so far just for me. And I knew Erin was losing money doing it by missing work. 'But I'm glad you did,' I added, wanting her to know how touched I was.

'Andrew made reservations at seven for some fancy place called Bistro de Margot. He made it for five people in case you and Daniel wanted to join us. He says Burlington is like a gourmet's field trip and this place is the best of the best.'

I sighed. I didn't know when Daniel would return from visiting his pals at the medical center, but I didn't picture him wanting to have dinner with my 'drinking buddies.'

'I'm not sure what our plans for dinner are yet, Erin. I'd better pass, but thanks. You'll love Bistro de Margot.'

I hung up to find John staring at me.

'I couldn't help but hear. You have friends who drove up from Boston? They must really care about you, Olivia. Too bad you can't join them for dinner, dear.'

We chatted for a few moments about the arrangements for the next day and where we should meet. I leaned over and kissed him on his scratchy cheek.

'Thanks, John. This isn't easy for either of us, but you've taken the burden for the ceremony off my shoulders and I appreciate it.'

I entered our room and switched on a lamp. It didn't appear Daniel had returned since we checked in. I looked at my text messages. Sure enough, he had sent a message, probably while I was talking to Erin.

'Hey, the guys asked if I'd like to join them tonight for a couple of beers and burgers like in the old days. You don't mind, do you?'

I didn't think the last line was a question, but then I saw he had sent another text. I was being too harsh again. Of course it was a question.

'Thanks for covering for me. I've been catching up with some buddies from medical school, so I'm not sure how she's doing. But she's with the dean of the medical school so if she decompensates, she's in good hands. I haven't seen any new signs of paranoia or delusions. Can't wait to get through tomorrow and back to you and Boston.'

I reread the message, which was obviously not meant for me. He was writing to Kayla. About my mental health. *How dare he*, I fumed. No 'new signs of paranoia or delusions' meant Daniel had reported seeing them in the past. My husband was having clinical conversations with his colleague, my former therapist, after I had discharged her.

I sent a text of my own. To Erin.

'Decided to join you at Margot's. Just me. See you at 7:00.'

EIGHTEEN

'Plebeians, that's what the three of you are,' Andrew said, after ordering cassoulet, while the rest of us played it safe with the steak-frites.

I laughed, feeling lighter than I had all day. Maybe it was the Old Square I was drinking, Margot's variation on an old-fashioned. The others had opted for the Stowe cider, which I'd had my fill of earlier at lunch.

'How's it going?' Erin asked after we'd ordered.

'OK. Mom made plans for her memorial service when she was first diagnosed, so there's little for me to do. Almost too little.' I realized I sounded maudlin so I quickly thanked everyone for taking the time to drive to Burlington just for Mom's service.

'No need to thank us. You'd do the same for us,' Erin said.

I wondered if that was true. I'd like to think I would, but I had so little experience having close friends I wasn't sure.

'Listen, I was glad to get rid of the ten heads on my schedule,' Andrew said.

'Excuse me?' I said, baffled by his statement.

Erin laughed. 'Andrew is one of the hottest hair stylists on Newbury Street, Olivia.'

I smiled, but was embarrassed. I should know what Andrew did for a living. I should have been interested enough to inquire. Caring for my mother seemed to cloister me from the world around me.

'True, and wouldn't I love to get my hands on each one of your heads, especially yours, Olivia,' he said, pointing to the knot I had pulled my hair into at the back of my neck.

'You're not getting near mine,' Ryan said to him and then turned back to me. 'You actually saved me from two homicides. My partner texted me and said I owe him big.'

'Really? Are you on the murder squad?' I asked, realizing now that the last time I had seen him in uniform had been in my home the day he escorted Mom back.

'My partner and I made the homicide unit a few months ago,' he said.

'It's a big deal. He just doesn't brag about it,' Andrew said, his high cheekbones flushed from the cider.

'Do you like it?' I asked. I wondered how it would feel to get up every morning and face the prospect of murder.

'It keeps me busy,' he said, making me think he had needed a distraction from the divorce he had mentioned the other night. 'What I really want to do is prosecute criminals and put them away, not just chase them.' I had wondered what motivated Ryan to go to law school when he already had a career in law enforcement. Now I knew.

Maybe that's what I needed. Something to get me out of my own head. It was fine to focus on my personal problems when I was with Dr Evans and to concentrate on finding answers to the questions about my past when I was doing research. But I didn't need to wallow in them the rest of the time. Otherwise, I might become a narcissistic bore. I hoped the legal clinic would help expand my interests and I'd do some good at the same time.

We chatted about school and the upcoming MPRE during dinner without anyone ever asking where Daniel was. I had prepared an excuse, but didn't seem to need one. I was relieved to be entertained by the convivial conversation rather than obsessing over where Mom got all of that dirty money and why my husband held such an abysmal view of my mental health.

Andrew talked me into sharing the crème brûlée with him for dessert, while we all ordered Rémy Martin VSOP as after-dinner drinks. I had laughed so much during dinner, especially at the stories Erin told about tending bar and the imitations Andrew did of his clients, that my stomach ached. It was a lovely ache, nothing like the bellyaches of my youth. I marveled that I was having more fun on the eve of my mother's memorial service than I could remember having, well, ever.

When they wouldn't let me contribute toward the bill, I welled up as I protested.

'Olivia, let us do this. We're your friends,' Ryan said, pushing the cash I placed on the table back toward me. I relented, knowing I was on the brink of insulting them.

I was about to ask for a ride home, when I heard a familiar voice behind me.

'There you are. John told me I might find you here. I was wondering what kind of mischief you were getting into, Olivia,' Daniel said, placing his hand on the back of my shoulder like a branding iron. 'How nice I finally get to meet your friends.'

NINETEEN

D aniel had little to say on the way home from the restaurant, other than he was glad he had chosen to do his residency in Boston rather than be limited by remaining in Burlington, which was code for 'I knew I was better than my buddies.'

I murmured my concurrence. I didn't want to engage in conversation that might dull the glow the evening had brought me. Even when Daniel suggested it was no surprise that my drinking buddies would never miss an Irish wake, I didn't take the bait. I didn't mention the text he had sent to me by mistake. I was saying goodbye to my mother in the morning. That was all I could handle for now.

'Tomorrow is bound to be difficult, Daniel. It's after midnight. I think I'd better hit the sack.'

I slept surprisingly well, showered, and dressed in my black wool suit and boots, while Daniel took a run around the campus. We drove to the medical school together in companionable silence. When we arrived, he reached across the console and took my hand, squeezing it in his.

'Lean on me today, Liv. This will be hard. I know. I've been through it twice.'

I looked over at him, adorable with his hair still slightly damp from his shower, his black knit bow tie speckled with a few polka dots poking out of his coat. He knew me so well, just what I needed at that moment. I smiled and knew whatever his text to Kayla had said originated from his concern when I had become hysterical about the missing moth orchid.

John met us at the entrance and took us up on the elevator to the rooftop garden where patients and their families could seek comfort and consolation. My mother's creation was a spellbinding labyrinth filled with flowering shrubs and scented herbs designed to fill the senses. The garden was still colorful with autumn blooms. Purple dome asters and towering Joe-Pye Weed towered over several varieties of sedum. Mom had conceived, designed, and made this sanctuary for patients and their families possible through her relentless fundraising. No one knew about the healing powers of a garden better than my mother.

The service was the perfect length, more crowded than I had expected. Not too many people spoke, but those who did shared tales with sincerity and personal regard for who Claire Taylor was. The music was mostly piano, which Mom had loved. The food and reception after the service was civilized and tasteful. People were kind. Daniel was ever at my side, while I felt John nearby whenever I needed something. I proudly introduced my law school friends to people. It was a perfect memorial. The only thing missing was my mother.

'Olivia, let's stay in touch this time. Before, it was almost too agonizing for me to call. I was afraid to hear your mother's voice, but know she was nowhere to be found, and I was too cowardly to deal with it. I'm sorry, dear,' he said, hugging me harder than he had ever before.

I knew the pain he had experienced from ambiguous loss only too well. I hugged him and cried, not for the first time that day.

'I'm here for you,' he said, releasing me, taking my two hands between his and pressing them.

'I know,' I said, kissing him on the cheek then running to the car.

Daniel was waiting for me in the driver's seat. We didn't speak for the first fifteen minutes of the drive. I needed that long to stop sniffling.

'It was a nice service, Liv. Claire would have liked it,' he said finally, looking over at me.

'She would have. She planned much of it, you know,' I said.

Daniel chuckled while I pondered whether I should tell him what else my mother might have been up to. I hesitated to reveal that she might have been involved in something dishonest. I was simply speculating. It was an enormous and unfair assumption without more to confirm it. Besides, there was no need to discuss it right now.

'She was a woman in charge,' Daniel said.

'Well, she had to be. Being alone all of those years. Fearing danger from my father, she needed to be aggressively defensive,' I said, wondering where Daniel was going. He had criticized my

mother in the past but always acknowledged her illness was responsible for her short temper or impatience.

'Yes, but you have to agree she took it too far. I mean, it's been
twenty-five years since all that happened, whatever "that" was,' he
said. 'She could have let go of the control and drama long ago.
Before she got sick, for sure, if she'd wanted to,' he said, slipping
a pair of sunglasses on as the late-afternoon sun hit the
windshield.

I perked up, no longer feeling drained by the emotion of the day.

'Are you saying my mother purposely instilled fear in me so she
could control me?' I asked.

'Are you seriously asking me that?' he asked, as if he were
flinging a dart toward a target.

'You don't know that she had any reason to stop worrying, stop
being protective, do you?'

'I just know that it's not normal to raise a child in fear. She taught
you to be cautious about everything. You can't even leave a window
open in the heat of summer when you go out of the house because
you're afraid it might rain. Maybe she had reason to fear for your
safety when you first came to Burlington, but I think she manipulated
you for years, maybe decades. Longer than necessary, in any event,'
he said very calmly for a man declaring war.

'Well, there's only one way to find out, isn't there, Daniel? I'll
investigate. Now that Mom's gone there's nothing to stop me from
finding out who my father was and why we had to hide from him.
Then I'll finally know who I am and whether my gene pool is too
defective for you to consider having children with me,' I said,
shouting so loud my own ears hurt.

'Calm down, Liv,' he said in that phony psychiatric tone that
didn't work on me and that I doubted would ever reassure one of
his patients.

'Don't you dare talk to me like I'm one of your patients,' I said
in a quiet voice, which I knew would alarm him more than my
screaming.

'Then stop acting like one,' he said.

'Daniel, I want to have babies. I want us to start a family. There's
nothing crazy about that.' This is what I had wanted to discuss with
him on our ride up to Vermont, but not like this.

'If I learn that my family of origin is no crazier than the rest of the world, there's no reason we can't have a family of our own, is there? Even if you don't want to research your birth family, your adoptive family was so stable, surely we'd be OK raising children,' I said.

'I don't want children, Liv,' he said, never taking his eyes off the road.

'Then I don't know if I want to stay married to you,' I said, remaining silent the remainder of the long way home.

TWENTY

Our bodies ignored our warring words and found one another deep under the covers in the middle of the night. It puzzles me why lovemaking is best when it's desperate, furious, and tender all at once.

I woke early and disentangled myself from a reckless sheath of sheets. I quietly found my way to the shower, not wanting to face Daniel. I didn't have words to explain how we had managed to mangle our marriage yet still found refuge in physical intimacy.

I grabbed a quick K-cup and slid into the silence of the conservatory, armed with a notebook and pen. I tried to make a grocery list since Sunday is when I do food shopping. But with Mom gone, Daniel working so much, and our weekly Sunday meal pre-empted by Josh's invitation for comfort food, I gave up without writing a single entry.

I was drawn to the plants I had ignored recently. My mother once told me that green is the color of hope. I believe her. Something magical happens when I am in this room where exotic tropical orchids, hibiscus and plumbago mingle with lowly commoners like spiders, pothos, philodendron, and rubber trees. I am drawn out of myself, forced to breathe in the scent of other living things, and reminded the world is more than me. I fussed, pulling dead leaves and blossoms, discarding them into a small bucket. I could barely look at the moth orchid sitting between the two jades. I still worried that I had moved it myself when I was at the edge of reality.

Daniel coughed as he entered.

'Morning. Shall I go grab some muffins or bagels?' he asked, the same question he poses any time he is home during a weekend. It should have felt normal, but it was awkward. We both knew how badly we hurt one another with our words the night before and how our bodies tried to make up for it.

'That would be great. I'd love a blueberry muffin,' I said, straining to sound normal.

We spent the remainder of the day circling each other in the house, each tending to our weekend duties, while struggling not to bump into one another. Around three, Daniel approached me sitting on the wicker chair in the newly ordered conservatory where I was trying to catch up on my family law reading. I didn't want to sound ignorant when I met with Professor Cohen the next morning at the clinic.

'I know it's a silly question, but should we bring red or white wine to go with the meatloaf tonight?'

I laughed.

'Well since it's beef, I'd go with red, but definitely plonk to go with the comfort theme. You can't go wrong with a jug of Carlo Rossi,' I said as he headed out the door on an unprecedented second errand of the day.

We left early for the drive to neighboring Brookline where Josh and Kayla had purchased a rooftop condo when they moved to Boston for her residency. Finding a parking space, even on Sunday evening, would likely take longer than the thirteen-minute drive from Moss Hill.

The condo was everything our home was not. On the tenth floor, it had a decent view of the Boston skyline. Sleek and modern, filled with soft leather chairs and couches, cool gray walls, and a stainless-steel kitchen sterile enough to perform surgery in. Kayla greeted us at the door and led us to the kitchen where Josh was wearing an apron that said 'Mr Goodlooking is Cooking.' He shook Daniel's hand and gave me a hug.

'Shit, I forgot the wine,' Daniel said, flushing a little with embarrassment. I found it painful to see how even a tiny mistake was unbearable to him.

'No problem, we have plenty of wine,' Kayla said, pointing to a wine rack that must have contained two dozen bottles.

'This was special. Do I have time to run home?' Daniel asked Josh.

'Of course. This kind of meal can't be overcooked. I'll put everything on warm and set out the apps while you're gone,' Josh said.

Kayla grabbed a set of keys off a hook.

'I'll drive you. If we take our car, we won't have to look for a parking space when we come back.' Josh and Kayla only had one car and insisted they liked walking over driving, but that hadn't stopped them from purchasing a parking space that cost as much as many homes in other sections of Boston's Hub.

Josh motioned for me to sit on a stainless-steel stool at the counter that felt cool to my touch as I scooted up.

'I personally could do without the wine. I'm going to have a bourbon while we wait. Care to join me?' Josh asked, a faint remnant of a southern accent barely detectible.

I nodded and watched him pull a bottle of Bulleit out of a cabinet. He had introduced me to bourbon on another occasion when he cooked us braised short ribs last winter.

'How are you holding up?' he asked, sliding on to the stool next to me. He placed a drink in front of each of us. I waited until I'd had the first sip to answer.

'One minute I'm fine, the next I'm a mess,' I said honestly. I'd found Josh was easy to talk to and understood why he had his own counseling practice in addition to teaching as an adjunct at nearby Northeastern University. I'd rather have seen him for counseling than his robotic wife.

'That's understandable. She was your mother, plus you're an only child. You've experienced what I did when my own mother died. I lost a whole family because after my father died, she was all I had,' he said.

'You had no siblings?' I asked.

'I lost a sister to leukemia when she was five,' he said.

'I'm sorry,' I said, wanting to change the subject. I had reached my weekly quota for sad stories.

'So what made you and Kayla buy this particular place?' I asked, looking around. The smell of meat and potato wafting from the oven felt incongruous with the antiseptic kitchen.

'Well, the location. You know, neither of us are fans of cars and would rather walk anywhere we can. We're close to the General here, not far from Northeastern, and the T stop is almost outside our door. But the particular building and unit was all Kayla. We rented a three-story row house in the Fells Point historic section of Baltimore when she was at Johns Hopkins, which I loved and she loathed. It was her turn to choose.'

'Is that where you met?' I asked as I watched him walk over to a stainless-steel Sub-Zero refrigerator that I personally knew cost close to ten thousand dollars. He pulled out a platter of deviled eggs and another with celery and carrot sticks with blue cheese dip.

'Wow,' I said as he deposited both in front of me, which was good because all I'd had to eat was the blueberry muffin this morning. I was beginning to feel the bourbon.

'I promised you comfort food, didn't I? No, Kayla and I met when she was an undergraduate at Emory. I was her professor.' Josh shrugged and put on an impish smile.

'Seriously? I thought those romances only happened in novels,' I said. We never could chat like this when our spouses were around. I hoped Kayla and Daniel hit traffic. I was fascinated by the woman I occasionally considered my nemesis. I wanted to learn more.

'I'd been teaching for a while, never married, and had a bit of a wild streak. I liked to drink and frolic with rowdy women. But when I met Kayla, that all slammed to a stop. She was so earnest, so intense—'

'And so beautiful,' I said, hoping the jealousy I had been trying to stifle wasn't apparent.

'Yes, stunning,' Josh said, ignorant of my envy, sounding a little dreamy. 'I was surprised she'd look twice at an old fart like me. I'm twenty-three years her senior, you know.'

I pretended I didn't but it wasn't true. Daniel had wondered more than once what Kayla had seen in a man so much older. I suspected it was his money, but kept my thoughts to myself.

I munched on an egg. It was fluffy, creamy while tangy, and tasted familiar even though I had never made them and my mother certainly hadn't.

'I like older buildings. Your home is so gracious, Olivia. It invites people to gather and celebrate or just live comfortably daily. I think when Kayla settles into her own practice, we may be able to find a home we both like. I know she thinks your place on Moss Hill is spectacular. Maybe she's had her fill of industrial-style minimalism. It's so severe.'

'I thought the house we bought would be a good place to raise kids,' I said, the bourbon becoming truth serum.

'I didn't know you and Daniel wanted children,' Josh said, chewing on a carrot he had dipped into the blue cheese dip.

'It's under consideration,' I said, not adding 'only by me.' 'How about you and Kayla?' I knew it was brazen, but he had opened that door.

'No. She says I already have a child: her. I'm too old to challenge her even if I thought I might like one or two.' I gathered he had considered the prospect but surrendered to Kayla's wishes.

'Besides, they're so damn expensive and inconvenient,' he laughed.

'That's true, but don't forget you're married to a doctor. Aren't they all filthy rich?' I chuckled, taking the last sip of the bourbon.

'Yes, but medical school has been an expensive drain on my assets and I'm closer to retirement than the rest of you.'

'Isn't Kayla a Mayflower descendant? Doesn't that come with some kind of dowry or bounty?' I remembered Daniel adding her lineage to the list of her endless attributes.

'Coming over with the Pilgrims didn't guarantee wealth. According to Kayla, her family was cheated out of a fortune.'

Laughter spilled in as the door opened and Kayla burst in with Daniel in tow.

'Wait till you see what a funny guy Daniel is, Josh,' she said, holding up a jug of red Carlo Rossi. 'You said comfort food and this is what he says matches that menu.'

I bristled, but said nothing about Daniel taking credit for my idea.

Josh took the jug from her, laughing as he placed it on the counter. Daniel handed him a bottle of Veuve Clicquot La Grande Dame. It was only the second bottle of it I'd seen. The first had been on our wedding night.

'Careful with this baby, Josh. She needs to go in the fridge,' Daniel said.

I was astounded. I knew it cost over $150. How did this fit in with the comfort theme Josh had created for me?

'Daniel bought it for me to celebrate the completion of my rotation at McLean. Isn't that sweet?' Kayla asked Josh.

'And because I know how much my wife enjoys French food and drink,' Daniel added.

'Ah, for *les deux grandes dames*,' Josh said, cheering Daniel on.

But I knew it was my punishment for dining with Erin, Andrew, and Ryan at Bistro de Margot.

TWENTY-ONE

The juxtaposition of delicious comfort food presented by Josh as elegantly as if he had cooked an exotic gourmet dinner worked its magic. My appetite surged as the smells of meat and potato combined.

'The silverware is gorgeous. Was it your family's?' I asked Kayla as I picked up an ornate fork that appeared to be antique.

'My family? My family was robbed of its money. The silverware belonged to Josh's parents. They were both corporate executives at Coca-Cola,' Kayla said, sipping from her goblet filled with Carlo Rossi, which turned out to be the perfect mate for the meal.

OK, no more questions about Kayla's heritage, I decided after hearing the bitterness in her response. The conversation grew intentionally light, avoiding any mention of my mother. I was fine with that, but when Daniel began to tease me about how I was overly conscientious in my studies, I grew uncomfortable.

'She obviously outranks her fellow students, but still she takes meticulously detailed notes and studies like she was at Harvard Law. Olivia is so organized you could probably publish her notebooks,' Daniel said. He'd had more wine than usual.

'I'm a research librarian at heart, Daniel. That's how we do things,' I said, wanting to add: 'Shut up.'

'And that's why I kept telling you to get an advanced degree at Simmons where you belong. Or at least you could have gone to B.C. Law where there's more prestige and your car wouldn't be getting keyed.'

Josh excused himself and returned with warm apple crisp laden with vanilla ice cream.

Kayla jumped up from the table. 'Champagne time,' she said.

By the time we'd toasted her good fortune at completing her tour at McLean and Daniel offered a tribute to my mother, I had sobered up enough to drive us home, which was fortunate because Daniel was sauced.

He went straight to bed. He was as intoxicated as I could ever remember. I remained in the kitchen where I had told him I needed to review 'my obsessively over-organized notebooks' for school the next day, even though I'd already completed my reading assignments earlier in the day.

I opened my laptop, now wired and awake. I had an email from Ryan saying he may have information on the Fairclough connection and to call him. Now I was really awake, but it was too late to call someone who was trying to help me and might be catching up on his own sleep.

I tapped my fingers on the desk. I decided I'd return to my research on Daniel's family and found where I located Chet and Barbara Buchanan's last address. I noticed a phone number and looked at the time. It was only 8 p.m. on the west coast. Why not call the number? I was sure it was disconnected.

On the third ring, a woman's voice said, 'Hello.'

I choked. I hadn't thought of what I might say if someone answered. I was going to have to learn to think on my feet faster if I was going to be a courtroom lawyer.

'May I please speak to Daniel Buchanan?' I was glad I had chosen the option to keep my number anonymous on my cell phone.

'Who is this?' the woman demanded.

'It's the alumni association. Does Daniel live there?' I asked.

'What alumni association? Daniel hasn't lived here in almost twenty years.'

'UVM, ma'am. I'm sorry to disturb you. Do you have a number for him? May I ask to whom I am speaking?'

'You are speaking to Barbara Buchanan and you'd better never call here again, do you understand? I thought my husband made that perfectly clear the last time you called looking for a donation.' I wasn't sure if the shrill of her voice was louder than the sound of the phone slamming. Clearly I was calling a landline.

Barbara Buchanan had spoken to me. Barbara Buchanan, Daniel's adoptive mother. She wasn't dead, that was for sure. And neither was her husband, Chet, who had admonished the alumni association when it had called soliciting a donation. Daniel had lied to me. I had no idea why he would do that. I couldn't grasp the implications readily. All I could do was sit and hold my head in the palms of my hands and wonder.

Whatever caused Daniel to fictionalize the deaths of his adoptive parents had to be awful. So heinous, he denied having any family and wouldn't consider having one of his own. This was why he didn't want children. Maybe he had been rescued by the Buchanans only to be abused by them. That had to be it. It was the only explanation why he had slammed the door on his past.

Daniel knew just about every skinned knee I'd ever had. I had revealed all of the injuries I suffered as a child, physical and emotional, during our intimate conversations before we were married. The most difficult one had come when I had shared with him about the breakdown I'd had when I was in high school.

'Tell me about it, Liv. What happened?' He held my hand while I told him how I could no longer cope with the secrecy and dearth of family history. I had no father, no siblings.

'Kids teased me when I wouldn't answer questions about my father or why I didn't accept invitations to parties. My social skills were pretty limited. I kept to myself, but that only made me an easy target for the bullies who taunted me daily. Eventually I refused to go to school. When I would no longer leave my room, Mom had no choice but to hospitalize me.'

I'd shared with Daniel about how I had recovered, but not without scars. I claimed I wanted to attend college in Boston, but I knew living in a city would terrify me after being raised in isolation. I had a therapist in college to help me adjust to a new environment. Although it made sense for me attend UVM where my mother worked and tuition was discounted, we both knew I would be swallowed by the size of the school. Ultimately, I'd elected to attend Marlboro College in Vermont, a tiny college, which allowed a self-designed curriculum.

I had bled all over Daniel. He knew every blemish I ever had. I felt wounded that he hadn't trusted me as I had him. It was an intimate insult. I hurt for him and whatever pain the Buchanans had inflicted upon him, but Daniel's sin of omission was a brutal blow to me and our marriage.

I went up to our bedroom. Opening the door, I heard him snoring an unprecedented alcohol-induced slumber. I undressed and slid under the covers on the edge of my side of the bed so I wouldn't awaken him. I didn't know what I would say to him. I no longer knew with whom I was sleeping.

TWENTY-TWO

D aniel was gone by the time I woke up, sparing me from the quandary about whether I should confront him about Barbara Buchanan's revelation. Instead, I discovered an unusual handwritten note from him on the kitchen island. 'Great dinner Josh cooked for you. Hope it was comforting. See you Wednesday night after school. We can order pizza in, if you're not going out with friends. Love, D.'

I was relieved I had three days before he would return from McLean, during which I could think things through. I would talk with Dr Evans, before deciding how to handle the information I had received the night before. My Monday was busy enough. I had to meet Professor Cohen at court for my orientation to the law clinic and then had classes in the evening.

But first, I had calls to make. I called Uber to schedule a pickup, so I could retrieve my Mini, which had been repaired. Next, I called Ryan to find out what he had learned about the Fairclough connection, but my call went straight to voicemail. I remembered there had been two homicides in Boston over the weekend and figured he was occupied with them. I left a message for him to call me when he had a chance.

The third call I placed was to Thompson House to check in with Terry. When I asked to speak to Terry Walsh, the snippy receptionist to whom I had spoken many times told me, 'She is no longer with us.' Startled, I was silent long enough for her to become impatient with me.

'Can I direct your call to someone else?' she asked. She had been the staff member to call me on more than one occasion to remind me I needed to either produce the papers giving me power of attorney over my mother's affairs or to get appointed by the court as her guardian. She was one of those little people who become intoxicated by authority.

'No, thank you,' I said, reeling with the realization about what she had said. Terry no longer worked at Thompson House, the place of employment where she didn't make great money and didn't like the administration, but where she could meet the needs of her son. Damn, she had probably gotten fired because she offered to nose around and find out what the night shift was up to. I should never have put her in that position. I knew when I spoke to her with my questions about Mom's death that she would volunteer to poke around. I didn't discourage her, even when I learned why she put up with Thompson House. She would never find a job that worked as well for her and Joey. This was all on me.

The arrival of the Uber interrupted my guilt trip. I grabbed my tan leather bag and went to place my family law notebook in it for reference while I was in court. I had no idea what to expect or if anything I'd written in the notebook would be of use, but it couldn't hurt. When I didn't see it on the desk, I waved out the door to the driver, signaling with my index finger I'd be there in one minute. I searched through the drawers, then the small bookcase next to the desk. No notebooks. None of my notebooks were there. I looked over to the kitchen island where I sometimes read over coffee. I tried to recall when I had last gone through the stack of notebooks. I had thumbed through them when I was reviewing for the MPRE exam. I remembered taking notes the morning before in the conservatory while I prepared for the week ahead. I raced into the moist fragrance of my little personal jungle, but no notebooks.

The driver honked. I looked at the clock. I had to be at the Suffolk Probate and Family Court in an hour and a half and it would have to be without my notebook. I hurried past the morning edition of the *Boston Globe*, which was rolled up in a plastic bag sitting on the driveway. I normally take it with me each morning, but I hadn't read it since Mom passed.

In the car, I chose not to talk to the driver who was already annoyed with me. I closed my eyes and catalogued the recent days in reverse, hoping to uncover where I had left the notebooks Daniel had described the evening before as 'worthy of publication.' He had been joking, but it was true I was a meticulous note taker, knowing the bar exam loomed at the end of my time at Portia Law. I strained to recollect where I been and what had I been doing in recent days. I realized that the past week had been a blur and that I would never be able to reconstruct it, let alone remember what I had done with the notebooks. I was relieved to get behind the wheel of my own little Mini and head downtown. I concentrated on driving and finding a parking space, ridding myself of thoughts about my complicity in getting Terry fired and my obsession over my notebooks. Even though I understood Professor Cohen would guide me, I was apprehensive about my first day in court. I wore the black pantsuit I had worn to my mother's memorial service. I wanted to feel she was with me. I had to pass through security and surrendered my cell phone when I entered the courthouse. A huge sign in black and red capital letters blasted the rules about what most people cannot bring into court. I read a footnote that attorneys are exempt. Had I known law students don't qualify for the exception, I would have left my telephone in the car.

I was relieved when I found Professor Cohen sitting on a wooden bench in a corridor waiting for me. He told me the other two students normally scheduled for the day would not be coming. One had a job interview, the other strep throat.

'You'll get all of the action today.'

I gulped and followed him down a long corridor and then into an empty courtroom. He showed me into the last row and began explaining how the clinic worked.

'Essentially, we are appointed to represent indigent clients who otherwise would be representing themselves because there are only limited rights to appointed counsel in civil cases. We get a fair amount of restraining order cases. You know, people who have been the victims of domestic abuse. We'll be covering that in class soon.'

I didn't tell him I had studied domestic violence on my own while researching what little my mother had told me about my father.

'It seems awfully quiet,' I said, noting only a few other people had wandered into the courtroom where a clerk now stood in front of the judge's empty bench sorting through a metal container bulging with different colored file folders.

Professor Cohen laughed. 'Be careful, Olivia. You don't want your first day in court to be baptism by fire.'

'All rise,' the court officer bellowed. We stood until the judge took the bench and sat down. I was struck by how much a courtroom and its rituals seem to mimic church. There were benches like pews for the worshippers, an inner court with railings around it like a choir for the lawyers, and an altar for the high priest, the judge. Everyone was told to be silent and that eating, drinking, and chewing gum were all prohibited.

I watched Judge Foley as she began to hear cases. I was surprised that she appeared to be only in her fifties and quite attractive. Her long auburn hair was pulled back from her freckled face. She wore a pin on her robe and dangly earrings. I had expected the judge to be more mature like Professor Cohen, whose thinning hair and furrowed brow seemed far more judicial to me.

The first couple of cases were quick uncontested divorces where no lawyers were involved. They were perfunctory, underscoring the sadness. After answering 'yes' to a series of rote questions posed by Judge Foley, the marriage was declared over, although she admonished them they could not remarry for another 120 days. I shuddered at the thought of someone plunging into the same deep waters so soon.

Next the contested motions were heard. Each lawyer strode with his or her client to a table in front of the judge and began to argue over minutiae I couldn't believe a court would be interested in. The father who refused to return the children's clothing to the mother after they spent a weekend with him. The mother interfering with the father's Facetime with the children. Arguments about whether books and travel count toward the college expenses the judge had ordered the parents to pay.

I was so engrossed watching the attorneys dramatize their clients' affronts that I barely noticed when the court officer tapped Professor Cohen on the shoulder and handed him a thin gray file. Professor Cohen took the file from him and opened it on his lap. He frowned, shut the folder, and beckoned me to follow him.

In a tiny windowless conference room with a table and four chairs, he handed me the folder to read. It was an emergency petition for a guardianship for a baby only two days old. His mother had been murdered while she was still carrying him. He was believed to be near full term and suffering from his mother's opioid addiction. Her name was Sophia Parro. She was nineteen years old. There was a brief report from DCF, the Department of Children and Families, charged with the care of children who needed protection. The father was at large, although it wasn't known if he was the mother's killer. The baby was referred to as 'Brady' throughout the social worker's intake because a tiny New England Patriot's tee shirt with 'Brady 12' had been found in a meager layette prepared for the baby's birth. Brady was at the Children's Hospital according to the notes written by the worker.

I looked up at Professor Cohen. 'Is this what you meant by baptism by fire?' I asked.

He nodded and looked up at me from over his black-framed glasses.

'Indeed. This is a very sad case, but I'm sure you know that from the news.'

I thought of the newspaper sitting unwrapped and unread on my driveway. I couldn't remember the last time I checked the news. I probably read the *Boston Globe* to my mother the day before she died. It was part of our daily routine, in part to occupy the time, but also to keep her as oriented as possible. I had been so absorbed by Mom's death, I was living in a current event coma.

'I'm sorry, but since my mother's death—'

'Of course, you're not up to date.' Professor Cohen provided me details that the court file omitted and explained our task was to fill out paperwork so that the court could appoint a guardian to make legal decisions for Brady, including some pressing medical ones. Brady would be physically placed with relatives or in foster care after he was discharged from the hospital.

I completed an endless pile of forms, seeking the appointment of 'a suitable person' to be Brady's temporary guardian until a permanent one could be determined, with Professor Cohen's patient tutelage.

We returned to the courtroom, this time sitting with the other attorneys waiting for their cases to be called. I was surprised when the Guardianship of Brady Parro was called right away. Rather than have us stand at the tables where I had seen other cases argued, the court officer ushered us up to the sidebar where we could have a hushed conversation with Judge Foley.

I watched while she read every page of what we had written. I saw now that the pin she was wearing was Tinker Bell from Peter Pan. I could tell she was a judge who cared about children.

'Terribly sad case, counsel. Could you please identify yourselves for the record?'

Professor Cohen stated his name and introduced me as a third-year law student from Portia. I mumbled, 'Good afternoon, Your Honor,' feeling privileged to be part of the proceeding.

'Do you have someone in mind to be Brady's temporary guardian, Attorney Cohen?' Judge Foley asked.

'No, no one comes to mind, Judge,' he said.

'Well, it should be someone who understands legal proceedings. This is bound to become complicated,' she said.

'I agree,' he said.

'Why not Ms Taylor then?'

Ms Taylor. That would be me. I doubted she was serious.

'Why not?' Professor Cohen said, beaming at me like a proud parent.

'Then Ms Taylor it is. Is this agreeable to you?' she asked me.

'I'd be honored,' I said. I wanted to add that I would also be terrified.

'All set then,' Judge Foley said, closing the file. The clerk's office will type up your appointment so you can take it to Children's Hospital.

Professor Cohen walked with me to the clerk's office where we sat and waited for the paperwork I would need to bring to the hospital while he explained my duties. Basically, I stood *in loco parentis*, which he explained meant 'in the place of the parent.' I already knew that but just nodded.

I was awed into silence. I finally had a baby to take care of, even if he wasn't my own.

TWENTY-THREE

I hurried to Children's Hospital to deliver the court orders and sign various authorizations for Brady's medical treatment so I wouldn't be late for class, although I knew Professor Cohen would understand. Driving past Mass. General Hospital, I thought about Kayla and Daniel practicing psychiatry just around the corner from the courthouse. Soon, we would be one snug little professional community.

I found my way to the NICU, which I learned was the Neonatal Intensive Care Unit. A nurse manager introduced me to Samantha, the nurse in charge of Brady's care.

'Poor little fella. It's a good thing he had a little weight on him or he might not have made it,' she said, going on to explain how a mother's opioid addiction affects a child in utero. Sophia's traumatic sudden death compounded Brady's medical challenges.

Samantha explained the various forms I had to sign.

'May I see him first?' I asked.

'Of course,' she said, leading me down a hall filled with beeping monitors and laundry carts. I was surprised to see a uniformed police officer sitting on a chair outside Brady's room.

I introduced myself, showing Officer Duggan my appointment and my license with my photo on it. He seemed old enough to be my father. I tried not to notice that the buttons on his shirt tugged across his bulging belly and hoped he would be able to protect Brady if need be.

'Someone will be here twenty-four-seven until we're sure this baby is safe. Whether that's from his father or someone else is up to homicide to figure out.'

I told him I went to school with Ryan Fairclough.

'He's on this case. He's a good kid. I knew his uncle and father,' he said as Samantha led me through the door to a sight I was unprepared for. The room was empty, other than various monitors, a rocking chair, and a crib with a tiny wailing body in its midst.

Brady didn't scream, he screeched 'wah,' like a warrior riding into battle. His back arched, while his fists were clenched tight as if holding on to dear life.

I drew back involuntarily and then murmured, 'Sorry,' to Samantha.

'Don't apologize. It's natural to be repelled. It's not how we think about babies,' she said, placing her hand on my shoulder, backing me out of the room.

Back at the nurses' station, Samantha gave me copies of the documents I had signed on behalf of Brady.

'Yours is really a legal function. There's no need for you to become personally involved with him. We've got plenty of staff for that.'

I took the papers and thanked her, for what I wasn't sure. She had been kind when I had recoiled at the sight of Brady. I ran to my car, grateful I had used the hospital valet parking, which spared me the time to walk to the horrid garage where my tires had been punctured just a few days ago.

Before class started, I told Erin about my day in court, omitting any reference to how meeting Brady had jolted me.

'I read about that case, Liv. They still haven't found the father. They don't know if he killed the mom or if someone was after them both after a bad drug deal. Ryan's on the case, you know,' she said. 'You sure know how to dive into the thick of things, don't you? How did he get the name Brady if his mother's dead and his father's missing?'

I remembered Erin telling me how she had been named, which explained why she was curious a baby would be named after Tom Brady, the Patriots' infamous quarterback who had left Boston for Miami for more money. Half the city still loved him. The other half of Boston would never forgive him for deserting them.

'There was an infant Brady tee shirt found with the stuff his mother had bought for him. Maybe the extended family will know what she planned to name him, but for now he's Baby Brady,' I said.

I only half listened to Professor Cohen's lecture on annulments and the distinction between void and voidable marriages. I had read and taken notes about the chapter the morning before in the conservatory. That started me obsessing about where I had placed my notebooks. I hated taking notes in class on the paper I had borrowed from Erin. She tore several pieces from a spiral notebook, giving me jagged-edged pages and leaving her with the same. No respectable librarian could deal with that kind of an affront to paper without reacting.

I wondered if I should text Daniel and let him know what happened in court. I knew my appointment as Brady's guardian might be mentioned in the newspaper. It was a matter of public record. I decided I should let him know, but then I remembered he had lied to me about the Buchanans. I tried to return my attention to Professor Cohen.

The sound of Brady's inconsolable wailing reverberated like an earworm playing over and over in my head. I put my pen down. Erin looked at me with alarm. I am always armed with a pen.

'Liv, are you OK?' she asked after class.

'Sure, I just need to catch up on my sleep. It's been a rough couple of days,' I said, folding the offending notepaper into half and putting it in my bag. I didn't mean to lie to Erin, but I didn't have the energy to explain the shame I felt for rejecting an innocent child. I just had to go.

Mary Ann Wallace, a younger police officer who now occupied the chair outside Brady's room, had replaced Officer Duggan. An older nurse named Carol had relieved Samantha. Neither questioned me when I told them who I was and why I was there. I took off the jacket to the black suit I had donned more than twelve hours before and began to put a johnny over my silk tee shirt.

'That will stain if he spits up,' Carol warned.

'I don't care,' I said and meant it.

'OK, you sit and I'll put him into your arms. He wiggles so much I worry about dropping him,' Carol said.

I sat in the chair, the lights in the room so dim I could only see the shadow of Carol carrying Brady to me. He screamed louder as she approached.

'You're sure you want to do this? You don't have to, you know.'

'I am and I know,' I said, cradling my arms so she could place Brady in them.

He felt like an electric jolt. He sprang erect and rigid and then arched his back while he shrieked. Carol was right. I thought I might drop him so I held him tighter and began to rock in the chair. Back and forth. I heard myself making hushing noises I didn't know I knew.

I hummed. I whispered. I talked nonsense. I rocked and rocked. My body was sweaty against his little brittle mass. But he smelled like I knew a baby should. And I snuggled him close to me like I would never let go.

Carol checked in periodically, once giving him medication I had authorized. I'm not sure when his wails turned into whimpers or when we fell asleep, but I woke to find the first light of day seeping in the windows while a baby slept tightly gripped in my arms.

After Carol finally lifted Brady from my arms, the warmth from his body continued to heat my chest and fill my heart. I wondered if this was what it was like to love a child. I removed the johnny damp with sweat and put my suit jacket back on. I should have been exhausted, but I felt more rested than I had in years.

I stepped into the hall to find Officer Duggan back on duty talking to Ryan Fairclough, who leaned against the wall, hands in his leather jacket pockets, speaking to him in earnest.

'Here she comes,' Duggan said.

'Olivia, Harry told me you were named as Brady's guardian. I hope you don't mind I tracked you down so I could buy you a cup of coffee and chat with you,' Ryan said.

I looked at my phone. It was 6:48 a.m.

'I know it's early, but we seem to have trouble catching up with each other.' He stepped away from the wall, slapped Duggan's shoulder a few times, and took me by the elbow.

'Hungry?' he asked.

'Famished,' I said. I realized all I had eaten since the dinner Josh had cooked was a hardboiled egg the morning before.

'Good. There's a spot I like just around the corner.'

It was a typical breakfast-only joint, quaint without being cute. Black and white checked linoleum floor, red vinyl booths, coffee Starbucks would be embarrassed to pour, but that I was delighted to drink.

I ordered the farmhouse breakfast with pancakes, scrambled eggs, sausage, and bacon.

'You weren't kidding about being hungry,' Ryan said after ordering blueberry pancakes.

'I tried calling you back,' I said, after the waitress took our order.

'I know. I'm sorry. When I got back from Vermont, they immediately assigned me to the Parro murder case. I found out you were named Brady's guardian before I had a chance to call you back. Now we can talk about both things,' he said.

He looked like he hadn't slept much since the last time I'd seen him. The crinkles around his eyes had darkened. I doubted I looked any better. I hadn't even combed my hair since I left Brady.

'Let's talk about Brady first,' I said.

Ryan told me that they hadn't made much progress on the case. Brady's father was a person of interest, but other than knowing he was also an opioid addict and dealer, they had nothing to prove he had killed Sophia Parro. Zack Laidlaw hadn't been found, nor had he turned himself in.

'Frankly, we're worried. There's a good chance whoever killed Sophia killed him. But if Zack is still alive, Brady could be in danger. That's how crazy this opioid stuff has gotten. We've got a cop assigned twenty-four hours to make sure nothing happens to that kid, but it's pretty clear Zack has pissed off some people high up in the drug business. That means you need to be extra careful too, Olivia. Your name was in the *Globe* this morning.' He stopped as the waitress put down huge platters in front of us.

I dug in, although I wasn't as hungry as I had thought before hearing how sinuous the young lives of Sophia and Zack had been. I knew I would need to let Daniel know about my appointment as Brady's temporary guardian – if he didn't already know.

'What about the Fairclough connection to me? You said you might have some news.' I wasn't sure what I could do about Brady's life, but maybe Ryan had information about my own.

He finished chewing on a piece of bacon.

'I called my dad. He and my stepmother are driving to Florida for the winter, so it took a little while for him to get back to me. He asked why I wanted to dig up ancient family history. I told him I had a friend who needed to know. He resisted answering, but finally said he was pretty sure his cousin Paulie was married to a Sheila a long time ago. They're both retired Boston P.D. He reminded me how sick Paulie is. He's at the V.A. Hospital in West Roxbury with a lung disorder he got in Vietnam.'

I winced. I could see I was causing consternation in the Fairclough family, just as I had cost Terry Walsh her job and created upheaval in hers. I was like a contagion bringing harm to families while I searched for my own.

'Maybe you should just forget about it, Ryan. I don't want to cause your family any problems. I'm sure it's pure coincidence that you have a Sheila Fairclough in your family. I have no business making waves on pure speculation,' I said. Privately, I hated abandoning the only lead to my identity I'd ever uncovered. But I'd already created enough trouble for Terry without now creating havoc for Ryan.

'It's OK. Paulie went on the Boston P.D. after he got home from Vietnam. I should visit him anyway. I'll let you know what I learn.'

'Listen, why don't I give you a photo of my mother to show him. That way we won't have to bother him if he doesn't recognize her.'

I opened my purse and pulled out a picture from my wallet of Mom and me at my college graduation. John had taken it and given it to me. I began carrying it when Mom started to lose her memory. I worried that she might disappear and I would need to show it in order to find her. At the time, I had been thinking that would more likely be in a grocery store than in a veterans' hospital. I gave the photo to Ryan, wondering if I was opening a huge can of worms. At best, learning Paulie's Sheila had no connection to me would be another disappointment. At worst, was I possibly about to open the door to a man who had tried to kill me and my mother?

I didn't resist Ryan's offer to walk me to my car. It was one thing to exaggerate an incident on a rotary or on a sidewalk while feeling anxious, but another to acknowledge the very real possibility someone may want to harm me because of Brady.

I drove home, still buoyed by my bonding with Brady. I pulled into the driveway, wondering how I would fall asleep for a few hours when it was such a sunny autumn day. I picked up the two newspapers now on the driveway and entered the code for the alarm. Once inside, I immediately noticed a pile of notebooks sitting on the stool at the kitchen island next to the one I normally sit on. I was flooded with relief at finding them, but furious at myself for overlooking them. I was simply overwrought and would have to ask Dr Evans what I needed to do to reel myself in. For now, I decided I would make a cup of chamomile tea and read the paper to make myself sleepy.

I took a mug of tea with the *Globe* into the conservatory. I plopped into the wicker chair, kicked off my shoes, and opened today's paper. I searched for the story that mentioned my name as Brady's guardian before I texted Daniel. I found it on the front page below the fold under a caption that read: 'Two Boston Mothers Dead in Unrelated Murders. No Arrests for Either.' Beneath the caption were two photos. One was of a very young woman with dark hair and hoop earrings as large as bracelets. The other was a file photo of a woman wearing a nurse's cap. It may have been thirty years old, but there was no mistake. The other mother who had been murdered was Terry Walsh.

TWENTY-FOUR

'She's no longer with us,' hadn't meant Terry no longer worked at Thompson House. It meant she was dead. The administration was using diplomatic doublespeak to convey a truth without involving Thompson House in a tragedy. Learning Terry's death had been ruled a homicide convinced me that my mother had also been murdered. I searched the article to learn how Terry was murdered, but only found that police were withholding details pending investigation.

I hated to think Terry's death was my fault. I'd felt responsible enough when I believed she had lost her job because I had asked for her help. I would never forgive myself if I had caused her murder. I thought about Joey and the tenderness Terry showed when she described him making their lunches each day. I wondered who would take care of Joey and hoped Terry had a supportive extended family.

I flipped through the paper to find an obituary for her, but saw none. I felt a terrible need to do something, anything that might atone for any part I may have played in Terry's death. I could send flowers, just as my friends had sent me the moth orchid. But flowers didn't sound like they would console Joey. I remember my mother baking macaroni and cheese, the one meal she had perfected, for families in Burlington when they had a death. I made a much better mac than Mom had. But I didn't even know where Terry lived.

I felt scattered. There were just too many things on my plate right now. I was now certain my mother had been murdered, although I had no idea about why someone would want to kill her. I knew Terry's death was connected. While I did believe in coincidences, neither of these two events could be one. I was scared.

I also knew my husband had lied to me about his adoptive parents being dead. I believed he may have had reason to want to consider them dead, but not sharing the truth with me seemed an irredeemable breach of trust.

While there may be a slight possibility I was on the verge of learning the real identity of my mother and me, I had no idea why she had nearly two million dirty dollars stashed in a safe deposit box in a credit union in Burlington, Vermont.

The emotions churning in me were confusing. I loved my mother, but wondered what she may have done in the past to require the dramatic flight she took with me when I was a child. I believed she wanted to protect me, but was angry she had gone to her grave never telling me the truth I deserved to know.

I loved the man I thought my husband had been when he rescued me from the life of a spinster, but now questioned whether that person ever existed.

All of those feelings I could share and dissect in Dr Evans' consultation room. But the one emotion in the pit of my belly I did not know how to deal with was fear. Two women were dead. My mother, and the nurse who believed she had not committed suicide.

'If you ever feel in danger, you must call Nikolai Wojcik.'

Was I in danger? I wasn't sure. I'll bet neither my mother nor Terry Walsh had believed they were in danger before they died. I wasn't going to chance it. I dialed Nikolai Wojcik's number and left him a message to return my call ASAP.

I texted Daniel next and told him about my appointment as Brady's guardian and assured him it was merely a legal formality so there would be someone to authorize medical procedures. I knew Daniel would get that and, with luck, think nothing more of it.

When my phone rang, I was sure it was Nikolai, which terrified as much as relieved me. But it was Ryan.

'Uncle Paulie won't answer my questions but said that if I bring you to meet him, you can ask whatever you want,' he said.

'Really? He wouldn't tell you who Sheila Fairclough is, if he even knows?' I asked.

'No, Liv. He was very firm about whose questions he would answer.'

'OK, you tell me when it's convenient,' I said. I was pressing my luck with Ryan, who sounded abrupt with me.

'Mornings are the best time for him, he said. How about first thing tomorrow? Where shall I meet you?'

'At Brady's room,' I said and hung up.

I closed my eyes and napped for an hour, long enough to fortify me for the rest of the day. I packed my notebooks carefully away and then pulled out my laptop. I searched for Terry Walsh's address and found several Theresa Walshes in Hyde Park. I then looked for Joseph Walsh and found an address on Winter Street that matched one of the addresses for Theresa Walsh.

I remembered Sugar Bakery in West Roxbury where I would buy whoopie pies and Oreo cupcakes as treats for Mom. I headed over there. I purchased a dozen different confections I hoped would ease Joey's pain and entered his address into my GPS.

I pulled up in front of a dilapidated single-family home on a street that the television crew from *Extreme Makeover* needed to visit. Terry had struggled hard to keep this rundown home for Joey, which made her death even sadder to me.

I got out of the car and walked up the front walk on to a porch with sagging planks in need of paint. I knocked on a door decorated with an autumn wreath adorned with miniature plastic pumpkins. No answer, although I could hear the sound of a television inside. I knocked again.

An older man yanked open the door.

'I've told you people I have no comment. Now go away or I'll call the police,' he said. It was obvious he thought I was a reporter.

'I'm not from the press. I was a friend of Terry's. She took care of my mother. I brought these for Joey,' I said, showing him the cardboard box with a string holding it closed.

He blinked, looked over his shoulder behind him.

'I'm Olivia Taylor and I am so very sorry about Terry,' I said.

He shifted from one foot to the other, and then surprised me by offering his hand.

'I'm Howie Walsh. Terry's ex. Joey's dad. Please come in,' he said.

TWENTY-FIVE

I stepped into a small hall with a maple coat rack covered with jackets. Howie led me past the darkened living room to the left where a television was blaring. I glimpsed at a mound on a reclining chair covered with a crocheted afghan that I assumed was Joey. He was sleeping, from the sound of the snoring.

We entered a small, dated, but cheerful kitchen that said TERRY with capital letters. A small maple table with captains' chairs sat in front of a window. Lime-green place mats were neatly arranged ready for the next meal, which for Terry would never come. A refrigerator filled with decorative magnets caught my attention. Signs and symbols from Cape Cod, the Red Sox, the Patriots, Dunkin' Donuts, and The Bowlarama covered the side-by-side fridge, much like the one Mom and I had many years ago. I pictured Terry and Joey taking field trips on their days off, bringing home a magnet from each as a souvenir. The counters were chipped green Formica, but clean except for a little clutter. The philodendron I had sent home with Terry sat on a paper plate, a ring of dried water surrounding it. I was on the verge of tears.

'Sit down,' Howie said, pointing to a chair with a tufted cushion that almost matched the color of the counters.

I collapsed into the chair, placing the bakery box in front of me. Howie took it and placed it on the counter next to the plant. He slid into the chair opposite me, giving me a view out the window behind him. I saw a rusted swing set in the small back yard that had yet to be raked of the autumn leaves. I wondered when Terry would have found the time to rake or whether Joey was capable of helping.

'Do you want some coffee or something?' Howie asked, jarring me from my thoughts.

'No, thank you. I didn't come to bother you or Joey. I just felt so bad hearing about Terry. I just learned she . . . I've been out of town at my mother's memorial service,' I said, silently asking myself why I was here. It had been impulsive to come, but I wanted to do something to help. Cupcakes seemed to be the extent of my support.

'I'm sorry about your mother. This is just so shitty,' Howie said, putting his hands over his puffy lined eyes. He had to be about sixty, with long stringy gray hair that sat on his thin shoulders but didn't cover his shiny bald dome. He was wearing a long-sleeve Grateful Dead Ship of Fools tee shirt that was lost on me.

'How is Joey taking it?' I asked.

'It's hard to tell. When someone comes to the door, he asks if it's Mummy, even though I've told him she's in heaven. I'm sure she is, poor old girl. After what I put her through and taking care of him.' He gestured toward the living room.

'She seemed like a devoted mother,' I said. I knew I couldn't ask the kind of questions I wanted to ask without listening to him. I was sure he and Joey had lost Terry at least partly because of me and owed him that much.

'We got married kind of late. I got her pregnant. I'm a musician. She used to drop by the bar where I played guitar a couple of nights a week after she finished the second shift at St. Margaret's. We got married and had Joey a couple of months later. It was pretty clear from the start something was wrong with him, but she didn't want to hear it,' Howie said, standing up and reaching into the refrigerator for a Sam Adams. 'You want one?'

'It's a little early for me,' I said immediately regretting how judgmental I sounded. 'Please, you go ahead. I know this can't be easy for you.'

'It's not me I'm worried about. Joey was Terry's life and vice-versa. They were like peas in a pod, if you know what I mean. We split when he was about five. The truth is, I couldn't hack it. His crying and whining. He was a twenty-four-seven job, and she already had a job. I'd come over and watch him while she worked, but I give her all of the credit for how well he's done. She got him into all sorts of programs at school. Fought the school board when they tried to cut off his eligibility for programs. She was a tiger. A spunky, good girl. I really did love her. I just couldn't handle it,' Howie said, draining half of the bottle down his throat.

I nodded, prompting him to go on.

'When Joey got too old for school, she put him in a workshop that taught him job skills. He got the job at the grocery store from there. He's had that job for thirteen years. Hell, I've never held a job thirteen months.'

'What will happen to Joey?' I asked because I needed to know. I hoped Howie was finally going to pony up.

'I don't know, but I'm going to do the best I can to do what I should have done a long time ago. I'll step in,' Howie said, draining the bottle and placing it on the placemat in front of him.

'She was good, and pretty patient with me too. She had us go to a lawyer a couple of years ago. We made mutual wills leaving everything we had to each other if something happened to one of us. Not to Joey. You know why?' he asked, looking at me like I might be judging him again.

'Sure, if you leave anything to Joey, the government will seize it to cover his benefits,' I said. 'I'm a law student,' I added.

'Yeah. He can't have anything in his own name. Poor kid. I'll move in here and try and take over. So far, he's been OK with me being here. I'm not sure how he'll do when we have the funeral.'

'When will that be? I'd like to attend. Terry was kind to my mother, who was another feisty woman. They hit it off,' I said.

'I don't know. The cops aren't telling me much. All I know is for some godforsaken reason, Terry left the house after Joey went to bed and never came home. Why she would do that, I'll never know. I mean, she'd run to the Cumberland Farms for milk or bread and leave him for a short time, but why would she end up in the parking lot at the Arnold Arboretum? Why would someone want to shoot her?' Howie choked back tears, while my eyes filled with them.

Terry had been killed in the Arnold Arboretum, the second largest link in the seven-mile-long network of parks and parkways in Boston known as the Emerald Necklace laid out by Frederick Law Olmsted. It was close to Moss Hill and Thompson House. It was another place I had taken my mother for long walks along the hills and brooks where we could pace ourselves while admiring species from all over the world. Terry's murder at a place that was sacred to nature lovers, including Mom and me, felt like a personal affront.

'Do they know who did it?' I asked, even though I was sure even if the cops had an idea who her killer was, they wouldn't share it with Howie.

'No, all they would tell me was that she died quickly and didn't suffer. She was shot in the back of the head, probably didn't know it was happening. Why would some bastard do this to her?' This time he couldn't hold the tears.

I stood and opened the refrigerator door, found another bottle of Sam Adams, and handed it to him. I was tempted to join him, but I knew I had to move on. I had to find out who had killed my mother and Terry. I was sure the same person killed them both. Why, I had no idea. I needed to think more about that. The motive might lead me to the answer. But one thing was clear. I owed it now to Joey.

'How about money, Howie? I know Terry worked hard to make ends meet,' I said. Since Howie had opened up to me, I felt comfortable raising the issue of money.

'It's not going to be easy. She still had a mortgage on this place. Joey gets social security disability payments, but it's pocket change. I can go on Social Security when I'm sixty-two, but that's not for another year. I won't be able to play any gigs if I have to be home with him, not that I have a lot these days,' Howie said.

'Mummy, Mummy. I want Mummy.' I could hear the anguished sound of Joey calling from the living room.

'I'll let you be,' I said. 'But I'll be in touch. I want to help.'

Howie rose from his chair, taking the box of cupcakes off the table.

'You already have,' he said smiling as he untied the string around the bakery box.

Not as much as I will, I thought as I walked to my car. I now knew where some of that stinking money would go.

TWENTY-SIX

I had two messages on my cell phone when I turned it back on. One was from Daniel, telling me to call him as soon as I got his message. Daniel rarely calls on his phone. He prefers the distance texting gives. The urgency in his voice told me he had something to say about my appointment as Brady's guardian.

The second message was from a woman who identified herself as Deema Zaheed, who said she was responding to the message I had left for Nikolai Wojcik. She asked me to please call her. I was far more interested in hearing what she had to say than listening to Daniel lecture me about the bad decisions I was sure he thought I was making.

Zaheed's telephone number was different than the one I had called looking for Wojcik. I couldn't imagine who she was or how she was connected to him, but I also had no idea why my mother had a stash of dirty cash in a safe deposit box. I dialed the number.

'Zaheed.' She had no trace of an accent, Boston or foreign.

'This is Olivia Taylor returning your call,' I said, trying to sound nonchalant, although I felt anything but.

'Ah, Ms Taylor. Thanks for getting back to me. I'd love to have a conversation with you, but I think it's better if we have it in person,' Zaheed said, sounding all business, yet friendly.

'I'm not sure I want to do that,' I said, because I wasn't. There was just too much bizarre stuff going on all around me right now for me to feel warm and fuzzy about meeting someone I hadn't placed a call to just because she thought it was better.

'I understand your reluctance, but a short fifteen-minute meeting, say at the bar at Legal Sea Foods across from Portia after class, should feel safe to you,' she said.

It did. I would be in a busy bar in the middle Boston's theater district where lots of theatergoers and even a few of my classmates would be jammed in having martinis and sushi. I figured why not. I had initiated the call. Only after I agreed and hung up did I realize I never told Zaheed I attended law school or had class that evening.

I decided not to obsess about it and moved on to returning Daniel's call. Of course it went right to voicemail. Daniel never picks up. He prefers to selectively return calls. I left a message telling him that I was on my way to school. If he couldn't call me right back, he would have to text me. If lucky, I figured I could avoid a conversation and confrontation.

My phone chirped. I was on his VIP list for the day.

'O-liv-i-a, what are you thinking?' he said, giving my name its four-syllable due.

'About what, Daniel?' I asked. About my mother's death, Terry Walsh's murder, or your adoptive parents being alive, I wanted to add, but I didn't.

'That child. The baby whose mother was murdered while she was still carrying him,' he said, sounding disgusted.

'The guardianship a judge appointed me to? What about it? It's part of my family law legal clinic experience.'

'That's not the point. That woman was murdered and her killer, which may be the baby's father, is still at large. Why would you accept such an appointment, knowing you could be placing yourself in danger? Olivia, you aren't thinking clearly. It's too soon for you after losing Claire. You're not able to make sound decisions,' he said in a more dramatic version of his regular lectures to me.

'Daniel, I am not at risk. Maybe Brady is. That's the baby's name. But he's under twenty-four-hour police protection at Children's so he should be fine, and so will I.' I was glad this was a telephone conversation. When Daniel and I argue in person, the intensity of his gaze reminds me of the bright lights used in police stations during interrogations and I have trouble holding my ground.

'You need to resign immediately. I know better about this type of situation. You are too fragile after your mother's death to make a good call here.' I noticed he sounded a little breathless. I waited a few seconds to respond.

'No, Daniel. I won't. This is my career we're talking about.'

'You can't seriously be planning to build a career dealing with the tawdry messes people like this create.' Daniel's comment momentarily jarred me. Yes, that was exactly what I planned to do.

'Isn't that what lawyers do, Daniel? We help people out of the messes they create in their lives. And don't psychiatrists help them cope with the internal fallout while they fix their lives? Lawyers help them out of the mess, while psychiatrists help them through it.' This was the first conversation we had ever had about the underlying missions in our chosen fields.

'Don't try to make this a philosophical difference, Liv. You know this could reflect on my professional status poorly,' Daniel said. 'I can't have my wife connected to gang murders if I want to join the upper echelon in psychiatry.'

I had no idea what the hell he was talking about.

'This is about my profession, not yours. I'll make my own career decisions, thank you. I appreciate your concern,' I said, waiting for him to blast me, tell me I needed to up my meds, but there was nothing. He had hung up on me. I had silenced Daniel. It was a first.

Erin was waiting for me when I arrived at my spot in the library. She was dressed uncharacteristically in all black. Stretchy black jeans, a tight turtle neck over her curvy chest, and black leather boots up to her knees.

'You have seen the newspaper,' she said, pointing to the *Boston Globe* she had spread open on the table before her.

'Yes. That's the nurse who took care of my mother.' I pointed to the picture of Terry. 'You met her when we were cleaning out Mom's room.'

'Liv, I don't want to be an alarmist, but you must realize that having your mother's nurse murdered and being appointed guardian of a baby whose mom was also murdered is like, a lot, a lot of shit,' Erin said somberly. 'Are you OK with it? I mean, you just lost your mom. Maybe I shouldn't have encouraged you to join the clinic so soon.'

I could bear Daniel doubting my professional choices, but not Erin, especially since she seemed to feel responsible for them.

'Erin, please don't second-guess yourself. I am going to love the clinic. I thought I wanted to practice family law, but sitting in the courtroom with Professor Cohen the other day watching the proceedings made me know, this is what I want to do. Besides, I won't officially start for a few weeks until the registrar clears my enrollment. It was just a fluke I was there to be appointed Brady's guardian, but I'm glad I was.' I slumped into the chair opposite her and looked at the photos of Terry and Sophia.

'Before your mother died, I worried that you were too isolated and wondered how I could help bring you out of your shell. Now I want to put you on a leash,' she said, chuckling. 'You do know you are always welcome to come and stay with me, don't you? Even just for the pleasure of my company.' She winked, threatening to drain the dam I was holding within me.

I wanted to tell Erin about Deema Zaheed and Paulie Fairclough, but I had burdened her enough. I would wait until the time was right, when I knew more about both situations.

'I'm OK, Erin. Maybe I'm just beginning to live my own life.'

'Well, OK, but don't get stupid about it. Ryan says they've got a cop watching over the baby twenty-four-seven. That should tell you, you need to be careful.'

'He told you that?' I asked. I was surprised Ryan would be discussing my need to be careful with my best friend. Now there were three people who seemed to think they could assess the risk I was under better than me.

'Chill, Liv. I called him. I was worried and knew he would know about the Baby Brady case, even if he wasn't on it, which he is. But you already know that. Don't go getting pissy about him again. He's a great guy,' she said, reminding me just how loyal a friend she was.

Andrew found us after class to see if we wanted to join him for a drink. I told him that I had already had plans to meet someone across the street at Legal Sea Foods. Erin gave me the look she is inclined to give when she feels like an overprotective mother, but said nothing.

The dampness of the past week had turned into a crispness that reminded me of Vermont. Soon it would be colder than even I liked it, but tonight I felt alive as the brisk air entered my nostrils as I crossed Stuart Street. I entered the Park Square locale of Legal Sea Foods, expecting to hear the usual buzz of conversation and laughter. Instead, it was nearly empty and quiet.

I looked around to find a dark-haired woman sitting in a booth waving at me. She stood to greet me. She was dressed in a boyish-cut herringbone pantsuit with three-quarter-length sleeves and pants that didn't quite meet her slender ankles. She wore a pair of Everlane bright-red day heels I recognized because I'd had a pair in my shopping bag online for a month but hadn't the fashion confidence to hit 'buy.' I'd felt comfortable in my jeans and a gray merino turtleneck sweater with ballet flats when sitting with Howie in his kitchen, but now was intimidated by stylish Deema Zaheed donning a bright smile outlined in lipstick that matched her shoes. She extended her hand, giving me a firm shake, and pointed to the bench for me to sit.

'Let's get you a glass of wine, or something, before we chat,' she said, gesturing for the waiter I knew was a second-year law student at Portia. Deema already had a glass of white wine in front of her. An order of Legal's jumbo shrimp cocktail, a favorite of mine, sat between us on the white tablecloth.

Once I had a glass of chardonnay in front of me, she began by pushing her card across the table toward me. I picked it up. Deema Zaheed was a member of the Federal Bureau of Investigation. As in FBI. How my telephone call to Nikolai Wojcik resulted in me having a glass of wine with an FBI special agent was beyond me. I hoped my mother hadn't been wanted for some crime. The dirty money must have come from somewhere illegal. I was beginning to regret what my telephone call may have set in motion.

'I want you to know who I am, and that you are safe talking to me,' she started. 'Please, help yourself to some shrimp. You must have had a long day. I remember what it was like when I was in law school. Eating was the last thing I had time for. Well, maybe sleep.' She gave me a sheepish grin, showing a mouth full of beautiful teeth.

I was on to her. The FBI always built empathy with people when they conduct interviews. I watched enough television to know that.

'I don't understand,' I said. Let her do the talking to start with, I decided.

'What don't you understand?' she asked. OK, she was better at this than I.

'Look, I called a number for a guy named Nikolai Wojcik. Why do I get a return call and visit from the FBI? Have I done something wrong?' I asked. I took a sip of the buttery chardonnay, wishing it were something stronger.

'Why don't you tell me why you called him?' Deema said, placing the tail of a shrimp she had consumed on a plate.

I plucked the index card I had found in the safe deposit box with my mother's instructions out of my jean pocket.

'Here,' I said. 'I found it with some of my mother's things. She just passed away.'

'So you're not feeling safe,' she said, reading the card.

'Well, not exactly. I don't know. I'm confused. So much has happened since my mother died,' I said, sputtering the obvious. I looked away from her gaze, not able to endure her scrutiny, when I noticed Erin and Andrew sitting a few tables away. My guardian angels. I wished they would come over and join us, but I knew Erin would only watch from afar, unless she thought I needed what she called an 'intervention.'

Deema said nothing. Shrinks aren't the only ones who know how to capitalize on silence.

'There are some questions about my mother's death. A few days ago, a nurse who took care of her at the memory loss center where she died and shared my suspicions was murdered.' Now it was my turn to be silent.

'I see. Do you personally feel in imminent danger, Olivia?'

I was tired of people asking me that. I must project vulnerability somehow.

'No. I don't think so,' I said.

'I mean, it's been more than twenty-five years, so it's unlikely, but not unheard of,' she said, draining her wine glass.

Twenty-five years? What the hell was she talking about?

'What's been twenty-five years?'

'Since you entered the program,' Deema said, like I should have known the answer.

'What program?' I knew I sounded guileless, even ignorant, but I didn't care. I knew I was on to something I had wanted to know for most of my life.

'You mean you don't know? Your mother never told you?' she asked, her thick dark eyebrows reaching up toward her ebony bangs.

'Apparently not. What are you talking about? Tell me.' I had raised my voice enough that our waiter looked over.

'WITSEC, Olivia. The witness protection program. You and your mother entered it about twenty-five years ago.'

I gasped and placed my hands over my mouth. I had never considered the possibility we were living under the witness protection program. It felt too exotic for my ordinary mother and me. We were just simple Vermont folk.

'I need to know more. I need to know it all,' I said, recapturing my poise. I wanted to know who we had needed protection from, if my father was an international terrorist, or a member of the mob. Most important to me was learning why someone wanted to harm my mother and me.

'And we may need to know more from you. But not with me. Agent Wojcik retired a few years ago, but he'll be the best one to talk to you. He'll be in touch, OK?' she asked, calling the waiter for our bill. Conversation over. I took a shrimp and gnawed on it just so I would feel like I had gotten something out of this meeting with my government. Something more than the knowledge I had been raised under the Witness Protection Program.

TWENTY-SEVEN

joined Andrew and Erin for a second glass of wine, shooing away their questions about who I had had my first with by telling Andrew I would let him do his magic with my hair, something he had continued to pester me about.

'Seriously? Oh, you won't be sorry. When? I want you to commit to a time and not try to get out of it later.'

I laughed and agreed to come to his salon on Newbury Street Friday afternoon, when we had no class. I was relieved to have company walking back to the parking garage where we set off on our separate ways. The drive to Children's Hospital was less than ten minutes with no traffic. I handed the keys to the parking valet and was on Brady's unit by 11:00, just as the nurses were changing shift.

I had telephoned Brady's nurse twice during the day to check on him. Carol waved to me to wait until she was finished giving a report to the oncoming third shift so we could talk. I sat watching the choreography that takes place when the second shift staff that covers 3 to 11 p.m. signs off to the third shift, aptly dubbed the graveyard shift. When the quiet bustle was over, Carol joined me on a chair at the edge of the nurses' station where I had been sitting, replaying my meeting with Deema Zaheed in my head.

After removing a pink stethoscope from around her neck, she took a piece of paper out of the front pocket of her scrubs that were decorated with Disney images and handed it to me.

'This is the name and number of Brady's DCF worker. Naomi Grenetier. They're doing a developmental eval. to see what Brady's needs will be for foster placement once he's stabilized here,' she said. 'She didn't ask for your contact information, so I don't imagine she's very interested in talking to you. I thought maybe you'd like to reach out to her.'

I hadn't expected planning for Brady's placement in foster care would start so soon. I knew what Carol was telling me. If the Department of Children and Families was involved with Brady,

I'd better be on top of it. DCF had a propensity for mismanaging the placement of children. After Brady's precarious introduction to life, he couldn't afford a bureaucratic mishap.

Besides, he was tiny and vulnerable. As I took him into my arms wrapped in a receiving blanket and sat in the huge rocking chair trying to soothe his writhing body, I vowed to be vigilant. I knew efforts were being made to locate relatives of Brady's mother. Maybe they would intervene. I looked at his tiny fingers, nails the size of a peppercorn. He opened and closed his fists in wretched uncertainty. This little boy was having a tough start he hadn't asked for.

I had planned to google WITSEC once Brady finally fell asleep, but I was so exhausted I nodded off with him. We dozed and awoke together periodically. When Brady whimpered, I rocked. When he startled, I drew him nearer to my body. When he screamed, I nestled his ears next to my mouth and cooed. A nurse brought a large blanket and covered us both.

Wednesday, October 22nd

By daybreak, I'd had enough mini naps to feel ready to meet Paulie Fairclough. I kissed Brady on his furrowed little brow and slipped into some fresh clothes I had brought in the yoga bag I keep in my car. In black yoga pants and shirt with my black ballet flats, I looked like an Erin wannabe, but I felt fresh as I set off to meet Ryan at the diner he had taken me to the morning before.

He looked freshly showered with slightly damp hair as I slid into the booth across from him. I thought I smelled a whiff of soap, but knew I must be imagining it. My senses seemed to be overly susceptible to this man.

'How are you doing?' I asked.

'OK. There's some good news. Zack Laidlaw, Brady's father, has been sighted twice, so he's alive. We've got a lead on where he may be currently hiding out,' he said, making me realize my visit with his uncle might be interfering with his investigation.

'Don't worry, we can't check it out until later,' he said, reading my mind. 'We think he's hiding from a drug cartel. That he and Sophia had plans to bolt with the money from the sale of a major heroin shipment after she had the baby.'

I struggled to eat some scrambled eggs, but my appetite had

waned. Ryan managed to tuck into a pile of blueberry pancakes that made up for it. We chatted about school and how neither of us would pass the MPRE if we didn't find more time to study.

I left my car at the hospital and rode to the West Roxbury Veterans' Hospital with Ryan. He explained his Uncle Paulie was his father's cousin, but he hadn't been to many Fairclough family events.

'Paulie retired earlier than my dad. He had health issues,' Ryan said as we circled the same rotary I had felt captive in a few days before. I was tempted to share my story with him, but was more interested in the Fairclough family history.

'I don't know Paulie as well as my father's other cousins. He was always kind of quiet. He still was when I visited him the other day, come to think of it,' Ryan said as we entered the VFW Parkway flanked by ancient trees. The autumn sun flickered through the canopy of golden leaves, making me miss Vermont and my mother.

The hospital parking lot was huge and full, even though it was barely 7 a.m. The enormous old red brick building was topped with an imposing spire and weathervane. Ryan parked in a spot reserved for those with 'official business.' I was suitably impressed we qualified and felt ready for my meeting with Paulie Fairclough.

'He said he'd like us to meet him in the library,' Ryan said as we walked through an entrance far more modern than the exterior of the building.

'How apropos,' I said. Ryan looked puzzled.

'I was a research librarian.' I was struck that a man who was taking me to meet his uncle where we might learn we were related did not know this much about me.

Ryan guided us through corridors and up elevators before we entered a surprisingly busy library. I inhaled the familiar scent of books and began to relax, aware of Ryan's hand on my back as he headed us over to a table in the corner. A frail-looking man with thick gray hair and bushy eyebrows watched us approach.

'Paulie Fairclough, meet Olivia Taylor,' Ryan said with warmth.

Paulie began to rise, but I put out my hand.

'Please sit,' I said.

'If you will join me,' Paulie said, in mock grandeur, smiling at me with yellowed teeth that suggested he smoked.

'And what about me?' Ryan asked, pretending offense.

'That's up to this young lady. Do you want him in on our conversation?' Paulie's tone had moved from charming to earnest, even conspiratorial.

I hesitated. Even if Paulie Fairclough was my father, he was too ill to cause me physical harm, so I wasn't afraid of him hurting me. But still, I had no idea what I was about to learn. I doubt it could stun me more than the revelation that I'd been in the WITSEC program. Part of me wanted to protect my privacy and shield my reaction to whatever Paulie was about to tell me from Ryan. He had already seen me emotionally raw at the hospital the night my mother died. But shouldn't someone bear witness if this was the big reveal?

'Please stay,' I said. Ryan shuffled over to a chair to the side of us and lowered his lanky body into it.

'So,' I started. Paulie laughed, coughing, which sounded like he had emphysema among his other maladies.

'So, you want to know who Sheila Fairclough is.'

'Yes, please.' My heart was pounding so loud I thought it might burst from my chest.

'Sheila Fairclough was my wife. My first wife. We went together in high school and got married a few years after I came back from Vietnam.'

He stopped. His shoulders stooped as he looked down at his fingernails. I looked over at Ryan who looked back at me then over to Paulie. Paulie wasn't going to tell me what I'd come to learn until he'd had his say. After waiting a lifetime for answers, I would have to be patient a little longer.

'Sheila was a pistol. Beautiful, auburn hair, not a lot of freckles. Just a couple across her nose. Enough to make her cute. And smart. She should have gone to college. The nuns tried to talk her father into it, but he said no one in his family went to college and they did all right. You know how that goes,' Paulie said, looking over at me. I nodded, not wanting to interrupt him.

'I got on the Boston P.D. after the war. There was preferential treatment for Vets, and our family has a history on the force, right, Ryan?' Paulie winked as Ryan gave him a thumbs-up and a grin.

'Sheila worked at the telephone company. Back then, that was the place to work for girls. We saved our money and bought a three-bedroom ranch over on Squantum with a VA loan, which was a little tricky because of the residency requirement at work. But I used my parents' address in Southie to get around it. Life was good. We decided to start a family. Sheila wanted three kids and didn't want to wait until she was too old to enjoy them.' Paulie paused, a little out of breath.

'Do you want some water?' I asked. I desperately wanted him to continue telling me what I was beginning to believe was my mother's history.

Ryan popped up out of his chair. 'I'll get it.'

'Do you want me to wait till he gets back?' Paulie asked.

'No, please go on if you're OK.'

'Not much happened after that. Sheila's sisters hadn't waited to buy a house before they started having kids. Sheila wanted to be sensible, do things in their proper order, which is why we waited until we had a house of our own. Sheila played the happy aunt to Eileen and Mary Beth's kids, patiently waiting for us to get pregnant. But it just didn't happen. After a few years, her doctor sent us into Boston for some testing. She was fine, but they had me come here. That was the first sign I had gotten something over in 'Nam. I was sterile, they said. It turned out it was a lot more than that, but back then that was what mattered. We were devastated.'

Ryan returned with three bottles of water, handing Paulie one first, and then giving me one.

'I was just telling Olivia that one of the thank-yous I got for Viet Nam was not being able to have kids.'

So I wasn't looking at my father across the table. I had doubted Paul Fairclough was my dad based only on instinct. He seemed nice enough, but I didn't feel a connection, although I realized that might be a silly thing to expect, another of my many childhood fantasies.

'I'm sorry,' I said, wanting to acknowledge his loss. Not being able to have children must be as painful for men as it is for women, although until now it had not occurred to me.

'Sheila didn't want to adopt. I did. We fought about it and then she decided she wanted a career. It was beginning to be a thing then. Women were going to law school and medical school. She hadn't gone to college, so she decided to get a certificate as a paralegal and see if she liked it enough to go further. I was OK with it. I mean, if I couldn't give her the one thing she wanted most, she could do whatever she liked.'

Paulie tugged off the cap to his water and took a big gulp.

'You sure you want to hear the rest of this?' he asked me.

'I not only *want* to hear it, I *need* to, Paulie,' I said with a reverence close to prayer.

I could see he was vacillating. These memories were painful to him and not worth enduring if they weren't relevant. He reached into his pocket and removed the photo I had given Ryan.

'That's my mother and me at my college graduation about eight years ago,' I said.

He frowned and then smiled. 'Why did she color her hair? It was beautiful in the sun when it was lighter. But yes, that's my Sheila, curves and all.'

I almost exploded with relief, while chuckling at the comment about my mother's curves.

'So my mother was Sheila Fairclough,' I said.

'It looks that way. Do you want me to finish?'

I nodded. *Please finish. Get to the part about me*, I implored him silently.

'OK, but first I have to hit the little boys' room.'

TWENTY-EIGHT

I waited to groan until Ryan had shuffled Paulie toward the bathrooms at the corner of the room. Even though he was obviously very ill, Paulie stood almost as tall as Ryan. Families. How I longed for one. But it was clear, the one I was getting might not be the one I had wished for.

I gazed around the library created for patients, many who required long-term treatment. It was cheerful, with informative displays featuring relevant books scattered around the room. Notices were posted for various 12-step programs, along with announcements for upcoming events.

Back at the table, Paul seemed tired. His breath was ragged and his color gray. I knew my window was closing, so I gently pressed forward.

'So my mother worked as a paralegal?' I asked.

'Yep. She went to work in Boston for a guy who had grown up with us in Southie, although we didn't go to school with him. He was a triple eagle. You know what that is, don't you?'

I nodded. I'd learned at Portia, being a triple eagle in Boston was an enviable credential, a triple crown of sorts. It meant you had graduated from Boston College High School, or B.C. High, as it was known, then B.C. College, and B.C. Law.

'She did real good working for Mickey Burke, raced right past the other paralegals and secretaries who'd been working for the firm for years. Sheila made more money and worked longer hours than me. We barely saw each other. That's when I started drinking. It didn't help the marriage, for sure.'

'You must have been lonely,' I said, knowing Paulie also must have felt a sense of shame for not being able to give Sheila what she wanted so badly. A family. It seemed inconceivable she hadn't understood how badly I wanted to know about my own.

'Not enough to leave, even when she asked me to. I kept thinking I could make it right. We pretty much led separate lives. I worked crazy hours anyway, so it was pretty easy to stay out of each other's way.' He stopped to take a sip from the water bottle. 'One night she waited up for me. I knew something was up. She was sitting at the kitchen table and asked me to sit down. I thought she was going to give me divorce papers. Instead, she told me she was pregnant,' Paulie said, swallowing hard as the words came out.

'With me?' I asked.

He nodded, looking down at his hands.

'So there was that. I had guessed there was someone else. I'd been bunking in what was supposed to be the nursery for a couple of years. Sheila was the kind of woman men flocked to. I had been lucky she picked me when she did. I didn't say anything. I got up and left and got as drunk as I ever had been or ever will be in my life.'

'I'm sorry,' I said, not knowing for what. Hearing that my conception was a source of sorrow to anyone was painful. It made me consider if it had been a precursor to how I would affect people throughout my life. I would bring joy to no one. I had been a burden even to my own mother.

'I sobered up. Talked to someone at A.A. and went home a couple of days later. I asked Sheila if the baby's father wanted to marry her. She said he was already married and not in a position to go through a messy divorce. I asked her if she loved him. She never said yes, but smiled in a way she had never smiled about me. I told her I was willing to stay with her and raise the baby as my own. Wasn't that what we both had wanted, I asked. Where we had gone off track?'

'You offered to raise me as your own?' I asked. I was astounded at his generosity, even if it had been motivated by his desire to keep my mother as his wife.

'She said she couldn't let me do that. She had screwed up my life more than I deserved, but she did let me talk her into us staying together until after you were born, so there'd be a certain amount of respectability about you coming. Quiet some of the rumors that Sheila had been having an affair with her boss. I agreed, thinking I'd have a chance to make it work. She'd see how great a father I'd be, well, you know.' He shrugged at his own innocence. I wondered how I would have turned out if Paulie Fairclough had raised me.

'You were a beautiful baby. You're still beautiful, young lady, but back then you had the softest blonde fuzzy hair and a button nose. I was crazy about you. Sheila reminded me not to get too attached, but I was as ga-ga about you as I was her, even though I knew I probably wasn't going to change your mother's mind.'

'What was my name?' I had imagined all sorts of names over the years. Jessica, Jennifer, Sarah.

'Ashley Ann Fairclough.'

What a beautiful name. Far more lyrical than any I had fantasized about.

'We stayed together longer than I had hoped. Had a couple of great Christmases. I got to take you skating for the first time after I gave you skates.'

'I skated all through high school,' I said, wanting to give Paulie something back, something that showed his efforts were appreciated and had an impact. He smiled.

'I thought we might go on forever, but things were getting dicey for your mother at work. Lots of pressure and some publicity about some bad stuff going down with some of the clients,' Paulie said.

'When did you leave?' I asked. I couldn't help getting angry with my mother. She had caused this man a lot of pain.

'A little after your third birthday. I painted your bedroom walls pink with white polka dots as your present. You loved your polka dots.'

I did love polka dots. I still loved them. Whether on Daniel's ties, a blouse or dress. I tried not to cry because I was certain Paulie would follow suit.

'Before I left, your mother drew up our divorce papers and a deed to the house she had signed over to me. She told me that she might not be staying in Boston and, if she left, I could record the deed to the house and take it back. She thanked me for what I had done for her and you.

'Even after that, I couldn't entirely stay away. I'd come over when she wasn't home and mow the lawn. My second wife told me I was addicted to Sheila. That I might have given up booze, but I had never been able to quit her. She was probably right,' Paulie said, no longer looking at me. He stared off in the distance to a time and a woman forever lost.

I knew he was done talking to me. I doubted he talked much

about this part of his life. Opening up had exhausted him. I knew I shouldn't press for much more, but I had one more question I couldn't leave unanswered.

'Is Mickey Burke my father?' I asked.

'I never made her tell me outright. I didn't have to. Yes, Mickey Burke was your father.'

Before I left, I gave Paulie a kiss on his reddened cheek and thanked him for stepping up when I was a baby and for telling me the truth I deserved to know.

TWENTY-NINE

I walked next to Ryan through corridors and down stairs in silence. The conversation with Paulie Fairclough had been surreal. Hearing about my mother's other life had been like listening to a story about someone I didn't know, which was probably true. I didn't know my own mother.

Once in the car, I turned to Ryan. I knew I should probably tell him what I had learned about being in WITSEC, but all I could think about was what I had learned from Paulie.

'Please tell me where I can find Mickey Burke.' In my heart, I knew what he was going to say, but I had to hear it and hadn't wanted Paulie Fairclough to be the one to tell me.

'Olivia, I'm sorry. Mickey Burke has been dead for years. He was killed in jail. I don't know all of the details, but he was a lawyer for the Irish mob and turned state's evidence,' Ryan said, looking at me like I might break.

'What am I supposed to do with all of this?' I said, pounding my fists against the dashboard. 'I finally get answers and all of the goddam people are dead. Where do I go with this? What good does it do now?'

My chest was heaving as I hyperventilated.

'I wish there was something I could do,' Ryan said.

We sat in silence for a few minutes. Then he put the car in drive and pulled out of the parking lot, turning up the VFW Parkway a short distance, where he crossed over and drove into another parking lot, but this one was nearly empty. I looked up at a sign that read: 'The Jim Roche Community Arena.'

'Come on,' Ryan said, getting out of the car.

'What?' I said, getting out and looking at him in puzzlement.

'You need to get out of your head for a while, Olivia.'

Inside the indoor skating facility, Ryan led me to an area where you could rent skates. He greeted a man sitting on a stool, who seemed to know him.

'Finally decided to join the Men's Hockey League, Ryan?' he asked.

'Can't fit it into my schedule at the moment, but we'd love to rent a couple of pairs and spin around while the ice is empty.'

'You got the place to yourself, until noon.'

I slid my feet into skates for the first time in about ten years. Even though they were rented, they felt like favorite old slippers. Ryan had his on before I was done and before I knew it, we were on the ice.

I took my time, slowly gliding forward and around the rink. I liked that Ryan left me on my own and was circling ahead of me. In short time, I lost any awareness he or anyone was around me. I started to skate faster, feeling my lungs expand with each rotation around the rink. Sweat began gathering on my neck, reminding me of one of the first contradictions in life I had learned. You can get hot skating on ice.

My legs felt strong, my face alive. I remembered how to stop then how to skate backwards, loving that I had the entire rink to myself. The world was mine. Skating backwards, I had the urge to do a jump, just as I had back in the day. I wondered if I could do at least a single Salchow, the most basic of jumps, or if I was too old, nearing the age of thirty. I could break an ankle.

Screw it, I thought, and went for it. I pressed back into the blade of my left skate, pushed off and sprung into the air for one simple spin that seemed to last a lifetime, until I landed on the outside of my right skate. I put my arms up in victory and skated over to the edge of the ice, where Ryan stood in amazement.

'Olivia, did you just do that?'

I grinned. I wanted to throw my arms around him and thank him for bringing me here where I could recover from the jolt Paulie Fairclough had dealt me.

'Thank you, Ryan,' I said, reining in my gratitude. I already knew how powerful it was to hug this man.

His cell phone rang, bursting the bubble, but I was ready to move on. I would research Mickey Burke, WITSEC, and see if I could trace my mother's relatives while at school.

I asked Ryan if he could let me run into my house on Moss Hill on our way to retrieving my car at the Children's Hospital parking lot. He sat in the car in the driveway as I dashed in to grab my MPRE book, which I had neglected during the past week. I popped into the house, turning off the alarm. I didn't want to take the time to change my clothes. Ryan had already spent two hours of his day on me that should be focused on Sophia's murder investigation. I tucked into the laundry room off the hall to the left where I grabbed clean jeans, a turtleneck, and underwear from a basket of clothes I had folded but had yet to put away. I passed through the hall into the kitchen and headed for my desk, when I sneezed. I breathed in, noticing the faint but distinct smell of cologne tinted with pear, one that makes me break into serial sneezing. I learned this when Daniel bought me cologne as a gift early in our relationship, which was when he moved on to buying me nightgowns. I could tolerate simple fragrances like lavender, citrus, and a few other herbs, but the more exotic scents sent me into a sneezing frenzy.

I sneezed again, paralyzed where I had been standing. I couldn't picture what we owned that would release that odor. I pulled the laundry I was holding in my arms up to my nose to confirm it had no scent. I used fragrance-free detergent because of my sensitivity to many smells. The laundry was odorless.

I raced over to my desk, picked up the MPRE manual, and then opened a drawer to get a fresh spiral notebook. I rushed out the door, embracing the pile, and jumped back into the car. Ryan was still talking on his phone. By the time we were on the Jamaicaway, I questioned whether I'd had some kind of panic attack because of the emotional morning I'd had.

'I can't thank you enough for this morning,' I said when he dropped me off in front of Children's.

'No need. You deserve to have answers, Olivia. Just remember, you get to live your own life. You don't have to live the one someone has handed you.'

I headed up to the NICU and over toward Officer Duggan, who sat like a potted plant outside Brady's door.

'You gotta sign in now,' he told me. 'They're beefing up security since they think the kid may be the lure to get the father out of hiding.'

I inquired at the nurses' station about signing in.

'Yeah, we don't usually make parents or guardians sign in, but they've toughened security up, so now you have to sign each time you go in to visit Brady. We're trying to get him on a bottle, by the way.' The NICU administrator handed me the same three-ring binder I had read earlier when I had first familiarized myself with Brady's history. It had grown several inches thick and was bulging with paper.

The front divider was labeled 'SIGN IN SHEETS.' I opened it and saw a long list of professionals who had signed in over the past few days. Each of the police officers' signatures had BPD next to it. There were MDs, RNs, Lic.SWs with DCF, and a number of other abbreviations that I didn't recognize. I scanned the list and noticed a familiar name. Kayla Vincent, MD had come to visit Brady this morning. I skimmed the notes contained within the various other dividers, but saw nothing bearing her signature. I wondered if Kayla might be part of Brady's developmental evaluation team. I hoped not. I didn't like the idea of her being anywhere near him.

I watched the nurse struggling to have Brady take a bottle so he could be weaned off intravenous feeding. I knew how challenging her task was. I had tried helping him accept a pacifier both of the nights I had stayed with him. But each time he would try to grasp on to it, it would fall out when he resumed crying frantically. I told her I couldn't stay now, but would be back later in the evening after class to try my luck.

At Portia, I discovered a first-year law student sitting at my table in the library with his stuff sprawled across it like it belonged to him. I wanted to take my forearm and sweep his book, pens, and forbidden Starbucks container to the floor and scream, 'Mine!' like a three-year-old.

Instead, I cramped into a library carrel unworthy of me and delved into the important questions I needed answered. I opened my laptop and began typing furiously. Michael Burke first, then I would move on to WITSEC. Pages came up, starting with his death twenty-three years ago. He was forty-two years old. I was seven. I felt my throat closing, knowing tears weren't far behind, and was now grateful for the privacy of the carrel. There were thousands of documents available to me. Trial transcripts, books, and more newspaper articles than I could read in a lifetime. What stopped me was his photograph.

This is where I got my wavy blonde hair. I couldn't see the color of his eyes, but I bet they were blue like mine and that he had been tall and slim. I had grown up wishing I had my mother's dramatic good looks. Now I knew I had inherited my father's Irish smile, fair complexion, and freckles. Maybe it wasn't a fluke I had entered law school. Wanting to be a lawyer may have been in my genes. I had so many questions, some of which could never be answered in news articles.

My phone vibrated. I picked it up, concerned I might miss a message about Brady as much as anything else.

'I'm over at Jacob Wirth having a bite of lunch if you'd like to walk over and join me,' a man said.

'Who is this?' I asked, impatient with someone who had probably called a wrong number.

'Wojcik. Nick Wojcik.'

THIRTY

I gathered up my belongings and headed out the door on to Stuart Street and down a block. I'd been by Jacob Wirth's countless times. The exterior old clock with the name of the famous German beer hall on it had fascinated me, but I could never persuade my law school buddies to visit a place so uncool it was for sale and had recently filed for bankruptcy. Apparently, Nick Wojcik didn't care.

The restaurant had the kind of decayed look I happen to like. Bentwood chairs that scraped the old wooden floors. A brass railing separating the bar from the eating area. Beers were listed on signs everywhere. I found Nick Wojcik sitting behind a half-finished one.

'How did you know I was across the street?' I asked before saying hello. I was tired of the FBI knowing where I was without knowing why.

'Just a precaution when you alerted us that you might be in harm's way,' he said, pointing to the chair opposite him. 'Please sit and join me for lunch. I wanted to be sure to have one more before the place is bought and turned into a Starbucks.'

I laughed and ordered a Reuben with corned beef and a Coke. I wanted to be alert when I heard what Nick had to tell me.

Nick ordered the Wiener Schnitzel with a fried egg.

'Promise not to tell my cardiologist.' It was beginning to feel like lunch with a long-lost uncle who was stopping through town. But it wasn't. It was the Federal Bureau of Investigation here to explain why I had entered the Witness Protection Program at the age of five when most children are entering kindergarten.

'Deema told me your mother never explained what happened,' Nick said, making me wonder if the FBI reads minds. 'I'm not really surprised.'

'She didn't. I grew up thinking we had fled my father who was violent and had threatened to kill us both. My mother refused to give me any details about him or where we had come from because she felt I might unwittingly divulge something and we would be found.' I looked at his face for a reaction. None. He was probably in his early sixties, with a full head of white hair, a little overweight, but attractive in that teddy bear way. What a disguise. A cuddly FBI agent.

'You must know she was under instructions never to reveal her or your true identity in the program or you'd both lose protection,' he said.

'I know nothing,' I said, imitating a Russian spy.

We both laughed at my absurd response. Daniel would call it 'inappropriate affect,' like laughing at a funeral. I didn't care. I was fairly sure there isn't an appropriate reaction to learning you had been consigned to WITSEC as a kid.

'You must know something. You met Paulie Fairclough this morning,' Nick said.

'Are you following me?'

'We're keeping an eye on you until we're sure you're safe. It's unlikely the people who really did want to harm you and your mother twenty-five years ago have reason to want to hurt you any longer. Most of them are dead or in jail. But we want to be cautious,' he said.

'Who are they? What did we do to make them want to hurt us?' I asked.

'Nothing, Olivia. You did nothing. Your mother worked for Mickey Burke. You must know who he is by now.' He put his finger to his mouth to hush me as the waiter brought our lunches. They were large enough to have prevented the Irish famine.

'I do. I know he was a lawyer. I know he was my father. I know he went to jail and died there. I was just looking him up when you called me,' I said. The smell of the Russian dressing and corned beef made me ravenous, but I didn't have the energy to pick up my sandwich.

Nick began a lengthy description of the history of organized crime in Boston during the past four decades. Some of it I knew from my work as a librarian. People were fascinated by the stories that had involved criminals who had not only evaded the FBI, but had also invaded their ranks.

'Your father was a very clever criminal lawyer. He started his practice representing a cop who had basically killed a black kid point blank – and he got him off. He quickly became popular with seasoned criminals and made a ton of money getting them off crimes they had committed. It wasn't long before he was on retainer with the top guys in organized crime. He became known as "Miracle Mickey." Your mother was his confidante and what we used to call "Gal Friday." I'm not saying she ever did anything wrong, but she got too close to what Mickey was doing.'

'What was he doing wrong, besides representing the bad guys?' I asked.

'Skimming for one thing. He wasn't just laundering money for the mob, he was taking some of it for himself. That's a major no-no with those guys,' Nick said, taking the last bite of his lunch while mine sat untouched.

'Eat some of that. You're too skinny,' he said, once again in my head. I took a bite obediently. 'They don't tolerate betrayal. One of the ways they discourage it is to go after the family of the traitor. They don't just let air out of tires. They get ugly. I won't subject you to the gory details while you eat, but girlfriends and wives are tortured, maimed, or worse.'

'They were coming after us? Why not his wife and kids? Wait, did my father have other kids?' Another question I hadn't had time to check out because the information was coming at a rate I couldn't keep up with.

'Yes, he had a wife and a kid about your age. They didn't threaten to go after them because they knew your mother and you were what counted most to him. Mickey would have already divorced his wife if so much shit hadn't been going down. They knew you were the "love child," – that's what they called you.' Nick called over to the waiter to bring us coffee.

I shook my head. 'I don't feel like the love child.' But I did feel an enormous weight lifted from me. My father hadn't detested me. He hadn't wanted to harm me and my mother. He had loved us both.

'You were. Mickey was nuts about your mother and crazy about you. He knew you were in jeopardy, which is why we approached him about copping a deal. We'd go lenient on him, get you and your mother into the program where you'd be safe. A happy ending.'

I frowned at him.

'We didn't live happily ever after, Nick,' I said.

'I know, I know. The program didn't turn out exactly like we planned. But you were safe all of those years. That's because your mother was smart and knew to follow the rules. She may have been the most compliant person ever to enter the program. She even made us send a linguist to help her ditch her Boston accent that people in Vermont recognized. Anyway, your father didn't want anything to do with us at first. I mean, what lawyer wants to serve time, even though it would only be a fraction of what he was looking at?'

'What changed his mind? How did it come about?' I asked. I would never be able to know what my father had been thinking first-hand or even from my mother. I may as well hear Nick's version.

'Your mother had separated from her husband, Paulie Fairclough. He was a Boston cop, so that had afforded you some protection while he was living there. But once Fairclough got the boot, you and your mother were vulnerable. The goons knew her from the office. She knew who they were. She started seeing them driving by your house slowly. She told Mickey. He knew he'd hit the proverbial fork in the road.'

My cell phone vibrated. Before Brady, hearing what Nick Wojcik had to tell me was paramount. Now, I had a baby who depended on me, at least for a while. I looked at the text message coming in.

'What would you like on your pizza tonight?' Daniel. Our pizza at home date had become a détente. 'Sorry,' I said to Nick, who put two raw sugars into his black coffee.

'We got the call from Mickey early one morning. Your mother had called him, hysterical. It seems she watered the plants for the neighbor who lived behind you when she went to Florida. Your mother took you over with her one morning to water them before she took you to daycare. When she looked out the window, the thugs who had been watching your house were going in your back door.'

I gasped. I couldn't imagine how terrified my mother must have been.

Nick described how my mother called my father in a panic. Mickey told my mother to sit still, not go near the windows, to be quiet, and that everything would be OK. He then cut the deal the FBI had been pitching. Nick and his partner arrived at the neighbor's home in a plumbing truck. They backed into the neighbor's empty garage.

'We waited a couple of hours, taking it slow like real plumbers.

I talked to your mother and explained what was happening. You never said a peep. Your mother fed you lunch out of a pink polka dot lunch box you were toting. I asked where she'd like to go. "Somewhere warm. California or Florida." I said pick between Wisconsin, Minnesota, or Vermont. No surprise she picked Vermont.'

I asked why he wanted to know her preference if he had no intention of granting it. It seemed gratuitously cruel to me.

'Because if she liked warm weather, where do you think they'd go looking for her first?' he said.

'How did she pack her things?' I asked.

'See, you're just like her. She wanted to know the same. I told her you don't. You come with what you've got. She said, "But that's nothing." I told her your daughter gets to take the lunch box.'

'What did she say?' I asked, picturing the terror my mother must have felt venturing into a new world with just me and a polka dot lunch box.

'She said, "Up yours. I'm not going anywhere without this plant." Then she picked up this little plant off the neighbor's coffee table and got into the back of the plumbing van with you.'

THIRTY-ONE

'Y ou got any more questions before I ask mine?' Wojcik asked, after I refused his offer of dessert. He'd ordered the warm apple strudel after explaining he didn't get to eat in the kind of restaurants Boston has since he retired to mid-coast Maine.

'Is this it? If I think of more questions, can I contact you?' I was overwhelmed by what he had told me, piled on top of what I had learned from Paulie Fairclough just hours before.

'Maybe. We'll see,' he said, with vanilla ice cream still in his mouth.

'Am I still in WITSEC? It seems like you people know everything I do.' On the one hand, it was comforting to think I was protected by an invisible benevolent force. But my keen sense of privacy overrode the benefit of being perpetually surveilled.

'Your case was on annual monitor after you went to college. That means we only did an audit of where you and your mother were and if there were any concerns. There hadn't been any ever because of your mother's compliance. The year we learned her house was for sale and why, I marked the case inactive. I was retiring and thought your protection could too. You were one of my success stories.'

Somehow being a WITSEC success didn't feel like an accomplishment to me.

'What was my mother's maiden name? I forgot to ask Paulie that. Where are her sisters? What are their names?'

He held up his hand and reached over for a plastic document pouch with a zipper. He took out a large index card.

'Mary Sheila Curran, born May 4, 1952. Ashley Ann Fairclough, born September 30, 1987. Nothing about the sisters here, but I do know one lived in Florida and another in California, which was another reason your mother didn't get located to either place.' He pushed away his empty plate and for a second I thought he was going to burp.

'Your turn, Olivia. Tell me about your mother's death and why you think it is suspicious. Why you think it may be connected to Terry Walsh's murder? What else has been going on in your life that made you pick up the phone and call me?'

I started with how my mother felt about suicide and how she loathed taking pills. I moved on to how I had enlisted Terry's help when I couldn't reconcile what the coroner reported and what I knew about my mother. I decided I might as well share the little calamities I had been experiencing, even if I sounded paranoid. I'd let Dr Evans deal with my mental health and report just the facts, as I knew them, to Nick.

He asked me some questions, taking a few notes on a fresh 5 x 8 index card. He gave me a fresh FBI calling card that had his name with 'retired' next to it.

'Call me if anything else happens,' he said. 'Deema or I will get back to you. For what it's worth, Olivia, your mother did a terrific job under the circumstances. Other people can't do what she did. They have to sneak calls or visits to people from their pasts, which pretty much undoes the protection we put in place for them. Sheila took the funding we gave her, not that it was huge, found a place for you guys to live, got a job in the medical field, even though she had been trained as a paralegal. She got it and stuck to it.'

As I started back toward Portia, my phone buzzed. I would have to respond to Daniel about what kind of pizza or he would be relentless. I looked at the screen and saw that it was only a reminder that I had moved my appointment with Dr Evans to today at 4:00. That was half an hour from now. I'd never make it if I went to get my car out of the garage, so I hailed a cab.

I was three minutes late for my appointment. Three minutes I couldn't spare, since I had so much to tell Dr Evans. I held up my hand and said, 'Let me fill you in.' He sat in his chair and gave me the floor for the next thirty minutes.

The stories fell from me like an avalanche. With each fallen chapter of my story, I felt my shoulders lighten, my breathing become more even. Dr Evans listened in silence, occasionally nodding or smiling, but never interrupting me.

'Well, what do you think?' I asked when I was done. I needed his wisdom and had only seventeen minutes to get it.

'I think you have done an incredible job in a very short time, Olivia.'

While I valued his praise, I needed more.

'What should I do?' I asked.

'About which part?'

'Any of it.' I was becoming frustrated. I had no time for a round of shrink questions.

'You know it's not my role to tell you what to do, Olivia, but we can talk it through so you can decide for yourself. Let's start with the present then. Your life with Daniel. Obviously, he has been less than truthful with you. Do you have any idea why?'

'Maybe the truth is too painful for him to share. Maybe he was abused by the Buchanans and doesn't want to relive it,' I said. 'But what I have lived through isn't exactly pretty either. I think I should tell him what I've learned about me and give him the chance to do the same. What do you think?'

'Will you be able to go forward with your marriage if you don't ask him? Will you be able to believe what he tells you, Olivia, after he's lied to you once?' One of his bushy brows leaped toward his wrinkly forehead.

I pressed ahead.

'What about Terry? What can I do to mitigate the damage I've done to Joey? I don't know if I can live with that. I just couldn't bear to let my mother's death be misinterpreted as a suicide.' I hoped Dr Evans had a remedy for the guilt I was feeling.

'Didn't Terry offer to help you? You only sought validation that your mother wasn't suicidal,' he said. It was true. I hadn't asked her to do anything. I just hadn't declined her offer to snoop around. She'd had her own misgivings about the third shift.

The clock was racing. I had a question to ask I had been afraid to even consider but I didn't have that luxury.

'Do you think the people who originally were intent on hurting my mother and me are actively coming after me? Or have I offended someone who is trying to send me a message through what amounts to criminal mischief? Or am I just freaking paranoid?'

He placed his hands on his knees and leaned forward.

'Olivia, I think the first two questions are better answered by law enforcement, but you do need to be very careful. You are not paranoid. I worry more about you dismissing your fears than inflating them. I'm not sure how helpful the FBI is going to be, from what you've told me. You may want to share more information with your friend Ryan than you have up until now.'

THIRTY-TWO

I left Dr Evans feeling validated but also concerned. I exited the creaky door to his home and looked for the cab I had asked to pick me up exactly fifty minutes after he dropped me off. To my surprise, he was waiting at the curb. I got in and thanked him effusively for service uncharacteristic of Boston cabbies. He told me he never left the spot where he dropped me off, deciding to chill for the fifty minutes instead.

'Hey, lady, you got boyfriend problems?' he asked me in an accent I couldn't begin to identify.

'What? No, why?' I asked, wondering where he was going. I hoped he wasn't thinking of asking me to meet him for a drink. That kind of thing doesn't usually happen to me, often because I'm too naïve to grasp when someone is coming on to me until after it's over.

'Just that some guy pulled into a parking space right after I dropped you off and sat watching the house you went into. He got out and walked around for a few minutes, looking at the cars parked on the street. As soon as you came out, he pulled out and left.'

I pulled up closer to the front seat so I wouldn't misunderstand what he was saying. Something made me look at the number of his cab.

'Are you sure?' I asked.

'Of course I'm sure. I got eyes, don't I?' He seemed irritated I would doubt him.

'What did he look like? What kind of car? Did you get a plate number?' I asked without waiting between questions for answers, something I have learned in law school is poor form.

'He was a tall skinny guy. Had a Red Sox cap on so I couldn't see him good. Sunglasses. This guy stalking you?' He sounded concerned.

We hit traffic on the way back to Portia. I assured him I had no boyfriend stalking me. What I didn't tell him was that I might have thugs chasing me for some twenty-five-year-old affront I didn't understand when I remembered my mother's smelly money.

I wondered if the money was the reason someone was pursuing me. Nick never mentioned money, other than my father had been skimming. A couple of million dollars might motivate someone to hunt my mother or me down. I had chosen not to discuss the money with Nick. Somewhere deep within me, I feared my mother had done something wrong to get it. I wasn't about to turn her into the FBI, dead or alive.

I was late for class. Professor Gomez glanced over at me as I slipped in the door, momentarily interrupting her lecture. I hate drawing attention to myself, especially negative attention. I looked at the back of the classroom for Erin and found someone sitting in my seat next to her. First my library table, now my seat. Nothing was sacred. I wanted to kill.

Perched in an unfamiliar chair at the edge of the last row, I was distracted throughout the lecture thinking about Paulie Fairclough, Nick Wojcik, and Dr Evans and what each had said. I abandoned any hopes about concentrating on the lecture material on the rights of individuals when confronted by ICE officials. I pulled out the fresh spiral notebook I had taken from my desk at home earlier and began taking notes about my life.

I made a few lists, trying to prioritize my concerns. Finding the real cause of my mother's death was number one. Second was confirming that Terry's murder had been connected. Finally, I wanted to determine if the person I now was convinced had been following me was a random nutcase or someone connected to organized crime trying to get back money my mother may have stolen. I added a fourth item: finding out why Daniel lied to me about his adoptive parents being dead. It dawned on me the last item was the easiest of the questions.

Barbara and Chet Buchanan were alive and could answer questions. Whether they would was an entirely different issue. Clearly, Barbara was not eager to speak about Daniel. She might be more willing to talk to me in person. For a fleeting moment, I considered flying to the west coast to talk to her face to face. But then I remembered I had a responsibility to Brady and commitments at school. There was also an underlying deterrent.

I had never flown in an airplane. My mother had insisted it was one of the easiest ways for people to be found with all of the documentation even a simple local flight required ever since 9-11. She had driven me to Washington when I did my internship at the Library of Congress that one semester during my junior year in college. I had postponed flying for so long, I was now terrified of it and felt like a freak. I added 'fear of flying' to my list of things to work on with Dr Evans.

By the end of class, I had five pages of notes containing lists, questions, and issues in my no longer virgin notebook. Instead of being exhausted, I was revitalized by organizing my thoughts. I was ready to tackle whatever I needed to do to reclaim my life, which Ryan had reminded me was mine and only mine to live.

I knew Daniel was waiting at home with pizza. On my way home, I dialed Barbara Buchanan's number.

'Mrs Buchanan, my name is Olivia Taylor,' I said when she picked up and said hello.

'What can I do for you? If you are selling—'

I cut her off. 'No, I'm not selling anything. Please don't hang up. I really need to talk to you. I am Daniel's wife. I need your help,' I said, my heart pounding as I drove down Huntington Ave by Northeastern.

'Oh God. What do you want from me? Has he hurt you? Or your children? Do you and Daniel have children?' Her voice rose with concern when she mentioned children.

I hadn't expected her questions.

'No, we don't have kids and he hasn't hurt me, at least not physically,' I said, wanting to keep the conversation going.

'With him, it's more psychological bullying, but still I always worried he might become violent,' she said.

'Barbara, may I call you that?' I didn't want to offend her but we had quickly entered an intimate conversation between two people who had loved the same person and it felt natural to call her by her first name.

'Yes, tell me about yourself and how you got tangled up with Daniel, Olivia.'

I shared how I had met Daniel and that we had come to Boston for his residency, bringing my mother who suffered from Alzheimer's to live with us.

'Tell me he hasn't been abusive with your mother?' Barbara nearly shrieked.

'She passed away last week. Daniel told me that you and your husband had died years ago. I need to hear what really happened. What did he do? Please tell me. I need to know.'

She started slowly, but became more animated as she repeated what Daniel had told me, that she and Chet had been unable to conceive and that they were given the opportunity through a local church to adopt Daniel privately from his birth mother. He had been a bright child, socially awkward, but essentially compliant when he was the only child in the family, until Barbara became pregnant five years later and gave birth to a daughter. Two years later, another daughter arrived.

'You hear about how this happens. You can't have a baby, so you adopt, and then boom, you're pregnant. We were thrilled. We had a boy and two girls, all healthy. It was a dream come true – until it became a nightmare,' Barbara said.

I pulled over near the Museum of Fine Arts on Huntington Ave and began taking notes. I didn't trust my memory alone to record what she was about to tell me.

'Please, go on,' I said. I needed to excavate the truth about Daniel's family history before I dared share my own with him.

'He began bullying the girls when they were toddlers. By the time they entered school, he was an adolescent and so enraged with jealousy that we couldn't leave them alone with him. He taunted them, played tricks on them, hid their things. He made up terrible lies about them to their friends. We took him to a therapist, sent him to private school where he would get one-on-one attention, thinking it would assuage his feelings that the girls threatened his place in our family. We tried everything. Chet would take him on camping trips alone, just to let Daniel know the girls hadn't replaced him in our hearts, that we had enough love for all of our children.' Barbara was weeping now.

'I knew this day would come,' she said. 'I knew someone would call and tell me he'd hurt someone.'

'When did you last see him?'

'At his high-school graduation. By then, he was boarding at a private school. We had to get him out of the house. He went off to college, which we paid for, Olivia. We paid every cent he needed for college, but he never returned. Chet says it's just as well, but he was my son. I keep thinking there must have been something we did, or at least could have done to make it right,' Barbara said.

'I'm having trouble absorbing this,' I said. I couldn't listen to her tell me unthinkable things about the man I had married for another second. 'May I call you again?'

'Of course. You sound like a nice girl. I'm sorry Daniel crossed your path.'

THIRTY-THREE

Barbara's words reverberated in my ears as I sat in my car trying to make sense of them. My Daniel had bullied his sisters to the point he had to be sent away to school. I didn't think that Barbara was exaggerating. Her words had the ring of truth, especially at the end when she expressed regret about not being able to help her son. I sighed, turning the keys in the ignition when flashing blue lights appeared behind me. Damn, I should have known better than to park here.

I opened my window, license and registration in my hand, as the uniformed officer approached. I fell on my sword.

'I'm sorry. I shouldn't have pulled over here,' I said, handing him my credentials. I was hoping for clemency by owning up.

'That's right, and there's a good reason for it. This isn't exactly a safe neighborhood at night.' He leaned down toward the window, close enough for me to smell coffee on his breath.

'I know. I'm sorry.' I decided not to tell him that I was on an urgent telephone call. Everyone's telephone calls are urgent.

'Yeah, well you're lucky the museum security guard saw the creep hiding in the alley, probably ready to jump in your passenger seat, and called it in. We had another carjacking here just a week ago.'

'I'm so sorry. I didn't realize,' I said, now genuinely stammering about my close call. 'Did he get the guy?'

'Nope. Scared him away. You better get going back to home to J.P. and find a better route home next time.' He handed me back my license and registration.

This day from hell would never end. I was either a magnet for creeps on the streets or a target for the sins of my father.

I pulled into the driveway next to Daniel's Fiat, relieved to see the lights in the kitchen ablaze. I had been so spooked by the strange smell in the house earlier I had been reluctant to come home. Knowing I wouldn't be alone in the house diminished my apprehension, although I dreaded the confrontation with Daniel I feared was about to ensue.

He sat on a chair at the kitchen island wearing a pair of plaid flannel lounging pants and a gray ribbed long-sleeved tee shirt. He was freshly showered, his wet hair flopped over his forehead as he read the *Boston Globe*. He looked up as if surprised to see me.

'I wasn't sure you were going to make it,' he said, looking over at the two pizza boxes and the bottle of pinot noir he had breathing next to them. 'I got both kinds.' I like white pizza without sauce, while Daniel is a red sauce guy with lots of garlic and peppers.

'I've been tied up all day. I couldn't get back to you,' I said.

He poured us each a glass of red wine and placed them on the counter.

'The pizza is in the warming drawer.' In addition to chopping vegetables, Daniel's culinary skills include warming pizza and other takeout items in our upscale Wolf stove.

'Let's have a glass of wine first,' I said, sliding on to my spot next to him.

He took my hand.

'Olivia, I want to acknowledge how hard things have been for you. I don't just mean your mother's death, but I know taking care of her for the past several years had to be exhausting,' he said.

I wasn't surprised he was being conciliatory to begin with. He often set me up like that, fooling me into thinking he was empathetic, then hitting me with criticism for what I had done wrong, saying 'although it was understandable under the circumstances.' Not tonight, Daniel.

'I'd rather we start an open dialogue about our family, Daniel, and not waste time with platitudes.' He flinched ever so slightly at my retort.

'Actually, I agree. I was starting to say that your mother's refusal to share vital information with you must have been difficult enough. Now that she has died, foreclosing any opportunity you have to learn about your father and extended family, you must be experiencing loss on a number of levels.' He looked earnest and adorable, but Barbara's words repeated in my ears like a bad song.

'And that's why I'm making bad judgments?' I asked, taking the bait as I had since I'd known Daniel.

'Well, it could explain why you aren't able to process information and reach sound conclusions.' He thought he had me.

'Stop the psychobabble, Daniel. Let's talk facts, not interpretations of them,' I said, draining my glass of wine and reaching for the bottle. 'You go first, then maybe I'll share what I've learned about my family.'

'I've asked you to respect my decision not to pursue finding my family of origin, Olivia. It is a personal choice I am entitled to and not one I made without agonizing,' Daniel said, sweeping his hair off his forehead. He sounded so injured I understood why I had backed off from difficult conversations with him in the past.

'Not your family of origin, Daniel. Your adoptive family. Tell me about them.' I thought I saw a look of panic flash across his face, but he recovered. I was just realizing how smooth he was.

'You want me to relive the memory of their deaths? Why would you want to put me through that?' He put his head in his hands as if I had wounded him for no reason.

'Why would you want to lie to me about it, Daniel? I know the Buchanans aren't dead. They're alive and recovering from the traumatic experiences they and their daughters had at your hands,' I said.

'You talked to the Buchanans? How dare you?' Daniel stood up and walked away to the far side of the island, turning his back on me.

I said nothing and let the silence work for me for a change.

'Do you have any idea how abusive those people were? Did it occur to you, I might have decided considering them dead was best for me so I could recover and try to live a normal life? That not telling you, when you already had so much baggage of your own, was an act of kindness on my part, even though by sparing you, it meant I had to bear the burden on my own?' He swiveled around to face me. I knew he hoped to see a guilty reaction to the trigger he had pulled.

He was a bully. A pathetic, cowardly bully. I saw that now and I was done.

'You need to leave, Daniel. I'm done,' I said, so softly I almost couldn't hear my own words. But I knew I had said them.

'Olivia, you don't mean that,' he said, starting to come toward me. I remembered Barbara saying she worried Daniel might become violent. I got off my stool and faced him. But there was no going back now.

'I do mean it. Please leave. Now. I'm done. We're done.'

'Are you saying you want a divorce? You're not thinking clearly. You have so much to lose,' he said, a little less emotionally than he had sounded a minute ago.

'No. I don't want a divorce. I don't need a divorce. I can get an annulment from you for fraud. You withheld information that goes to the essentials of marriage, Daniel. You lied about who you are.' I was shocked to find myself thinking on my feet, reaching into my legal knowledge about what renders a marriage invalid. I felt buoyed as I went head to head with my husband for the first time ever without being manipulated or intimidated.

He snapped.

'Don't spout that legal bullshit you learned at a third-tier law school, Olivia. I'm not leaving. This is my house and I am entitled to be here. If you want out of the marriage, you're going to have to leave, sweetheart.' The snarl on his face removed any trace of adorable that had been there when our conversation began.

'Excuse me, but this is my house, bought with my mother's money, in her name and mine. You are not on the deed, Daniel.' I stopped short of stamping my feet.

'If you're as smart as you think you are, you know in Massachusetts it doesn't matter who holds title to the "marital home" during a divorce.' Daniel used both his index and middle fingers to create quotation marks around 'marital home.' I knew then that he had already consulted a lawyer. I just didn't know why.

'There won't be a divorce. In an annulment, there is no property division.'

'By the time I've finished describing the extent of your mental illness and the cognitive deterioration in your lunatic mother, no one will buy your allegations of fraud. I should have listened to Kayla's concerns more seriously,' he said, calmly folding his arms in front of him, wearing a demonic smile that I knew was genuine. I had a lot I wanted to say about Kayla, but again I resisted his effort to provoke me.

'I'll leave tonight, Daniel, but you'd better be gone tomorrow when I return,' I said, heading toward the door. I didn't feel comfortable about grabbing a few things from our bedroom upstairs. I knew he would follow me and continue his tirade until I broke and reacted. I remembered the overflowing basket in the laundry room filled with clean, folded laundry I hadn't found time to put away, from which I had grabbed some items earlier in the day. I picked it up, walking into the kitchen where Daniel was munching on a piece of pizza.

I took the pile of his folded clothes and threw them at him.

'You'll need these when you go,' I said, furious to see he had an appetite. 'Remember, be out of here tomorrow.'

'In your dreams.'

THIRTY-FOUR

Thursday, October 23rd

I started shaking once I was in the car with the doors locked. I had an absurd thought that I should run back in and get my notebooks, but I knew better. I had crossed a line I never wanted to traverse again.

I pulled out of the driveway and wondered where I should go. It was midnight. I gravitated toward Children's Hospital where I had spent the last several nights. I was surprised to find Brady sleeping lightly in his crib. Although I missed holding him, I didn't want to disturb him. I sat on the rocking chair and opened my laptop.

I was exhausted but edgy. Daniel had infuriated me, but it was my own naiveté and neediness that had enraged and appalled me. He had taken enough of my time and energy. I decided I'd focus on learning about my own family, such that it was.

I eased into the search, focusing on the Currans. There were a ton of them in Boston, many with the same or similar first names. It wasn't until I looked up Mary Elizabeth Curran that I caught on. My mother and her sisters all had the first name Mary. I assumed that was a traditional Catholic practice, honoring the Blessed Virgin Mary. I might normally find that a fascinating topic to research, but I didn't have time to get sidetracked.

I couldn't find either of my aunts in California or Florida, probably because I didn't know their married names. I would need a more sophisticated data source. I did establish that both of my maternal grandparents died long after my mother left Boston. I wondered if they knew why she had disappeared. It saddened me to think they may have died believing their daughter didn't care about them.

I moved over to the paternal side of the family. Again, I was swarmed with information about my father, the Irish thugs in Boston he had represented, his testimony against them later, and finally how he had been stabbed in jail.

His obituary fascinated me. He was described as a rogue, but with a reverent tone. His wife was listed as Patricia 'Trish' (Alden) Burke of Milton. He had a daughter, who was unnamed.

I had a sister. Well, a half-sister, but that was more than I had until yesterday. I wondered if she lived in Massachusetts and how her life had been affected by our father's infamy.

I looked for Patricia Burke in Milton without luck. I found one born around the same time as my father in Boston and narrowed my search to that date of birth. Bingo, I found one in Hyannis on Cape Cod just as Brady began whimpering, which turned into wailing in less than a minute.

I focused on him and the bottle the nurse had persuaded me to try giving him. No one had had much luck, but I gave it a try. Brady resisted, first grasping the nipple into his tiny mouth, and then opening his lips in a cry that made it fall out. I didn't have much better luck than the nursing staff, but I tried. By daybreak, we'd both had a few naps, but not much more.

I knew I was living on adrenalin and that I couldn't go much longer without sleep. I decided I would text Erin and take her up on her offer to curl up on her couch. I needed a clear head. I don't do well with sleep deprivation or without food.

I was famished, having only eaten a few bites of my Reuben with Nick the afternoon before. I should have taken the white pizza Daniel had bought for me, but I should have done a lot of things that I hadn't. I was thinking about the diner I'd been to with Ryan when he walked in the door of Brady's room wearing a paper gown over his clothes.

'Did you come to relieve me?' I joked. He pulled a chair over across from me but said nothing.

'Liv, we may need to move Brady to a different hospital. He may not be safe here. We'll need your permission, of course.' He sounded grim.

'Not safe? He has twenty-four-hour police protection,' I said.

'Brady's father is still at large. We've thought we knew where he was a couple of times. Our information is that he didn't kill Sophia. I guess there's small comfort in that, but the people who did are looking for a shipment of heroin that Zack was supposed to distribute. We know they're threatening him through his kid. They're hoping to smoke Zack out. Too many people know Brady is here. It was in the press. We just want to transfer him over to the NICU at MGH,' Ryan said.

'I see.' The first thought that occurred to me was how unkind it was to make this little tortured creature I had grown so fond of adjust to anything more than he had. The second was that I hated the prospect of running into Kayla at MGH. I knew that Daniel would be joining her at the General in less than two weeks after his rotation at McLean ended. My hesitation seemed to irritate Ryan.

'Look, I shouldn't be telling you this, but we think someone unauthorized already got in to see Brady. That's why we tightened up the sign-in sheet procedure. It may actually have been Zack. We can't be sure, but we've verified everyone on the list is legit except this one person who signed in so illegibly you can't decipher the name,' Ryan said, looking at me with bloodshot eyes that begged for sleep.

'OK, but why Mass General? Why not Tufts Medical Center?' I was no expert in medical care for kids, but I had read Tufts had a great reputation, second to Children's in Boston.

'Because that's exactly where people would expect to find Brady if he were transferred. And actually, that's where we need your help.'

Ryan explained they were fairly certain the hospital unit was being watched, perhaps by an employee connected to Zack or the people after him. The police wanted to fake a transfer to Tufts, while actually transporting Brady to Mass General. All I had to do was exit the front door of Children's carrying a bundle in my arms that was supposed to be Brady, get into an ambulance with a uniformed cop, and ride over to Tufts. I'd leave the ambulance as visibly as I entered it and walk through the main door of the Tufts medical complex where I would proceed to Tufts Children's Floating Hospital.

'Could you do that, Olivia? I know you had a rough day yesterday, so if you're not up to it, I'll understand. We'll figure something else out.'

'Of course I'll do it. I'm not fragile. I would never refuse to do something that might keep Brady safe. I wish I could have done the same for my mother. Or her nurse for that matter. I would never put anyone I care about in jeopardy,' I said.

'That's great. I'll go tell the staff to start the paperwork if you can wait around . . . Wait a minute. What was that about your mother and her nurse? Sweet Jesus, don't tell me your mother's nurse was—'

'Terry Walsh,' I finished for him.

'Holy Christ, you have got to be kidding. Why didn't you tell me?' He sounded more than exasperated. Ryan's words sounded accusatory. He sat erect, no longer leaning toward me, and then stood up.

'I just haven't had a chance to. I was planning on telling you, asking you for your help,' I said, aware that Brady had arched in my arms as the tone in my voice changed.

'Ask for my help? What about giving yours? What else do you know, Olivia, that you haven't shared with me?'

The formality of Ryan calling me Olivia wasn't lost on me, nor was the wounded look on his face.

'OK, you take care of Brady while I get the transfer in motion. You're going to have to talk to Costa, the homicide detective in charge of Terry Walsh's investigation. You can probably do that while you're at Tufts. You'll be stuck there for a couple of hours to make it look like you're visiting Brady. We'll deliver your car home later.' He was all business, reprimanding me with his tone, just as he had the day he decided I had let my mother wander off.

'No, don't do that,' I said over Brady's bawling. I stood up, meeting Ryan's angry gaze squarely. I had to take charge of my life. The last thing I needed was for cops to bring my car home, giving Daniel another opportunity to bolster his argument I was unstable.

Ryan looked at me curiously, but said nothing.

'Put it in the garage at school. It will be more convenient.' Tufts was two blocks from Portia.

'Fine,' Ryan said, leaving the room, not giving me the chance to tell him I had talked to the FBI about Terry Walsh.

'Fine' was right. I'd save it for Costa.

THIRTY-FIVE

The charade would have seemed comical, were it not intended to protect Brady from abduction or worse. Two receiving blankets were rolled into a third to make it look as if I was swaddling him. Officer Duggan in full uniform stayed at my side. We exited through the main entrance to Children's Hospital where an ambulance with two attendants awaited us with a bassinet on wheels. I tenderly placed my lump of blankets in it. Once the bassinet was in the ambulance, one of the attendants extended his hand and pulled me up from the small step at the rear. When Duggan followed suit, they closed the doors and we were off, but at a snail's pace.

Inside, Duggan and I sat on benches opposite one another, saying very little other than him grunting, 'At least I get to go home after this. You got an appointment with Lou Costa. Good luck with that one.'

I pictured Lou Costa like Andy Sipowicz on NYPD Blue, one of the few cop shows my mother ever watched when I was a kid. I was exhausted, starving, and in no condition to talk to a homicide detective. I was ragged with sleep deprivation and without nourishment to draw on for reserve. Playing decoy had zapped what energy I had left. I thought about catching a nap at the Floating Hospital before Detective Costa interrogated me. Surely they would have cots for parents there.

We continued with Act Two once we arrived at the hospital, where Duggan got out first. We were greeted by a nurse, who helped take the lump out of the transport bassinet and placed it in another, which I assumed belonged to Tufts. 'Take one side of the bassinet and push it slowly with me,' she instructed. I did what I was told, hoping Brady was getting at least as much attention during his actual transfer. I looked dutifully at the pile that was supposed to be Brady. The nurse led us through a lobby to an elevator we rode to the ninth floor together with Duggan and one of the ambulance attendants. Once off the elevator, we all paraded toward a room with a sign on the door that said: 'Clinical Conference Room (No food or drink allowed)' where a woman who looked to be about my age waited.

The first thing I noticed was that she looked more tired than I felt. Her round green eyes had dark circles beneath them as if someone had colored them with charcoal. Her tussled short blonde hairdo looked more like I-need-a-shower than bedhead. The seasonless stretch black suit I knew had been chic when she put it on now bagged a bit at the elbows and knees. Her white V-neck tee shirt had a small coffee stain. She was still striking. When she rose from the chair where she sat at a long conference table, I was surprised that she was shorter than me, but built solid with curves.

'Louise Costa,' she said, putting out her hand. Just what I needed. Another female contemporary to make me feel dowdy. Bring me Andy Sipowicz. Please.

I introduced myself while Duggan greeted the 'nurse' who had escorted us into the hospital. She apparently was another cop who was now arranging to take Duggan home.

'You take care, Olivia,' Duggan said, clapping me on my right shoulder.

I thanked him, taking my backpack from him, which he had kindly toted for me.

Costa pulled out a chair for me as she resumed her position at the head of the long table. No mistaking who was in charge here.

'You could probably use some coffee. Can you guys grab us some before you go?' she said, looking over at the nurse-cop.

'Sure thing,' nurse-cop said, leaving the room with Duggan to fetch some for us.

Once we each had a cup of black coffee in front of us and had seen the last of Duggan and nurse-cop, Costa started in.

'Fairclough tells me you knew Terry Walsh. Tell me how,' she said. I noticed she wasn't asking.

I explained that Terry was the medication nurse at Thompson House and that she and my mother had hit it off, even though my mother was suffering from Alzheimer's disease, which had made her less social. Not that Mom was ever exactly social. Her some-what abrasive exterior had worked well at keeping people at a distance. I now understood her motivation.

'Why do you think they hit if off?' She strained her neck to look over at me. Her question surprised me. I didn't understand why that would matter.

'They were both very smart, but not overly emotional women. Neither suffered fools gladly,' I said, taking a sip of the lukewarm black liquid I was supposed to believe was coffee.

'Tell me a little about your mother, how long she'd been in Thompson House, her history, you know.' She had pulled an iPad out of a black tote that had been sitting on the floor next to her.

I shared my mother's medical history with her and how when Daniel began his residency at Mass General, we had to persuade Mom to move with us. I skipped the part about Ryan and good cop finding her circling Jamaica Pond in her bathrobe and slippers. Then I went on to chronicle her admission to Thompson House. Costa yawned.

'Look if I'm boring you,' I said, ready to leave. I took Criminal Procedure and got an A. I knew my interview with her was voluntary.

'Sorry, I'm just trying to connect Terry Walsh's murder to why you think your mother's death may not have been suicide. I know some weird stuff has been happening to you. Fairclough told me. I'm trying to connect the dots. Listen, let's try this,' she said and bent over to her right, reaching for something where she had gotten her tote.

I stared as she lifted the laundry basket I had tossed in my car the night before so I'd have clean clothes to wear.

'What are you doing with my laundry basket?' I asked. Even though it was filled with clean, folded laundry, I felt exposed.

'Hang on. Fairclough thought you'd want it.' She reached into it and pulled out a couple of clear zip-lock bags. She held out one that had the gray cashmere glove filled with the white pills. I had tucked it under the passenger seat the afternoon Erin and I had cleared out my mother's room so that Daniel wouldn't see it. I had forgotten it was there. I had never gotten around to checking if the pills were Xanax, but I was almost certain they were. How my car had four ruined tires replaced without some mechanic at the garage finding the pills was pure providence.

'Let's start with these,' Costa said.

My cheeks burned with outrage.

'Let's start with why you're going through my car without a

search warrant?' I said, thinking I might need a lawyer and should shut up.

'You gave us permission to transport your vehicle. These were in plain sight,' Costa said, with a slight smile. Oh no they weren't, but it was my word against the police and I knew how that went. I had a decision to make. I could stop talking to Costa and get a lawyer involved. But that would only complicate and delay resolving the situation. My whole purpose for involving Terry had been to disprove the allegation my mother had committed suicide and to find out what had really happened.

'Look, those pills are what raised my suspicion. My mother hated taking pills and was hoarding them. Where did she get the pills she supposedly took with alcohol to kill herself?'

Costa put the glove in the baggy on the table and listened as I recounted how there had been an empty Dunkin' Donuts Coolatta container on her nightstand the night she died. I explained that I had discovered the pills concealed in the glove in her drawer the next day while clearing out her room. I went on to describe how hypercritical my mother was about people who commit suicide. 'It's the easy way out for them, but not the people they leave behind,' I said, quoting Mom.

'Where does Terry Walsh fit in?' she asked, no longer seeming bored.

'I needed validation that my mother was still, you know, my mother. That she hadn't softened her views about suicide, hadn't become so desperate and depressed about her illness that she might kill herself. I went to see Terry, who was just as aghast at the suggestion my mother committed suicide as I was. She talked about some odd things going on during the third shift. My mother had described being visited by someone she called Dr Nightmare. She also spoke about a kind researcher who visited her at night who was looking for the cure. I think one of those people gave my mother a jade plant, which is my only proof he or she existed,' I said, noticing I had emptied the horrid coffee.

'What else did Terry say?' Her cup was empty too.

'That she'd poke around, see what she could find out. I tried to check back with her after I came back from Vermont where we had my mother's memorial. I thought I'd gotten her fired when I called Thompson House and they said she was no longer there. I didn't know they meant she had died, had been murdered. I haven't kept up with the news.' I was babbling as if the putrid coffee had been truth serum.

'I didn't mean for her to put herself in danger. She's got a disabled son, for God's sake. I wouldn't have asked her to do that.' I choked up. I would never forgive myself for what had happened to Terry.

'We don't know if that has anything to do with her murder, Olivia. Don't go blaming yourself just yet. I take it your mother had a sense of humor,' Costa said, looking at the glove with its middle finger standing erect. She reached over for the other two plastic bags and placed them in front of me on the table. One held a black plastic item the size of the palm of my hand. The other contained a gray metal object, the same shape, only a little larger.

I waited for her to say something. I think she was doing the same.

'Am I supposed to know something, say something about these?' I said, blinking.

'Do you know anything about them? They were both found on your car.'

No wonder I'd felt like someone was stalking me. Someone was.

'I take it they track where I'm going,' I said, giving nothing more. 'But why two?' I asked.

'Exactly, why two? Do you know why someone would be tracking you? Maybe your husband? How's your marriage?' Costa looked less tired than she had when we first started talking. She was dogged.

'My husband? I don't think so.' Daniel was not technologically savvy. A tracking device wasn't his kind of thing. He would be more inclined to control what I did by manipulating me.

'Are you cheating on him?'

'What? No, of course not.' I didn't appreciate Costa's interrogation becoming personal. Her question was insulting.

'Well, how is your marriage? You didn't answer me about that,' she said, folding her hands in front of her.

'I'm, we're separated,' I said. It was the first time I had thought about what had happened the night before in those terms. Saying them felt foreign and made me feel ashamed. I had failed at marriage, the foundation for building a family, and I had to admit it to this bitchy cop.

'When did you separate?' she asked. I could see she was not inclined to let it go. I caved.

'Last night. I guess it was coming, but the strain of my mother's death didn't help.' I felt like I had entered a confessional. 'But I don't see him using something like that.' I motioned toward the plastic bags.

'Well, one of these is commercially available. You can buy it on Amazon, so it's not like a tracking device is hard to find.'

'It's just not Daniel's style,' I said, and believed it.

'Well, who then?'

I shrugged my shoulders. I had no idea why anyone would want to track my whereabouts, unless it had to do with Brady. I suggested that possibility.

'Maybe. What about the other one, Olivia? That one looks more like a government-issued device. Any idea about where that one came from? Because I know it isn't Boston PD.'

'If you say it's connected to the government, that's easy,' I said. I could see I had surprised her with my plucky retort.

'Oh, yeah? What government agency is tracking you?' she asked as if I had inflated my importance in the world.

'The FBI.'

THIRTY-SIX

'And exactly why would the FBI be interested in where Olivia Taylor is going?' Costa recovered with the same sass she had shown since we began talking. I don't know how to talk to people the way she did. She combined a genuine sense of interest with hard-hitting tenacity. I wanted to please her, gain her approval. I also wanted to kick her in the shins.

'Because they may have reason to believe I am at risk,' I said.

'At risk of what? From whom?' The exasperation in her voice was unmistakable.

'The people my mother and I ran away from when I was a child. We were in the Witness Protection Program,' I said. This time I yawned. I was depleted. Costa could ask me anything. I had nothing left.

'You grew up in WITSEC?' Her question dripped with incredulity. I understood.

'Apparently,' I said.

'What do you mean "apparently"?'

I explained what I had learned from Deema Zaheed and Nick Wojcik.

I know my mother intended to shield me under a blanket of secrecy, but the cost of her protection had been exorbitant. I never felt as if I belonged. I didn't know what 'normal' was. Being on the edge of the world made me feel freakish, as if I didn't deserve what other people take for granted. Now I had the opportunity to cast away the shame years living like an alien had cost me. Being raised in WITSEC explained why I was the way I was. I told Costa everything.

She listened without interrupting while she pounded furiously on her tablet. I chronicled my mother's early life with Paulie Fairclough, her affair with Mickey Burke, and my birth. I referred her to the same news sources where I had learned about my father's life and death, if she didn't already know them. I told her how I had encountered a number of close calls in my car and the vandalism.

When I was done I was out of breath, spent, but exhilarated by a sense of freedom.

'Wow, that must have been one hell of a childhood. You had *no* idea you were in WITSEC?' she asked.

'None,' I said, sharing my mother's version of fleeing her violent husband.

'You got cards for those FBI agents?' I handed her the two cards. She grabbed her cell phone and placed a call.

She told someone to 'Get over here quick with a printer,' while she examined the cards. When she hung up, she took photos of the cards with her phone and handed them back to me. Then she started pounding on the iPad again. Costa was a machine in her own right.

She asked me questions about what I had told her, clarifying information I had been vague about. I realized she was compiling a statement from what I had told her.

A knock on the door told me the printer had arrived. A short man carrying a small portable printer and two new cups of coffee from Starbucks set all three on the table.

'Did you bring paper?' she asked.

'I'll get some from the nurses' station,' he said, racing out the door.

'Jesus,' Costa muttered, shoving one of the Starbucks coffees toward me. She called Zaheed and Wojcik next, leaving each a detailed voicemail.

I sat silently watching her do three things at once, marveling at how she had rallied. She was rejuvenated and had climbed over the wall she seemed to have hit when we first met. I checked my own cell phone to see if I had any messages. I wondered if Daniel would ask me to reconsider my decision to leave him, but my only message was from Erin who texted: '*Mi casa es tu casa*. Come on over.' I was touched by her welcome. I needed a friend.

'OK,' Costa said, as she pulled two single-spaced pages from the tiny printer. 'Read this and see if it accurately reflects what you've told me. It's in plain language, so don't go getting all lawyerly on me.'

I laughed. 'I wouldn't think of it,' I said, enjoying the lightness of the moment. I read through the document, finding the spare, factual representations to be accurate and unexaggerated. I saw a place for my signature at the bottom of the second page.

'It's fine,' I said.

'Go ahead and sign it then. We'll be using it first to get a few search warrants. I want to look at the employee records at Thompson House. I'm telling you this so you know we are investigating your mother's death as well as Terry Walsh's, so there is no reason for you to start playing Nancy Drew again.'

'I promise I won't, but will you let me know what's going on?' I didn't want to regress into the darkness of ignorance ever again.

'Sure, although Ryan Fairclough may be the one to talk to you since you're on the baby case and talk to him routinely. I'll fill him in and explain you only found out about WITSEC two days ago. He thinks you were holding out, playing games.'

'I never had a chance to tell him. Everything just kept coming at me at once,' I said.

'Yeah, well I've been telling him he needs to work on his active listening skills for a while,' Costa said, packing up her evidence bags and handing me my laundry basket.

'Does he work for you?' I asked, wondering if I had gotten Ryan into an awkward situation with his boss. I knew he was new to Homicide. It was evident Costa was not.

'No,' she said, chortling. 'He's my ex.'

THIRTY-SEVEN

t was nearly noon before I left. I considered walking the two blocks over to Portia and waiting until class. But I was tired and in desperate need of food and a shower so I headed to Erin's. Costa had advised me not to drive my car for a few days. I concurred with her judgment and took a cab to Powder House Square in Somerville where Erin lived in a two-story Philly-style apartment.

'Nice luggage,' Erin said, greeting me in a foyer with two stained-glass windows and a shining dark oak hardwood floor. She took the laundry basket I was lugging out of my arms.

'Shut up,' I said back. I followed her into a spacious living room with three tall windows with a cushioned window seat beneath them, a towering ceiling, and a fireplace that looked functional. The trim was dark oak. I had expected hot fuchsia walls, lime-green trim, a wildly covered futon, and exotic posters. Instead, I walked into a sedate shabby chic cloud of white on white. Only a splash of slate blue in the Oriental rug that sat between a three-cushioned couch and two cushy club chairs interrupted the sea of whiteness. The windows had ivory macramé lace panels that let the October sun in, but gave an element of privacy. There were pillows everywhere. Books were stacked neatly on the coffee table next to a cloche, which covered the flowering African violet I had given Erin from my mother's window. Botanical prints hung on the walls.

I gushed.

'Erin,' I said, gasping as I twirled around.

'I know. It's my dirty little secret,' she said. I worried I had insulted her as she stood next to a display of stacked antique suitcases with a birdcage on top. Erin was dressed in jeans, aqua Chuck Taylor high tops, and a matching aqua hoodie that said, 'In my defense, I was left unsupervised.'

'It's fabulous,' I said. The tranquility in her apartment relaxed me. I was fascinated about the incongruity between her public persona and her private quarters.

'Sit, tell me what's going down,' she said, placing the laundry basket on the floor.

'Could I shower first? I feel gross,' I said. She led me through the living room to a bathroom that continued with whiteness. Thick towels, a seersucker shower curtain around a clawfoot tub, and a tufted cotton bathmat. The scent of lavender and lemongrass everywhere. I felt like I'd arrived at a spa.

When I opened the bathroom door and emerged in clean jeans and a fresh turtleneck, I smelled the unmistakable fragrance of melting butter. I didn't know what Erin was up to, but I knew I would love it.

She brought me a plate with two grilled cheese sandwiches bulging with melted cheddar cheese and sliced tomatoes. Next to the sandwiches, which were arranged on a blue and white Willow ware plate, sat five baby gherkin pickles. I took a wine goblet filled with ginger ale she offered and placed it on the coffee table. If this was what I had been missing by not having girlfriends in my life, I planned to make up for lost time.

I repeated everything I had told Louise Costa and then filled Erin in on the details about Daniel.

'He lied about his parents being dead? Liv, you and I are both real orphans. That's just not something you lie about,' Erin said, when I described the painful conversation I'd had with Barbara Buchanan. But I knew better than Erin that people tell lies for all kinds of reasons, survival being one of them.

When I got to the part where Daniel refused to leave the house, Erin became incensed.

'We all knew he was an asshole that night when he came to get you after dinner. And there was that issue with the missing orchid. I knew something was up. We've got to get him out of your house,' she said.

'I don't have the energy to deal with Daniel. I haven't slept a full night for days. I'm worried about Brady and can't even visit him. I'm being stalked and don't know by whom or why. And the FBI has just told me I grew up in the Witness Protection Program. It's exhausting,' I said, chomping on the last pickle. Baby gherkins had been my mother's favorite pickles.

'You're right. You need a nap. Right now. Come with me,' Erin said. She motioned up a flight of bare oak stairs. I dragged my weary body, now logy after lunch, past a bedroom that appeared to be a continuation of Erin's fondness for all things white. She led me into a small study with a white secretary desk with a hutch filled with books I recognized and also owned. There was a white Jenny Lind daybed with a thick white puff, half a dozen pillows, and a gray tabby cat.

'You have a cat?' I knew it sounded critical.

'Now you know all of my secrets, Liv. I'm a cat lover. This is Daphne. I can put her outside the room and close the door.'

'No, don't. I love cats. I was just surprised,' I said, falling on to the daybed, careful not to squish the cat that had barely noticed my presence.

I made Erin promise to wake me in time for school and was out for the count within minutes. At some point, Daphne crawled up on my hip and continued her nap. I woke when she jumped off some time later. I decided to use the bathroom. I looked out the window to see darkness had fallen and knew Erin had made an executive decision to go to school without me and to let me sleep. I trudged to the bathroom, and then went downstairs to find more ginger ale. The pickles had made me thirsty.

About halfway down the stairs, I sneezed. I stopped still, paralyzed by the same pear fragrance I had smelled in my house the day before. I inhaled, confirming the scent. Maybe Erin liked pear, just as she did lavender and lemongrass. But I had never smelled it on her and I'd sat next to her in all of the classes we've taken together for three years. I moved down the rest of the stairs and went into the living room.

I saw a note in Erin's sloppy scrawl on the coffee table. 'Couldn't wake you. You need sleep more than school. I'll take SUPER notes. Xo, Erin.' I agreed. I did need sleep more than school, although I wasn't convinced her notes would be super. But I was warmed by her generosity and turned to get some ginger ale when I saw a small jade plant sitting next to the birdcage.

THIRTY-EIGHT

I grabbed my backpack out of the laundry basket that still sat on the floor behind one of the club chairs. I made certain my wallet and cell phone were in the outer pocket and then I ran out of the apartment on to the street, looking up and down for signs that someone was waiting for me.

I headed toward Davis Square, which I remembered was the T location Erin used before she bought my mother's car. I had driven Erin home a few times but had never been inside her apartment until today. That hadn't seemed odd to me since I had never invited her into my home until recently. I couldn't believe Erin had any part in a jade plant appearing next to the birdcage. She had been terrified by the African violet, which she was certain she would kill. 'All I am capable of is spider plants and philodendron,' she had said.

I could still smell the repulsive scent of pear as I hurried toward the T, glad to see people out enjoying the restaurants. Soon the smell of barbecue, Thai, and burgers replaced the pear odor. I hurried down the stairs to the T with a group of other people. Once on the platform, I listened to a man playing the harmonica while I considered where my destination should be.

I couldn't go home, unless Daniel had gone to work. He should be doing one of his last shifts at McLean, but I wasn't sure that he might have called in sick so he could guard the 'marital home' like a fortress. If I had my car I could drive by. I couldn't go to see Brady. If I went anywhere I should show up at Tufts under the pretense I was visiting him. Classes at Portia were over and the library would close soon afterward.

I wondered now if I had panicked over the presence of a room fragrance Erin might simply have sprayed. I had been exhausted when I arrived at her apartment and might not have noticed the jade plant in the living room. Or Erin may have watered it in the kitchen sink and then put it back in the living room when I was napping.

I worried that I had become a paranoid wreck. But Dr Evans had assured me that was not the case. I wished I could talk to him now. I knew if I called his number, I would get a message to leave a voicemail and that if it was an emergency, I should go to my local emergency room. No, that wouldn't work.

At Park Square, where all of the trolley car lines converge, I transferred to the Green Line simply because it was my local line. I got off at Copley Square, knowing it was the stop for the Boston Public Library, one of my favorite libraries in the world. I looked at my phone. It was 9:05 p.m. It had just closed. I felt dejected.

I glanced over at the Copley Plaza Hotel where Daniel and I had splurged and stayed when we came to Boston looking for houses before he began his residency. It had been an elegant and exciting preview of our new life. Now I stood on the precipice of the destruction of my dreams.

The temperature had fallen enough to make me shiver. I remembered there was a Marshalls right up the street and dashed for it. I would have about ten minutes to grab a jacket, underwear, and fresh clothes for the morning, which I would need wherever I went since I'd left my trusty laundry basket at Erin's.

Rushing up and down the aisles, I found more than I needed. It was a pleasant distraction from being nearly homeless. I warmed up as I filled my carriage with underwear, a pair of pajamas, a North Face jacket, and a pair of boots. Two sweaters, a pair of jeans, and four pairs of socks later, I was in business.

The illuminated sign from the Lenox Hotel shined like the star of Bethlehem. I remembered reading that it was one of Boston's charming boutique hotels. I entered the lobby with my Marshalls bags in tow. When the clerk at the desk greeted me warmly without even glancing at them, I decided this was my new temporary home. I had credit cards and the money to pay for them. There was no reason not to check in, or not to choose one of the executive rooms with a working fireplace.

A porter offered to escort me and my 'luggage' to the corner suite. He lit the fireplace while I perused the in-room menu. In half an hour, I was in my new pajamas eating short ribs with macaroni and cheese and drinking a double martini in front of the fire. I felt safe. No one knew where I was. Not the stalker, nor the FBI, BPD or Daniel. I felt a little guilty about Erin, so I texted her that I was safe. I cautioned her that someone knew I had been at her place and for her to watch out. It was the best that I could do at the moment.

THIRTY-NINE

Friday, October 24th

I wasn't sure if it was the alcohol, exhaustion, or the fact I turned my cell phone off, but I had the best night's sleep since my mother had died. Maybe I should permanently live in a hotel paid for by my father's laundered money.

I ordered breakfast in my room at 6 a.m., allowing the porter to relight the fireplace. If it was as cold outside as it was gray, I needed to fortify myself. I had no school on Fridays. I couldn't visit Brady, although I would stop briefly at Tufts pretending I was. I knew Erin worked doing billing at a law firm in Cambridge on Fridays where she supplemented her income from tending bar during the weekend evenings. All I had scheduled was an appointment with Andrew at 5 p.m. to give him a chance to rehabilitate my hair.

I ordered a rental car after finishing off my crab cakes Benedict and fresh orange juice. I rechecked the address I had found for Patricia Burke. After showering and putting on my new sweater and jeans from Marshalls, I finally turned my cell phone on. A cacophony of pings ensued. I sat in front of the waning fire, sipping coffee as I tore through the text messages.

Erin's message was frantic. She had no idea where the little jade plant had come from and was staying home from work that morning to have her locks changed. Where was I, she asked. Then I listened to a voicemail from her. 'Liv, I thought we were friends. Don't you trust me?' I did, I just couldn't be sure I was safe anywhere – or worse, that I wasn't endangering her.

'Where are you?' Two separate texts from both Deema and Nick, my friends at the FBI. 'Checking in with you, Olivia, after our chat today,' Costa said in a voicemail. 'Call me.' All of these people may have been properly motivated when they contacted me. But none of them were being stalked. I replied to no one.

Ryan's voicemail sounded a lot different than the tone he had used when he chastized me during our last conversation about Terry

Walsh. 'Liv, I need to talk to you. Brady's OK. Please call me.' I was glad to hear Brady was OK. I didn't need to hear anything more than that from Ryan.

The rental car arrived in time for me to make a brief stop at Tufts, ride the elevator to the ninth floor, circle the hall for fifteen minutes and then leave for Cape Cod before 8:30. If anyone was watching, they'd think I'd had a proper visit with Brady.

I felt a little wild, like I was playing hooky, something I never dared do as a child. I was driving a black Jeep Wrangler Unlimited, the kind of vehicle I imagined people driving to Cape Cod found suitable. I passed the inbound commuter traffic stuck in gridlock as I sailed by on the southbound side of the Expressway. In an hour I was on the other side of the Sagamore Bridge, which divides Cape Cod from the rest of Massachusetts. I realized I didn't have a game plan for approaching Mrs Burke. For all I knew she was at her winter residence in Florida, if she had one.

I got off at Exit 6 in Hyannis and found a Starbucks next to a Trader Joe's on a commercial strip looking nothing like the quintessential Cape Cod photos in ads luring tourists. I bought a cup of coffee and picked up a map from a display filled with brochures about everything Cape Cod. I saw I wasn't far from Craigville Beach, followed directions, and arrived in less than ten minutes. The long expanse of sandy beach on Nantucket Sound was nearly deserted, other than a man walking a yellow lab and an elderly couple huddled on a bench.

I got out of the car and drew a breath in. The grayness I had seen from my hotel room in Boston was deeper here where it was difficult to tell where the ocean ended and the sky began. A faint mist fell on my face. I pulled the hood from my jacket over my head.

I began walking toward the water then along its edge. I forgot I was supposed to be planning what I would say to Trish Burke. Small frothy waves lapped at my feet as I stepped on fragments of seaweed and small white rocks. The sound of the undulating sea soothed me. I was simply a woman taking a walk on a beach on Cape Cod.

I remembered the dream or memory I had repeatedly, where my mother and a man are sitting on a blanket on the sand leaning into each other while watching me build castles at the edge of the water. I smelled the salt in the air, heard the seagulls crying out to one another, and never wanted to leave this beach.

But I had to. I pledged I would return to the sea and rediscover the part of me that feels tethered to the ocean. I got in the silly car I'd rented, which had nothing to do with the ocean no matter what the ads said. I decided I would wing it with my father's widow.

I punched the address into my cell phone, fairly confident Trish Burke lived in one of the silvery gray cedar shingled cottages I passed on my way to the beach. I imagined her living in one of the grander cottages. To my surprise, the directions led me back toward Starbucks to a street about one block from Main Street in Hyannis. The address was for a large captain's house that had been converted into public housing for seniors with an addition at the rear. Each of the ground-floor units opened on to a long common covered porch. The condition of the complex was somewhere between pristine and rundown.

The address I had for Patricia Burke didn't mention a unit number, which is why I expected to find her at a single-family home. Now I had to determine which was her unit. I noticed two women huddled at one end of the porch on a couple of plastic chairs. One was smoking a cigarette.

'I'm looking for Mrs Burke,' I called over from the sidewalk.

'And who are you?' asked the woman who was smoking.

'Olivia Taylor,' I said, knowing it would mean nothing to either of them.

'What do you want her for?' the smoker said, putting her butt out in a cup I imagined had water in it to douse the ashes.

'I'm looking for her daughter,' I said.

That got her attention. She rose from her chair. The non-smoker looked up at her. 'I didn't know you had a daughter, Trish.'

'I don't,' she said. 'You'd better step into my apartment before I catch pneumonia.' Her voice was raspy and her tone hostile. What was I getting myself into here?

I came on to the porch and met her at Unit 3. She opened the door and let me in to a combination bedroom-sitting area. There was a lumpy floral print couch at one end of the room with a maple coffee table stacked with newspapers. At the other was an unmade single bed. Off the sitting area, I could peek into a small kitchen where I saw a pile of dirty dishes sitting in the sink. The smell of stale beer and rotting garbage was the perfect complement to the décor. I wanted to gag.

'Who the hell are you?' she asked in a hiss as soon as she closed the door. 'I value my privacy. I don't need nosy neighbors knowing about me or my family.' She held on to the wall as she stepped toward the sofa and plopped down. She sounded worse than Paulie Fairclough and was wheezing enough to alarm me.

I stood in the middle of the room facing her.

'I told you. My name is Olivia Taylor. I came to ask you about your daughter—'

'I heard that. Why would you want to know about her? What's this about?' The years had not been gentle to Trish Burke. Without her jacket, I could see she was too thin. Her face had deep wrinkles, especially around her mouth, likely the result from years of smoking. Her hair was a combination of thin and greasy gray. I remembered she was my mother's contemporary, but would have guessed her to be close to eighty had I not known.

I knew our meeting was doomed. I needed to find out what I could and get out.

'Mrs Burke, my mother was Sheila Fairclough,' I began.

'Sheila Fairclough? Your mother was that cheating whore? Wait, are you the "love child"? Her name wasn't Olivia. Was she your sister? What the hell do you want from me?' Trish snarled like a caged animal at me.

'My name was Ashley, before we moved away,' I said.

'Moved away. You mean ran away, don't you? With all of my husband's money.' She was baring yellowed teeth at me, ready to pounce. I knew she couldn't hurt me physically, but her words were painful to hear.

'I was just a little girl,' I said softly, hoping to calm her down.

'Yeah? Well, so was my daughter. The one your father chose not to protect. The one he left me with to support after we'd lost our house in Milton because we had to pay lawyers a lot smarter than he was to try and keep him out of jail. It didn't matter. He'd sold out so you and your mother would be safe, never thinking about what it would do to his wife and daughter.' She had to stop to catch her breath. I didn't know what to say to her so I defaulted to an apology, although I was as innocent as my father's other daughter.

'I'm sorry,' I said.

'You damn well ought to be. We went from living in a six-bedroom house with tennis courts on Brush Hill Road to a unit in Dorchester smaller than the in-law apartment over our three-car garage. I had to get a job. Mickey blew through every dime I'd inherited and he still went to jail. And you know what? He never apologized. Never worried about what would happen to me and his daughter, his legitimate daughter. He just kept saying, "Trish, I did what I had to do." He wasn't worried about our safety because he knew they'd go after the people he really cared about. That was you and your slut mother.'

I'd about had it. I got that the supreme insult to Trish was that the thugs knew her husband cared more about his paramour and their child than his wife and daughter. But this woman was making me angry in a way I had never been angry before.

'Just so you know, Mrs Burke, I didn't exactly have it easy growing up. I didn't even know who my father was until two days ago. My mother's dead. I have no siblings. I just thought if I had a half-sister, I would reach out to her,' I said, less concerned about Trish's breathing than I had been at the beginning of our conversation.

'She was his namesake for Christ's sake and he let her suffer for his sins. No wonder she was a screw-up. Shoplifting, lock-picking, drinking and drugging. But she was smart, as smart as he ever was, and once I got her into Fontbonne Academy, she settled down. I worked damn hard to put her through that school.' Trish was gazing past me into a time and place long gone.

'I'm sure she appreciates it,' I said, starting to edge toward the door. This was going nowhere good.

'The hell she does,' she screeched at me. I heard someone knock through the wall next door.

'Where is she now?' I asked, the last question I intended to ask before I ran out the door.

'How the hell do I know? I haven't seen or heard from her since she went off to that fancy college down south. She doesn't even know I finally lost the cottage on Craigsville beach I tried so hard to save. For her. Those summer renters paid for Fontbonne. She doesn't know if I am alive or dead. She doesn't care. She's just like her son-of-a-bitch father.'

That was it for me. I left without saying goodbye. I couldn't blame my half-sister for never returning home again.

FORTY

I fled to the Jeep, started the ignition and drove down the street until I found an empty parking lot where I could sit and calm down. I could not remember ever meeting anyone as bitter as Trish Burke. While she had valid reasons to steep in resentment and anger, the result seemed only to exacerbate the harm originally done.

I checked my phone for text messages and saw that Deema, Nick, and Ryan had all repeated their requests for me to contact them. They could wait. They already knew more about me than I knew about myself.

Rain pelted the windshield. I wanted to roam Cape Cod from beach to beach and explore it in solitude without the masses that invade it during the annual summer invasion. I felt safe away from Boston, far from the husband who had betrayed me, and the unresolved mystery of my mother's death and my father's life.

But I am dutiful, if nothing else, and I knew I would have to return. I had obligations to Brady and a silly appointment with Andrew for a haircut I had promised to let him give me.

I could barely see the Sagamore Bridge as I drove over the Cape Cod Canal smothered in fog. I tried not to think about Trish Burke's words. She had chosen to ignore that I was a victim as much as her daughter, my half-sister my father's namesake was. I guessed her name was Michelle. We were innocent children, unable to launch after our parents' lives misfired. I wondered how Michelle had fared. She had grown up at least knowing the ugly facts. That may have been more difficult than being raised under a maze of lies and omissions. The prospect of comparing our miserable childhoods gave me an odd sense of comfort.

I got off at the exit for East Milton Square to refuel the rental Jeep. I looked around while pumping gas at a station in a town where my father and half-sister had lived. My father may have bought his gas at this station. I wondered how far his house was from where I stood. I considered taking a detour to peek at it and

Fontbonne Academy, which sounded like a Catholic school to me. I decided I didn't want to be rushed when I explored my family's roots and pushed forward into the sluggish traffic on the Southeast Expressway. A lot of people had places to go at two o'clock on a Friday afternoon. I felt left out.

At the hotel, I handed the valet the keys to the Jeep.

'Did you love it?' he asked.

'Of course,' I said, thinking how silly we are to confuse who we are with what we drive. I walked to the registration desk to sign paperwork to return the car.

'You have someone waiting to see you,' the clerk said, gesturing toward the sitting area in the lobby by the fireplace where coffee, tea, lemonade, and cookies were served in the afternoon. Deema Zaheed waved to me from a red chair next to a low burning fire. I hated that she had found my hiding place.

I walked over and turned to the table, taking a tea bag from the tea caddy. I took my time pouring hot water into a cup, dipping the bag in it, and placing two lemon slices on to the saucer. I sat across from her, noticing she had chosen black coffee.

She looked as stylish in jeans, a black turtleneck sweater, and black Hunter boots as she had the night I met her at Legal Sea Foods. She had a yellow slicker draped over the back of the chair. Her half smile was annoying. I had no energy to guess why she was here. I knew she would make me ask so I wasted no time.

'Nice to see you again too, Deema. What brings you here? I don't suppose I need ask how you found me.'

'Olivia, if we're going to make sure you're safe, we need to know where you are. You must understand that.' Her logic was flawless yet annoying. I was fed up with people knowing more about my life than I did.

'Am I in danger?' I asked. That was why I had called Nick Wojcik.

'Well, not from any of the sources you were when you entered the program, from what we can tell. We've checked to see where the people who were threatening your mother and you through your father are. Many are dead. Some are in prison. A few seem to have been rehabilitated. There doesn't appear to be any activity that would suggest you are in danger. The case has been dormant for years. The only unresolved issue is where the money Mickey Burke skimmed went.' I saw she was holding a small file and wondered what was in it if there was no new information to share.

'Where did it go?' I asked, pretty sure it was the same stinky money sitting in a safe deposit box in my name as my mother's survivor in the New England Federal Credit Union.

'We don't know. We don't really care at this point. We suspect your father diverted it to your mother and that's what she supported you with.'

'My mother made an excellent salary at UVM Medical School and she was a very savvy investor,' I said, which was true, but I didn't think she could have gotten where she was without having been financially seeded.

'Whatever happened to the money, it is unlikely anyone is still looking for it or we would know. We are officially closing your WITSEC file, although we're monitoring the situation regarding your mother's death. Nick wanted you to have this,' Deema said, handing me the manila file I had been watching. 'It's the information we have regarding your history before the program. Medical, statistical, you know.'

'Thank you,' I said, opening the file. The first items I saw were my mother's and my names and dates of birth. The ones Nick had told me about at Jacob Wirth's. I had been so overwhelmed I hadn't realized I had missed my birthday. I was already thirty.

FORTY-ONE

I was furious that I had missed celebrating my thirtieth birthday, which I had pledged to share with my mother. I clutched the file to my chest and went to my room. The birthday was a milestone for most, but for me it was more. I had promised myself it would be the day when I finally acknowledged that my mother was gone. I would succumb to the ambiguous loss her illness brought and release us both from the illusion her condition would improve. But only after a suitable birthday party where we would share a birthday cake with candles and ice cream.

Inside the room, I put the file on a table between the two tufted velvet sapphire blue chairs on either side of the fireplace. I sank into one, thinking I should stop sulking and do something constructive like research my half-sister on my laptop. My eye caught sight of a plant on the desk next to the MacBook. I stood up and confirmed I was staring at a white triple moth orchid, like the one my friends had sent me when my mother died. I saw my name typed on a card on the plastic pitchfork. It was exquisite and from Winston's. There was no note, no signature.

I called the front desk to ask if there was any information about who sent it. The nice clerk who had helped me return the Jeep rental placed me on hold. When she came back on the line, she said she could only confirm that it had been delivered by a Winston's van and asked if there was a problem. I told her no, it was a beautiful plant and that I just wanted to thank the person who sent it.

I plopped on to the desk chair and glared at the plant, tempted to turn it upside down into the wastebasket on the floor. But it was a splendid plant, one I admired. It bore no blame for its arrival in my room. Maybe Erin had sent it as an expression of camaraderie after declaring us both orphans last night.

I opened my laptop and Googled 'Michelle Burke.' There were slightly fewer than twenty-three million results that included an obscure movie actress. I sighed and closed the laptop. I was restless and had two hours before I was due to meet Andrew at the salon on Newbury Street, one block away. I got up and flopped on the bed. I could nap, but the sight of the moth orchid had my adrenalin surging on high alert.

I stared at the ceiling. I couldn't decide whether I was Ashley Ann Fairclough, born September 30, 1987 or Olivia Rose Taylor, born December 29, 1987. I would need to decide if I should change my name back to Ashley or continue being known as Olivia and when I should celebrate my birthday. I couldn't imagine anyone else in the world had to agonize over these dilemmas or confront them alone.

That was the dark part that frightened me. Even though my life as Olivia had been predicated on a lie, I had my mother, John, and eventually Daniel to fill the void. Ashley had no one. Now Olivia only had John. I was torturing myself, on the brink of calling Dr Evans, when my cell phone rang. It was Ryan Fairclough apparently no longer content to wait for me to return his multiple text messages. I still felt annoyed at how he had dismissed me, but I needed to hear another human being's voice. Besides, he could be calling about Brady, so I gave myself permission to answer.

'Olivia, why haven't you responded to my text messages? Are you OK?' He sounded genuinely concerned without a tinge of judgment in his voice.

'I was going to. I've just been preoccupied,' I said.

'I know. I can't imagine. Can I come talk to you? Please.' I detected urgency in his words.

'Is Brady OK?' I asked. I hadn't seen him for more than twenty-four hours and didn't know if his condition had changed.

'Yes, but we need to talk. Can I come up?' he asked.

'Ryan, where are you?' I asked, expecting him to say exactly what he told me.

'I'm in the lobby of the Lenox. I won't take up too much of your time.'

While I waited for his knock, I pondered how he had discovered I was staying in a tiny hotel where I had kept a low profile. When the knock came, I opened the door.

'Is the Boston Police Department following me? Am I a suspect in Terry Walsh's murder? Or my mother's? Why does every law enforcement agency in Boston know where I am?' I stepped away from the door to let him in.

'No, of course not. You're considered to be more of a person at risk. Listen, I can understand how it must feel to have cops and FBI agents on your tail, especially after what you learned about being in the WITSEC program—'

'I'm sorry. I should have told you about that and that Terry Walsh was my mother's nurse. I meant to, I just kept getting distracted,' I said, going over to one of the blue chairs and sinking into it.

Ryan walked over to the other chair facing me and sat down.

'Olivia, it's more than understandable you didn't get around to it. You were being barraged by information and events that rocked your world. I'm the one who should apologize. I should have asked more follow-up questions, explored some of the information with you that you were learning. Hell, some of it came from my own uncle. I am sorry. I own this.'

He looked like hell. The brown leather jacket had been replaced with a black L.L. Bean windbreaker. His eyes were bloodshot and his mane of thick hair matted. It broke my heart. We were too young to be so beaten.

'You're not responsible for what's happened, Ryan,' I said.

'No, but I didn't have to add to your problems. Basically accuse you of withholding information, of thwarting a murder investigation, when I could have just asked you to share what you knew. Instead, I go judgmental and banish you to Costa, knowing what she'd say. I didn't listen. I didn't ask the questions I should have or I would have known what you had to offer days ago. And she's right. Once again.'

'I'm sorry. I know she's your ex-wife. That can't be easy.'

'No, especially since she has outranked me the entire time we've been on the force. I was lucky to get assigned to Homicide. She was already on. After the divorce, there wasn't any reason not to have us on the same division, as long as we didn't get in each other's faces. Lou and I are very professional, so it hasn't been a problem, but I knew I had screwed this up and she would be all over me. That's why I jumped on you, instead of supporting you. It was a shitty thing to do.'

'Did Costa give it to you bad?' I asked. I could appreciate how difficult it might be to deal with a former spouse when the emotional buttons each knew how to push hadn't been fully disengaged.

'No. She was a class act about it. She said Terry Walsh's murder was a cluster – you know. How, where, when, and why it happened made no sense. She thought your mother's death might be connected, but she wasn't there yet. She's combing through employee records at Thompson House. When she found out the FBI was following you and that you had been in WITSEC, she decided she had been cast in a bad movie no one would pay to see, it was so unreal. She said she got why I didn't follow through when so much was going down.'

'Sounds like you two turned a corner,' I said.

Ryan laughed. 'If you only knew. Lou and I have been around our share of corners. She never thought she was good enough for my family. I was always trying to prove to her I was her equal. Our relationship was more like a competition than a marriage. We'll be better friends divorced than we ever were married.'

'I wish it could be like that for Daniel and me. We've separated,' I said.

'I know. I'm sorry. Erin and Costa told me. Don't be mad. Erin's worried about you and Costa's running a murder investigation. Listen, Liv, do you think Daniel might be responsible for some of the things that have been happening to you?'

'Two weeks ago, I would have told you that was crazy. Today, I don't know.' It hurt my soul to think I could have misjudged and married a man who would want to hurt, even destroy me.

'OK, then. Brady's doing about the same as he did at Children's. There was a little adjustment after he was transferred. He's still a tiny wretched creature, poor little guy. And the news about his father isn't good. We thought we knew where Zack was hiding. We planned a raid on the apartment in Brockton, but when we got there, it was empty. So Brady is still considered at risk for abduction or worse.' Ryan stood to leave.

'Can I see him?' I asked.

'That's one of the reasons I came. They need paperwork signed by you at the General. Authorizations, and that kind of stuff. I have a plan to sneak you in after your haircut. Would that be OK?' he asked.

I started to bristle. He even knew about my haircut. I saw him grin.

'Erin told me. Honest. I'll pick you up. Text me when you're done, OK?'

'Sure,' I said, standing in front of him, aware of how tall he was, relieved we had patched things up.

'Am I forgiven?' he asked, stepping toward me to give me one of his hugs. I nodded, letting him wrap his arms around me. He held me a little longer than an apology required, but I didn't mind. Only when he left did I realize I had forgotten to tell him about the moth orchid.

FORTY-TWO

killed the time until my appointment with Andrew searching for my mother's sisters in California and Florida on Facebook. It seemed everyone over sixty with grandkids was on Facebook, but since I didn't know their married names, I hit a wall.

I moved back over to my Michelle Burke search, forgoing Google, opting instead to search websites designed to find classmates, reunions, and other alumni-related information, including yearbooks. I became engrossed in how much the classmate industry had grown since I had left my job as a research librarian at UVM. I researched my own records, just to get a feel for how it worked. Most of the better sites cost money. When I decided which one would most likely get me to my half-sister's yearbook, I paid my $9.99 and waited for it to load. I became impatient and looked at the time. Even though Andrew's salon on Newbury Street was only a block away, I was pushing my luck. My research would have to wait.

'I thought for sure you were going to stand me up,' Andrew said, as I walked to the back of Cerebral, which Erin had told me was one of the top-ranked salons in Boston. At 5:30 on a Friday afternoon, the salon was emptying, but a few clients remained. A woman brought me over a flute of prosecco, while Andrew circled me, inspecting my hair, and occasionally raising a tress as if something was hidden beneath it.

'It's really not that bad, we just have to untame it and capitalize on the color. Add a little makeup and you'll be gorgeous, not that you aren't already a natural beauty.'

'Untame it? Don't you mean the opposite?' I asked. Andrew chuckled.

Sitting in his chair with a large plastic bib draped over me, Andrew walked around me, cocking his head at different angles as he continued to inspect my hair. He put his hand through it, holding it up under the light. The blonde highlights predominated the light red.

'Do you know how much people pay me to create this color? And you got it as a birthright. You have to be pure Irish, sweetheart.' He shook his head in mocking disbelief. The bright LED lighting reflected off his bald dome.

'Pretty much so, according to Ancestry.com,' I said, remembering how infuriated my mother had been when I spit in a cup and sent for my DNA results.

Andrew brought me over to a sink, explaining I didn't need to have my hair colored, but he would put a rinse in that would bring out the shine and natural highlights. I sat in the chair, leaned back to let my neck extend on to the cool porcelain, and began to relax. I closed my eyes and listened to Andrew fussing next to me. He turned the warm water on and soaked my scalp when I started sneezing.

'Stop,' I said, sitting forward, ready to leap out of the chair.

I sneezed a few more times, while Andrew reached for tissues.

'What's wrong?' he asked, handing me several.

'What is that stuff I smell?' But I knew. Whatever it was, it was pear scented.

'The shampoo? La Poire et L'Avocat. Pure pear nectar with avocado mash. Organic. It's just in. It's the rage. I've got oodles of samples for you,' Andrew said.

'No thanks,' I said. 'I must be allergic.' I blew my nose a few more times.

'Too bad. We'll go with lemon mousse. Here, smell it before I almost kill you again.' It smelled so good I almost asked for a spoon.

Andrew massaged my scalp until it felt like my brain had gone to the gym for a workout.

When I was back in his chair, we reached the moment of truth.

'Well?' he asked.

'Well, what?' I asked back, but I knew what was coming.

'Do you want to tell me what you want or do you trust me to tell you what you need?'

Maybe I didn't need Dr Evans to help me with my issues and I should just see Andrew regularly. I knew from Erin that doctors, lawyers, and television personalities paid huge money to have him do their hair. So much so, she said she teased about him taking a pay reduction when he becomes a lawyer.

'I am all yours,' I said, letting go.

Instead of watching in the mirror what he was doing to the hair I ignored more than styled, I asked Andrew questions about his family, deflecting any interest he might have in mine since I knew he must know about the separation. I learned Andrew had a sister and two other brothers. He went to culinary school before entering a hairstyling academy, both after flunking out of Catholic Memorial.

'It wasn't that I'm not smart. I am. Very. But I was practicing a little civil disobedience after being bullied. Even back then it was pretty scary to be a gay adolescent in Boston.'

I felt ashamed that I was trying to keep Andrew from prying into my life by probing into his. I had been raised under a shroud of secrecy and to fear the intimacy friendship brings. I had to learn to trust and reciprocate.

I told Andrew about my own painful adolescence. How I had grown up in isolation with my mother and when I reached the age when you naturally gravitate toward your peers, I had imploded.

'I'm sorry about Daniel, Olivia,' Andrew said. The kindness in his voice was like a salve.

'I am too.' I was surprised to feel tears coming down my cheeks. Andrew stopped clipping and handed me a tissue.

'That night in the restaurant, it was very clear the man didn't appreciate you. You deserve someone much better. And the way you're looking, you'll have no trouble attracting him.' I looked at the floor and saw a circle of tufts of my hair surrounding his chair. When he put the scissors in a cup on the granite counter in front of us, I sighed and looked in the mirror. My eyes looked larger and a deeper shade of blue.

'You can text Ryan and tell him I need ten more minutes.'

Andrew waltzed around me as he drew my hair around a circular brush while aiming a blow dryer at me as if it were filled with magic. Long after it was dry, he sprayed little spurts from a plastic bottle. Soft waves rested above my shoulders making me look playful, almost mischievous. For once in my life, I felt stylish, hip.

'There you go. I left enough hair for you to squish into a ponytail if you start to panic.' He kissed the top of my head, pulled the cape off me and rushed me out the door before I could pay him.

FORTY-THREE

Ryan was waiting for me at the curb, standing outside of what I guessed was an unmarked police vehicle. It was a clunky old Ford, the kind old people tend to drive. The rain had abated but a constant drizzle combined with the streetlights to turn Newbury Street into a hazy Impressionist print. Ryan opened the door for me. It almost felt like a date.

But my 'date' never mentioned my new haircut or the conversation we had a few hours before. He was all business.

I was surprised at the number of people out walking about in the mist, spilling into bars and restaurants or just crawling home on a Friday night. Since I don't have class on Friday, I usually spend the day catching up on laundry and playing and pruning in the conservatory. I try to read something other than the law. Daniel almost always has to work, so I sometimes go to the Dedham Community Theater in the evening where they serve popcorn with real melted butter and feature the movies most people skip. Being in the city on a Friday night gave me the opportunity to see what I was missing.

'We need to move your car from the law school garage to the one at Tufts first,' he said, pulling away into the night.

'OK. Is that so the people after Zack will think Brady is still there?'

'Yes, it's more important than ever. The search for Zack has become urgent. What we found where he was staying in Brockton was alarming,' Ryan said, turning on to Stuart Street toward the garage.

I knew better than to ask what had been found. I also understood the longer Zack was at large, Brady's risk of harm increased.

'Do you want me to go to the ninth floor after I park in the garage?' I asked.

Ryan looked at me.

'You'll have earned a badge of your own after all of this is done. Yes, please. If you could wait for about fifteen minutes, then exit through the emergency room entrance, I'll be waiting for you.'

'How do you know there aren't any new tracking devices on my car?' I asked.

'Because we've been watching your car since I brought it over from Children's,' he said, grinning at me. 'And yes, we've paid the garage, so you can exit and drive over to the next block.' He handed me what I knew was the card you placed in the machine as you exit after paying at a station on each floor.

Getting into the Mini felt foreign, it had been so long. I felt a pang of disloyalty for having taken the Wrangler to the Cape in the morning. I pulled out of the garage on to Charles Street, took a right on to Stuart Street past Portia, and then a right on to Tremont Street, past the Wang Theatre, and into the Tufts garage where I had occasionally parked when the law school garage was full. Within a few minutes I was in the hospital on my way to the ninth floor after checking in at a central desk where a woman said, 'OK,' after I said who I was.

I checked my phone while I killed fifteen minutes. No more messages from the FBI. Erin left a text to 'please, please call her,' which I did.

'Liv, you have had me crazy. Are you OK? Don't be pissed I told Ryan and Andrew what's going on. They're your friends. And Ryan is the police, you know.' Erin spoke so fast I had trouble absorbing what she was saying, but as usual, she made me laugh.

'I'm OK and I'm not angry. I got worried I put you in jeopardy,' I said.

'I got new locks and added a security system to my cable services, which already costs too much. But I'm safe and so is the cat. And so far, I haven't killed the mystery jade plant, but I might like to kill its donor,' she said, chuckling.

I saw a flash on my telephone that told me Chester Buchanan was calling.

'Erin, I've got to go,' I said and hung up.

I expected to hear Barbara Buchanan's voice, but no, this was the real deal. Chet Buchanan wasted no time telling why he was calling after he identified himself.

'Your husband telephoned here a little while ago. Fortunately, I was the one to answer the call. I gather from what he said you have told him you want out of the marriage. Apparently, he thinks that Barbara and I are the reason for that. He has threatened to take legal action if we ever speak to you again.' I could hear Chet wheeze as he paused.

'I'm so sorry, Mr Buchanan. I never thought he would contact you, or worse, threaten you.' I felt stupid at not realizing the Daniel they had known and was now crawling out from under a rock would make them vulnerable to him again.

'You wouldn't. Until you cross a line with Daniel, it's hard to imagine what he's capable of. I'm not blaming you. I know you're just another of his victims. From the sound of his voice, college and medical school didn't do anything to temper his viciousness. The last thing Barbara and the girls need is to have him back in their lives. I've called our family attorney and he advises me I can't get a restraining order because there's no threat of imminent physical harm. Just like when he tortured his sisters. He's slick, I'll give him that.'

I wasn't sure why he was calling me. Chet didn't seem to be blaming me for setting Daniel in his direction.

'How can I help?' I asked. 'I am sorry if I triggered this.'

'Oh, I'm not calling to ask for your help, although you are very kind to offer it. Barbara said you sounded like a nice young woman. I'm sorry you got mixed up with him. You really are much better off without him. No, I'm calling to alert you. Barbara said we should let you know how volatile he sounded when he called. We both remember how bad it was when he got to that point,' Chet said.

'I see,' I said, gulping. They were calling to warn me. I thanked him and promised to be in touch if I needed their help. I asked them to do the same. I hung up and rushed toward the cop waiting for me.

FORTY-FOUR

When we pulled into the parking lot at Shriners Children's Hospital, I was confused.

'Did they move Brady again?' I asked. Ryan placed his index finger over his lips in a 'shhh.'

'Come on,' he said. We got out of the car and walked into the entrance to the hospital emergency room. From what I had observed recently, cops spend a lot of time around emergency rooms which, for them, are like doors into a labyrinth.

In companionable silence, we passed the waiting area for the emergency room, walked down a long cream-colored corridor, turned on to a longer blue hall, and then got on an elevator and went down two floors. There we opened on to a windowless green corridor. We had seen a few medical professionals in the halls before we hit the elevator, but no one was to be found on what I guess was a subterranean passage.

'Are we in a tunnel?' I whispered.

'Olivia, you keep showing promise in law enforcement,' he said.

We reached an elevator and got on. Ryan pressed for the fourth floor. We got off and walked through an empty room filled with chairs and a large sign that said 'Pediatric Gastrointestinal Motility Clinic.' I shuddered to think what kind of problems kids brought here. We walked down another corridor to another elevator.

'Last one,' Ryan said, pressing the button for the sixth floor.

When the door opened and I saw the sign read 'NICU', I felt a rush of relief. Ryan pointed to a long, curved counter much like the one at Children's Hospital. I walked over and identified myself to a woman who was sitting on a stool and asked where Brady was. She looked up, past me, and at Ryan.

'OK, I'll need some ID and your guardianship documents, please.' I gave her both out of my purse, and waited while she went to make copies. When she returned, she had Lettie Johnson, RN, in tow.

'Hi. I thought there was a new guardian in place,' she said, offering me her chilly hand, which if the saying was true meant she had a warm heart.

'Not that I've heard,' I said. I hoped I hadn't been so neglectful by not seeing Brady for almost forty-eight hours that I was being removed. Professor Cohen would be horrified. But I reeled myself in and remembered I wasn't obligated to see Brady regularly, only if there was a problem. Visiting him had been purely voluntary.

'It's just that Dr Vincent said the team had decided along with DCF that a graduate mental health professional should be guardian,' Lettie said.

'Dr Vincent? It's the first I've heard of it. Tell me about the team and what role Dr Vincent has on it?' I asked. The tone in my voice must have alerted Ryan, who had stayed a diplomatic distance from the nurses' station that sat behind the counter. I sensed him not far behind me now.

'Sure, she's part of the Developmental Team that's been started to help transition the babies who are born to mothers addicted to opioids. They're conducting a study with Harvard. But listen, you're here. You've got the credentials and Detective Fairclough to back you up. Come, you can read the updated chart and sign the authorizations we prepared,' Lettie said.

I followed her behind the nurses' station to a desk where she pulled out a chair on wheels. I lowered myself into it as she presented me with a chart that had grown exponentially each day since Brady was born. I read the doctors' progress notes, the nurses' notes, skipped the lab reports, which I couldn't understand, and found Kayla Vincent's name nowhere. Then I noticed a tab marked 'TEAM' and dug in. There wasn't much, except a handwritten notation that Brady had been determined eligible for the study and DCF recommended his participation, pending him no longer requiring police protection. 'A mental health professional with advanced degree should replace current law student guardian.' The signature, though barely legible, was that of Kayla Vincent, MD.

I was incensed. I wanted that viper off the case, as far away from Brady as possible. And for the moment, I had the power. I checked the authorizations clipped to the front of the chart with a Post-it note for 'Guardian to sign.' Three were for medications. The last was for Brady to be admitted to the TEAM study, pending no longer needing police protection. I signed the first three.

'There's a fourth,' Lettie said. She'd been watching me as she leaned against a tall cabinet with multiple closed doors, each labeled for its contents.

'I know. I'm not signing it,' I said.

'But the TEAM,' she said.

'I'm getting my own developmental expert for Brady.'

'But the TEAM's publicly funded. Brady is indigent,' Lettie said, losing patience with me.

'But I'm not. I'd like to see him, please.' Ryan and I followed her down another corridor into a room where a nurse sat.

'Fairclough,' she said, getting up to shake his hand. I got it. Another nurse-cop. I was getting good at this.

Lettie handed me a paper hospital gown and got one for herself. I couldn't imagine Brady nestling into the stiff, crinkly material. But I shut up and went with her into a smaller dark room where Brady lay in an incubator. He was attached to an IV and was just as miserable as he had been the first night I met him. His dark hair was sweaty from crying, his extremities were frantic. I went to the sink and washed my hands. I found a pile of receiving blankets and took one to wrap him in.

'Is this thing running right now?' I asked Lettie, gesturing to the IV.

'No,' she said as she unplugged it.

I scooped Brady into my arms and started walking with him around the room, swaying him a little from side to side.

'You've done this before,' Lettie said.

'Yes, I spent nights with him at Children's. I just couldn't come here until now because . . .'

'I know, security. It's so sad. His mom's dead, his father's being pursued. The social service egotists want him for their own glorification. Why does it have to be so complicated?'

I sensed I might have an ally.

'You mean DCF or Dr Vincent?' I asked.

'Both, but Dr Vincent seems driven to make Brady part of the study. I suppose his notoriety would bring attention to it. Nothing like a front-page case study. She really is intense.'

I almost said, 'No kidding,' but remembered I hadn't disclosed I knew Dr Vincent.

'Do you have rocking chairs?' I asked.

'Sure, would you like me to get you one?' Lettie asked, as I continued to rotate around the incubator, sensing Brady sinking a little deeper into my arms.

'For the morning. I can't stay. Detective Fairclough brought me here. But I'll be back in the morning and can spend the whole day.' I had already figured I could walk from the Lenox in less than half an hour and enter through Shriners just as Ryan and I did. I was excited to be back with Brady where I felt I might do someone some good.

'That's great. We have volunteers who rock the opioid babies, but we can't use them for Brady because of the security issue.'

Ryan and I retraced our steps back to the car. I tried memorizing the route for my trip back in the morning, which I knew I had to divulge to him. I hated to break the quiet contentment that had come over me since holding Brady in my arms. I could still feel the warmth of his body in my chest twenty minutes after I had left him.

'Ryan, I plan to walk here from the Lenox tomorrow morning to spend the day with Brady. Do I need to walk to Tufts first or can I come directly?' I asked. Giving him an 'either/or' question was cheating, which we both knew from Evidence class, but I wasn't above it.

He looked at me out of the side of his eyes. 'I got an A in Evidence, Liv.'

'I tried,' I said, putting both palms up. 'I figured I would go the same way we did tonight. Through Shriners.'

He laughed. 'There are a lot more tunnels under the hospitals in the city and under the harbor, you know.'

'One tunnel at a time, please,' I said.

'Call me in the morning and I'll see how things stand. It's probably a good idea to stay at the hotel for the weekend, Liv. Between your husband and all of this stuff with Brady, a little hotel security can't hurt,' he said more seriously.

Copley Square had emptied by the time Ryan pulled in front of the Lenox. The doorman looked over at us like an impatient father waiting for his daughter to return from a date.

There was an awkward moment before I opened the door.

'Thanks,' I said.

'Liv, I meant to say, great haircut.'

I smiled and closed the door. I almost skipped to my room. I had seen and held Brady, whom I would protect from the evil Dr Vincent. Ryan and I were friends. Erin and Andrew were my friends. The Buchanans cared enough about my safety to warn me. And I had a great haircut.

Shit. I'd forgotten to tell Ryan about the call from the Buchanans and the moth orchid. It wasn't that I wanted to keep information from him. I just had been programmed for so many years by my mother to keep personal information sealed that it was my default setting. Even Daniel had been forced to pry information from me early in our relationship.

I would tell Ryan when I called him in the morning about seeing Brady. I would write it down so I would remember.

I slid the plastic hotel key into the door. Before I opened it, I could smell the fireplace burning. I guessed I had the staff trained. They knew I wanted an evening fire and when I would return.

With the door opened wide, I saw the flames burning low in the fireplace. Daniel was seated on one of the elegant blue chairs wearing one of the plush white hotel robes I hadn't ripped the plastic cover off. He was sipping what I was sure was brandy from the wet bar.

FORTY-FIVE

'What are you doing here?' I asked, closing the door behind me, but staying close to it.

'Liv, come in. Put your feet up by the fire. How did you find this delightful spot?' Daniel wasn't as drunk as he had been the night we had dinner with Josh and Kayla, but he was definitely in his cups. His face was flushed and his hair uncharacteristically disheveled.

'Who let you in? How did you find me?' I walked closer to him, but didn't sit down. Chet Buchanan's warning rang in my ears. I knew I shouldn't engage with Daniel, but I was incensed. I felt violated that he had discovered my sanctuary and invaded it.

'The hotel staff let me in. I am your husband and I had my credit card for the account you used to charge the room. If you didn't want me to find you, why would you put the room on our joint Visa, Liv?' He smiled through whitened teeth as phony as he was.

I had put the room on our joint account thinking it was safer than using a credit card in my individual name. I hadn't factored in that I might need protection from the man I shared it with. I could see him charming the hotel staff, telling them he was joining me for a weekend escape.

'You need to go home. You wanted to stay in the house. I left. Go back. Now,' I said. I was biting my tongue. I wanted to excoriate him for all the hurt he had caused the Buchanans and me, but this was not the time to do it.

'I can't. The house is swarming with cops. Some butch detective from the Boston Police Department showed up a few hours ago with a search warrant. Said it was connected to the death of your mother's nurse. Funny how Claire can still be a pain in the ass even after she's dead.' Daniel took a swig of Courvoisier. I could see he'd brought an entire bottle, which was sitting on the table next to him. I'd never seen him drink my favorite cognac before.

I knew he was baiting me with the remark about my mother. He was counting on me losing control so he could gain it. I would not yield and remained silent and standing. I tried reminding him of his professional obligations, which he never ignores.

'Daniel, you must have to be at McLean tomorrow. You need to go to another hotel and get some sleep.'

'Don't be silly, Liv. I'm already here. Come have a drink. Sit. We'll order room service and then tuck in. You look a bit of a wreck. I don't suppose you've been sleeping. And what happened to your hair?' He patted the empty chair next to him.

Don't take the bait, don't take the bait. My new mantra. I saw how easily he had controlled me. He would show kindness and concern, then comment on how pathetic I was without explicitly saying so. I'd be grateful that he cared and paid attention and would be malleable to his every whim. He had been all I had, other than a mother who was disappearing more each day.

'Why don't you call Kayla? I'm sure she and Josh could put you up for the night,' I said, veering toward a line I didn't want to cross. Learning Kayla was attempting to inject herself into Brady's professional care had alarmed me. I had to be careful not to let my repugnance for her spark my own temper.

Daniel laughed. 'No, Liv, that's definitely not a good idea. I can't believe I actually considered starting a professional partnership with her. She definitely has some boundary issues of her own. And now that she's been disciplined, I could never consider her as a partner.'

He had me. I was curious and could not resist asking why she had been disciplined.

'It was stupid really. Apparently, she was taking time off from her shifts. An hour here, an hour there. I wasn't surprised. Occasionally I'd have trouble finding her and she was always borrowing someone's car. She told the administration she was taking breaks to counter the stress from the residency. They said she should have reported she needed time off. Stupid on her part, but now she's switched to research, so the administration is less concerned. Josh bailed her out, like always. Told them they overwork us to the point of breaking us and they would have a lawsuit on their hands if they dismissed her. He is as devoted a sugar daddy as they make.'

I flinched at the description of Josh. He had been so kind to me.

'But she and Josh are still your friends. You could go there. Everyone has problems, Daniel. You're a psychiatrist. Why can't you see that? Kayla has work-related stress. You have marital problems. We're all human,' I said, wanting to scream at him for being so robotic. He seemed to think he was above having the kind of issues he was trained to help resolve.

'No, it's worse than that. Kayla seemed to have misunderstood our relationship. When I confided in her that you were blaming our marriage for your personal internal problems and were considering divorce, she suggested something very inappropriate.' Daniel reached for the bottle on the table and filled his glass. Then he filled the one next to it and handed it toward me.

'Here, Liv, I bought this for you. It's not bad,' he said, taking a sip.

I walked over and took the glass, not intending to drink more than a sip, but I was spellbound by what he was telling me about Kayla and wanted him to continue. I sat in the chair next to him. I kept my jacket on.

'What was she suggesting?' I tried to remove any edge to my words.

'That you didn't appreciate me. You don't,' he said. I kept my mouth shut.

'She thought we would make a formidable combination professionally and personally. She was coming on to me. Proposing she leave Josh, that she and I could become the most elite psychiatric couple in Boston. There are so many of us in psychiatry who marry within the profession, it wouldn't sound crazy if we both weren't already married. Then there was the part about the house on Moss Hill. Kayla had all sorts of ideas about what she'd do to it when we were together. She said she'd finally have everything she was entitled to. It came right out of left field.' Daniel was looking at his glass as if it held the memory of his bizarre conversation with Kayla.

'What did you say?' I asked. Even though I no longer wanted him, some part of my ego buried deep within felt triumphant that Daniel had rejected Kayla.

'I told her to stop acting like one of the nutcases we treated and walked away. I suppose I'll have to smooth her feathers at some point, but frankly I was unnerved. Until that conversation, I considered Kayla to be the most rational contemporary among my colleagues.'

Poor Daniel, he would never get it. He was missing a chip when it came to human relationships. Even when a woman threw herself at him, he didn't get it. Worse, there was that dark side of him that the Buchanans and I knew too well.

I put my glass down and stood up. I walked over and grabbed my Marshalls bags out of the cherry wardrobe closet. I unplugged my laptop, grateful I had never shared my password with Daniel, and placed it in my backpack.

'Where are you going?' Daniel looked bewildered.

'It doesn't matter. You stay here for the night. Thank you for sending the moth orchid,' I said, placing it in the crook of my elbow, edging toward the door. I couldn't leave it with Daniel.

'Don't be ridiculous. Why would I send you another plant? You already have more than you can keep track of.'

I stood with the door opened a crack, arms loaded, ready to run. But I had something more to say.

'Daniel, if you ever call, contact, or communicate with Chester and Barbara Buchanan or their daughters, I will report you to the Massachusetts Board of Medical Registration and do everything I know how to make sure you never practice psychiatry ever again.'

I slipped out the door, kicking it shut along with my life with Daniel Buchanan.

FORTY-SIX

I went down to the front desk and explained I needed a room. The confused clerk reminded me I already had one.

'Yes, but you gave my estranged husband who has been stalking me access to it so I need another,' I said.

In twenty seconds, the manager appeared, full of apologies. I accepted. No one knew better than I how smooth Daniel was. But I did suggest they should be more careful.

'Of course,' the manager told me as he tucked me into a limousine that would take me back to Newbury Street where I had been given a complimentary room at the luxurious Newbury Guest House.

I stashed my belongings in the charming room, which sadly was missing a fireplace. I decided I needed food and to be in the company of normal people, so I headed down to the Roost Bistro in the small hotel where I ordered a Caesar salad, traditional Boston baked scrod, and a double lemon drop martini. I watched couples dining together, observing them like a clinician. I wanted to know how normal couples behave. Some shared bites of their dinners. Others barely spoke. The ones who dived into each other's plates laughed more. The silent diners peeked at their phones.

I was clueless about how Daniel and I might have appeared to observers on the rare occasions when we dined out. I didn't remember ever spearing a bite on to a fork and placing it in Daniel's mouth. I didn't remember much laughter either.

I indulged in a piece of vanilla crème roll, deciding that if I ever did get into another relationship with someone else, he would have to love food and drink. And fun.

I returned to my room, put my pajamas on and hopped on the huge feathery bed I had all to myself with my laptop. Satiated with a full belly, I basked in the satisfaction I had stood up to Daniel and that I had been right, as had my mother. Kayla did have her sights set on him. I worried about Josh and how he was being used. I suspected he knew and had been willing to pay the price.

I turned on the television and found the local news. When my mother lived with us, I had watched the Today show with her every morning. Since then I got my news online or in the newspaper I still preferred to read in print.

A female anchor I didn't recognize, wearing a sheath that looked like a cocktail dress, stood holding a pile of papers she never looked at. Brady's father was still at large, considered a 'person of interest' although related to drug crimes, not the murder of the mother of his child. She looked over at her male counterpart, dressed in a suit that looked too small for him. He appeared to have forgotten to shave, possibly because he had spent so much time slicking the tuft of hair above his forehead. I remembered why I read rather than watch the news. He somberly reported that Terry Walsh's murderer had not been taken into custody, but that a search warrant focusing on employees of the health care facility where she worked had yielded helpful information.

I switched off the television and clicked on the laptop. I was too wired to fall asleep. I checked my email and noticed one from the yearbook site I had joined earlier in the afternoon. I clicked on the link and went searching for my half-sister. I guessed she was a year or two older than me, so I headed for the Class of 2003. No luck, no Burkes graduated that year.

There were three Burkes in the Class of 2002, but none of them fit the profile. It turned out 2004 was my lucky year. I found Michaela Patricia Burke listed as a graduate. So she wasn't a Michelle. I flipped through the pages of photos of lay teachers, nuns, glee clubs, until I reached the graduates. I started wading through them, stalling because I was nervous to meet my half-sister, even on paper. Each graduate had a quote beneath her photo and a list of the clubs, sports, and activities she had participated in.

There were no clubs, sports, or activities listed below Michaela's photograph. Only the quote, 'Don't get mad, get even,' attributed to Joseph P. Kennedy. Michaela was a striking young woman with smooth, straight, shiny hair, the color of midnight. Her features were perfectly symmetrical. She had a beautiful full mouth, although she did not smile. Above those pouty lips sat a beauty mark.

My half-sister was Kayla Vincent.

FORTY-SEVEN

The idea that Kayla Vincent was Michaela Patricia Burke was hard to absorb. Kayla had obviously taken Josh's name when they got married and Burke was her maiden name. Kayla was a nickname for Michaela.

One thing was clear. They were the same person. I'd spent too many hours staring at Kayla during sessions to not recognize her. I wondered if she had known who I was. She must have. There was no other explanation for her intrusion into my life with Daniel, and now with Brady.

Brady. Dear God, Kayla had unfettered access to him. All I had prevented was his admission into the study. I had to protect him. I had to call Ryan.

'Fairclough.'

'Ryan, it's me, Olivia. I have to talk to you about Brady,' I said. I was taking off my pajamas while I spoke. I needed to get dressed and to the hospital.

'Olivia, how did you hear? I was just calling you,' he said.

'Hear what? What's happened?' Whatever it was, I could tell by Ryan's voice it wasn't good. I had never heard him sound so somber. I prayed he wasn't going to tell me Brady was dead.

'He's gone. We don't know who took him, only that he or she was dressed like a nurse or a doctor. The cop on duty was in the restroom. It happened in a minute or two. We're doing an Amber Alert right now. We'll get him back, Liv.' I heard him choke up.

'Ryan, I'm pretty sure I know who took him. Her name is Kayla Vincent. She's a doctor at MGH, a psychiatrist. She's actually Mickey Burke's daughter, my half-sister. And she's more than a little crazy,' I said.

'Why would she take Brady?' he asked.

'I'm not sure, but I can guess. I'm coming to the hospital. Or the police station. I don't know. Where am I supposed to be for Brady?' I was crying.

'Stay where you are, Olivia. We don't need any more drama than we have on our hands now. I'll send a cruiser over to pick you up. Stay in your room. Don't go to the lobby. We don't know what we're dealing with here. I don't want anything to happen to you,' he said and hung up.

I put on the pair of jeans and second sweater I had bought. I jammed my feet into the boots. I felt so helpless. I needed to do something. Anything. I just didn't know what.

It came to me. I hated to do it, but I had to call Josh. He understood what a mess Kayla was. If anyone could intercede, it would be Josh.

As soon as he picked up, I could hear Brady crying in the background. The dinner I had eaten began doing somersaults in my stomach.

'Josh, what's going on? Is that Brady I hear? The baby I was appointed to be guardian for?' Who the hell else would it be? But I had to say something.

'It's Olivia,' I heard him say, but not into the receiver. I heard him mumbling while Brady's cries turned to whimpers. Josh came back on the phone.

'Yes. Yes, it is. Kayla says if you don't want her dropping him on his head from our balcony, you'd better get over here fast. And don't bring any cops,' Josh said. His voice quivered.

'I'm on my way,' I said, grabbing my jacket and purse as I ran out the door.

I hailed a cab, which fortunately at 11 p.m. outside a Boston hotel on a Friday night on busy Newbury Street wasn't difficult. I had to look up the address for the condo in my phone for the cab driver, using time Brady might not have. The condo in Brookline was fairly close to where we were, but maybe not close enough to get there in time to save Brady. I told the cabbie to step on it. I had a family emergency.

My phone rang. I picked it up.

'Liv, where the hell are you? My guy just went to your door at the hotel and was told off by your drunken husband. Are you OK?'

Damn, I never told Ryan I left the Lenox. Or why. I had done it again.

'I'm sorry. Daniel followed me there so the hotel found me a place on Newbury Street where I'd be safe. I was in a panic about Brady and forgot to tell you. Ryan, she's got him. Kayla. Kayla

Vincent. The psychiatrist from MGH. She's got him up in her condo on Longwood and is threatening to throw him over the balcony on his head . . .' I couldn't finish the sentence.

'Are you on your way there? Jesus, Liv, don't go in there. Wait for me. What's the address on Longwood?' Ryan asked.

'I'm almost there,' I said as the cabbie pulled up to the front drive. I gave Ryan the address. I handed the cab driver a fistful of bills I didn't bother to count and jumped out of the backseat. I wasn't sure why, but the door to the lobby was wedged open with a newspaper, removing one obstacle to my entry. Inside, I looked at the intercom and buzzed unit 1009.

'Yes?' Josh said, while Brady continued to wail in the background.

'It's me, Olivia,' I said.

He buzzed me in. I flew through the second set of glass doors over to the bank of elevators, furious I had to wait for one to come down. Finally, the elevator door opened and I took a slow ride up to the tenth floor. I didn't know what Kayla was thinking or how I could bargain with her. If Daniel hadn't already rejected her, I could have offered to step aside. I was sure his dismissal of her must have enraged her. He had no diplomacy.

The door to the condo was also ajar. I wondered if Josh had done that to make it easier for help to enter. Brady's cries sounded muffled from where I stood. I stepped through the threshold into the foyer. I could see Josh through the living room standing in the dining room where he had served a meal designed to comfort me less than a week before. He looked over at me and then back toward the sliding glass doors I knew were on the far side of the condo leading out to the small balcony where he had told me he grew herbs in the summer.

His face was pale. His stance was tentative, as if he were poised to intervene. He gestured for me to come in. I walked through the living room and into the dining room where Kayla stood in front of the sliding glass door, which was opened about an inch. She held Brady against her body with her left arm as if he were a bag of potatoes. In the other hand, she held a pistol. I hadn't expected a gun. I stopped and said nothing.

'Well, if it isn't little Ashley Ann,' Kayla said. Her eyes, wild and widened, darted from me to Josh. For once, her perfectly smooth head of hair was matted. She was out of control. She was wearing purple scrubs.

'I didn't know until just days ago,' I said, looking at Brady. I wished Kayla would support his neck while she held him, then chided myself for thinking she would care when she was threatening to throw him over the balcony.

'Little Miss Innocent to the end,' Kayla snarled.

'Look, Kayla, we can work this out. I can handle it, just like I did with the hospital administration. Give the baby to Olivia.' Josh didn't seem to dare to move from where he was standing any more than I did. We looked at each other quickly. I sensed a silent agreement between us to try to use words first.

'Don't be ridiculous, Josh. You can't finagle me out of this. And why would I give this baby to her? She's taken everything I ever had or wanted from me. Now it's her turn to see what it was like to lose everything,' Kayla said. She pointed the gun at Josh for a second for emphasis, but not long enough for me to leap for it. The escalation in her voice made Brady howl.

'Shut up, you little mongrel.' Kayla's admonishment sounded like a loud jeer.

'What do I have that you want? You can have anything, just don't hurt Brady,' I said.

'What do I want? Plenty. Things you can never give back. How about my father, for one? You stole him from me, just like your slut mother stole his money. Even before he was killed, he was in jail. My mother took me to see him once a month, but he didn't have much to say to either of us. I don't suppose there was much he could say. "I chose a whore and our love child over my family." "Sorry you had to leave the nice family home and move into a dump in Dorchester." "Too bad you're being bullied at school, not because your father's a criminal, but because he's a turncoat." He never said he was sorry about any of it and you know why? Because he wasn't. He knew my mother had become a bitter alcoholic after what he did to her. He protected you and left me alone with the woman he destroyed. You can never change that and neither could your slut of a mother.'

Kayla was screaming, which had the odd effect of quieting Brady. I didn't know how to respond to her indictment of my mother and me. I didn't want to anger her, although I would have loved to let her know how lonely and void our banishment to Vermont had been. But I knew it was not the time for a contest about whose childhood was more miserable. I glimpsed at Josh who gave a tiny shake of his head in confirmation. I needed to engage Kayla in a dialogue that didn't enrage her more and would buy time. Ryan knew where I was. Surely, the police must be headed our way.

But I heard no sirens. I didn't see the flash of blue lights beyond the balcony. The police had to be en route. I needed to stall Kayla. I risked enraging her and asked a question.

'How did you know my identity when I didn't?' I asked. I knew Kayla considered herself brilliant and decided to play into it.

She smiled like a cat ready to pounce on a mouse.

'Your husband. Dear Daniel. He couldn't shut up when we began our residencies. He bragged about the house on Moss Hill, "his" house, he called it. But I knew better from your therapy sessions with me. He talked about his mother-in-law, whom he was determined to put in a home. He talked about her mysterious past and her flight from an abusive husband. Daniel was sure Claire was afraid her husband would come after her because she'd taken all of his money when she left. He said Claire could never have earned all of that money on her own.'

But she had. Between her salary and investment income, my mother had become a wealthy woman in her own right. It was clear most of the money she had gotten from my father remained in the safe deposit box. I clamped my teeth together. My task was not to defend my mother, but to save a baby's life. Brady seemed to be dozing at the moment. I hoped he wasn't traumatized and unconscious. I had no choice but to ask another question to buy time.

'But how did you connect Daniel's comments with your father?'

'I began to wonder. The timing seemed right. Your age and your mother's, the time you had arrived in Vermont coincided with the time your mother split. I knew everything about my father's downfall. I kept an album filled with newspaper stories. There had been mention of his mistress leaving Boston with her child. I just needed confirmation. Daniel had spared no details about what a mess you were. Claire had seen to that, he said. I teased him about marrying his case study and offered to help by seeing you for therapy. No cost, of course. Just professional courtesy.' Kayla laughed, pointing the gun at me for emphasis. I swallowed. I was terrified it would go off, the way she was jerking it around.

I felt my face flush with humiliation. I was mortified by Daniel's betrayal of me, the reduction of our relationship to a clinical study. But I felt more ashamed that I hadn't listened to the inner voice I had heard repeatedly, warning me about Daniel and Kayla and their conspiratorial treatment of me. At some level, I had known I was being used, diminished, and abused, but I didn't have the skills, stamina, or spirit to confront Daniel. Until I fired Kayla, I reminded myself. Until I told Daniel our marriage was over. I was strong now.

I peeked over at Josh. The pain on his face was visceral. I expected him to double over if Kayla revealed more of her chicanery, which she soon did. She couldn't seem to stop.

'You weren't exactly forthcoming in therapy, but I did manage to get enough biographical details out of you to support my contention you were little Ashley Ann reincarnated. Your mother was a much better source of information,' Kayla said, shifting Brady higher against her chest, making him whimper, which I knew from experience was the prelude to a full-blown wail. I was grateful that he remained quiet.

'My mother? I don't understand.'

'I knew none of this,' Josh said, breaking the silence I knew he should keep. We didn't need this getting any more complicated than it already was. I was struck by how quiet the night seemed, save for the drama ensuing in front of me. No cops. Not even any partygoers. This was Brookline, for God's sake, where no one eats until nine or goes home until the wee hours.

'Of course you didn't, Josh. Your middle name should be Clueless. You never bothered to ask the right questions, you were so busy playing super-husband.' Ouch, I cringed hearing her berate Josh.

'My mother?' I repeated.

'More than a little liquor, some liquid Xanax, all poured into a Dunkin' Donuts frozen drink and she would get so chatty during our night-time talks,' Kayla said, smirking at the memory. 'All I had to say was, "Tell me a little about Mickey Burke," and she would babble enough to share the racy parts, but I could never get her to tell me about the money.'

I was outraged. Terry and my mother had been right. The third shift at Thompson House had been corrupt. I snapped.

'How despicable,' I said.

'Well, how else was I going to be sure I had found Sheila Fairclough and could make it right? That house on Moss Hill was going to be mine. The money Sheila stole from my mother and me and whatever it had earned? Mine. And, while I was at it, that cute little brainy husband of yours who could be a little dense about relationships? Mine. Too bad it all got derailed by that nosy nurse.'

Brady had started crying again. Kayla looked at him in exasperation. 'Anybody got something I can stuff in this kid's mouth?'

Josh and I looked at each other.

'He's just a baby, Kayla. If you don't want to give him to Olivia, hand him to me,' Josh said. I was afraid he might begin to howl. I decided to distract Kayla. Brady had difficulty breathing as it was. When he cried he got congested and would often need to be suctioned by the nurses at the hospital.

'Tell me about Terry Walsh,' I said.

'She should have stayed out of it. What went on during the third shift was none of her business. Good thing you got me this so I'd be safe leaving the hospital in the middle of the night,' Kayla said, pointing the gun at Josh, who had tears streaming down his cheeks. I could see he was at breaking point and wasn't surprised he lunged toward the gun, extending his hand to grab it.

She shot him.

FORTY-EIGHT

J osh fell to the floor behind the table with a thud following the blast from the gun. The smell from the gunpowder made me gag. Brady was now howling. Kayla looked at the gun and then at me.

'Don't move,' she said. I didn't. I could see we were at the point of no return.

'Kayla, give me the baby. I'll give you money, all that I have. I'll send it to you wherever you want. You can have Daniel,' I said. There was panic in my voice I could no longer disguise. I wondered if Josh was dead.

'That won't work and you know it. Daniel's made his choice. I'm making mine. I can't get back the things you stole from me, but I can make you watch me take down the one thing I know you want more than anything in this world. This kid and I are going down together.'

Kayla turned, pushing the sliding glass door open with the gun wide enough for her to fit through. The balcony was about four feet deep. I rushed to the door, grabbing Kayla's right shoulder from behind, grasping Brady around his belly with my left hand. Kayla lifted her right foot to kick me from behind with the force of a horse's rear kick. I twisted away from her right shoulder, while clinging to Brady with my left hand. The sickening scent of pear fragrance filled my nostrils. I willed myself not to sneeze.

Kayla lifted her right leg up over the waist-high wrought-iron railing. I didn't know if a ten-story drop would kill her, but I was sure it would be lethal for Brady. I remembered a move I had learned in the self-defense class I took in college where you place your thumb and index finger behind the knee of your attacker and dig into the flesh with all your might. The back of Kayla's right knee was placed on the railing. I planted my fingers in position and jabbed with everything my heart, soul, and brain could muster. I heard her groan and felt Brady release into my left arm. I let go of Kayla with my right hand and grasped him close to my body as she began pulling her left leg up. I could see she still had the gun in her right hand. Just as I was about to kick at it, I heard a shot and felt my right thigh burn. Another shot rang out.

The gun flung from her hand. I heard shouts and saw movement from the neighbor's balcony next to us. I heard someone yell, 'Oh, no!'

I pulled back toward the sliders and into the dining room where I slammed into a cop wearing a Kevlar vest. He pulled Brady and me into the room and then went through the sliding door followed by three more cops. I ran past Josh, who was being attended to by another cop. I dashed toward the front door, wanting to get Brady out of that damn condo, when a female police officer told me to sit on the living-room couch.

'You're safe here. We've secured the building.'

I did as she said. I placed Brady over my shoulder and rubbed his back up and down, while he sobbed and drooled. But he was alive and breathing freely.

A stretcher pushed by a paramedic arrived through the front door. Another followed. The first went through to the dining room. The second stopped in front of the coffee table beyond the couch where I was holding Brady.

'Can you hobble over here or do you need some help?' the paramedic asked.

'Me? I don't need a stretcher,' I said.

'Ma'am, you're bleeding,' she said, pointing to a watery red stain on my right pant leg.

'Oh,' I said, realizing that the first bullet must have grazed me.

'Here, let me take the baby. We'll take good care of him,' she said.

'Not on your life. I'm never letting this baby go, ever again,' I said, hobbling over to the stretcher with Brady in my arms.

FORTY-NINE

B ut I had to let him go. He belonged back at Children's Hospital where he had begun to thrive. I spent the night at the Brigham, where my mother had died and where Josh was undergoing surgery for a gunshot to his chest.

I had been admitted and given medication that had made me very sleepy. I remembered hearing voices around me. Ryan and maybe Erin. I may have been dreaming.

I woke before sunrise, restless and filled with questions about what had happened. A doctor visited me to answer my medical questions. I had a flesh wound on my right leg from the bullet brushing my skin and muscle. I would need a course of antibiotics and anti-inflammatory medication, but after some rest I would be fine. She advised me to get some counseling for PTSD and offered to give me a list of local psychiatrists, which I declined.

Instead, I left a message for Dr Evans, telling him I planned to make my standing appointment for Tuesday.

It was still dark. I was hungry. I missed Brady. A nurse told me the *Boston Globe* hadn't arrived yet when I asked, thinking I would find answers in the newspaper. I had so many questions I need to have answered. I hoped Ryan would be the one to provide them.

He was, but he arrived in my room accompanied by Lou Costa, laughing together like old buddies. They both looked exhausted but exhilarated by the night's excitement.

'You look pretty good for a hero,' Ryan said.

'That baby wouldn't be here if it weren't for you,' Costa added.

'Aw, shucks,' I said on cue. 'Now tell me everything.'

'Kayla is dead. She died from injuries after falling or jumping over the balcony. I managed to shoot the gun out from her hand, but I couldn't get to her before she went over,' Ryan said, pulling up chairs for him and Costa.

The half-sister I had desperately hoped to forge a relationship with was gone and so was any opportunity I had to salvage my family. Even though she had nearly killed Brady, I couldn't shake the feeling that I might have succumbed to bitterness and desperation had I been in her circumstances. I understood how the absence of family could affect who you become.

'Josh?' I asked, needing to move on.

'We're not sure. He has internal injuries to his chest cavity and was still in surgery the last I heard. From what we can tell, he had no involvement in Kayla's plan. Although by covering for her, he enabled her plot to some extent,' Ryan said.

'He's a nice guy. Just another of her victims,' I said.

'That's why I'm here, Olivia. To fill you in on Kayla's victims,' Costa said, pulling her chair closer to the bed.

'She killed my mother, didn't she?' I asked. I already knew the answer, but had to hear it officially.

'She did, and Terry Walsh. The same gun she shot you and Josh with was used to kill Terry. Kayla lured Terry to the Arnold Arboretum with a message about her son and shot her in the back of the head. It happened after Terry left Thompson House the night she went to check and see what was going on during the night shift. Denise, the night nurse who it appears was drunk during most of her shift, gave Terry a message to go to the parking lot in the Arboretum. Apparently, Kayla had been visiting your mother at Thompson House, telling her she was an Alzheimer's researcher. Denise had been the beneficiary of some "drug therapy" by Kayla and kept quiet. She slept most of the third shift, according to Caleb, the aide who has cooperated and given us as much information as he knows.'

'I will never forgive myself for getting Terry involved,' I said.

'The way I understand it happened was that you asked Terry if she thought your mother was capable of committing suicide. She volunteered to poke around, Olivia. Terry sounds like the kind of woman who did what she thought was right,' Ryan said.

'We interviewed Daniel, Olivia. It's clear he shared his car, keys, and information about you with Kayla. She's the one who's been stalking you. Daniel didn't hesitate to share that Kayla had been disciplined for leaving work while on duty. She also had access to your house after Daniel gave her the alarm code when he asked her to pick up something he'd forgotten to bring to McLean.'

'Was she trying to kill me, too?' I asked, but I already knew the answer.

'We think originally she wanted you to have an "accident." But my sense is she was frustrated and her plans had escalated. I think she would have liked to see you have a breakdown and then stage your suicide, like she did your mother's,' Costa said.

'She didn't know about the FBI and WITSEC as far as we can tell. She was just obsessed with you and what you'd taken from her. We could hear what she was saying through the wall of the condo next door where we placed a listening device,' Ryan said.

'It's just so sad. All I ever wanted was to have a normal family,' I said.

'There's no such thing. That reminds me. Your house is cleared,' Costa said.

'You mean there are no cops there?' I asked.

'No, I mean there is no Daniel there,' Costa said, chuckling, looking over at Ryan who was laughing.

'You need some sleep, kid,' Ryan said.

'So do we,' Costa added. I didn't particularly like the way 'we' sounded so close to the word 'sleep.'

They put their chairs back up against the wall and started for the door.

'Wait. What about Brady? When can I see him? Is he still under protective custody?' I asked.

'All set, Olivia. You can see Brady whenever you'd like. We found Zack's body last night right before I called you. They got him. No one will be after Brady now.'

FIFTY

Sunday afternoon, December 29th

I was considering celebrating my birthday on September 30th in the future, but since I'd already missed it this year, I threw myself a thirtieth birthday party on December 29th.

I decided I would continue using the name Olivia Rose Taylor. I wasn't really a Fairclough and not quite a Burke either. The aunts whom I had connected with urged me to become Olivia Rose Curran, my mother's maiden name, but I had earned the name Olivia Rose Taylor and wasn't keen on giving it up. I just wished my mother had trusted me enough with the story behind it.

I'd invited people who knew my story to celebrate with me in the dining room I had long hoped to fill on Moss Hill. Ryan, Erin, and Andrew had helped with the plans. We were also celebrating that all four of us had miraculously passed the MPRE earlier in the month.

Paulie Fairclough hadn't been able to make it, but sent me flowers. I've been visiting him every week at the VA after I go skating.

John Miller had driven down from Vermont. Howie and Joey Walsh came. I invited ten more of my Portia classmates for the party. Josh was still in rehab but promised I could cook him a comfort meal as soon as he was discharged.

Noticeably absent was Daniel, who had agreed to an annulment and to waive any interest in my property after I hired the top domestic relations lawyer in Boston, but not until he tried several times to reconcile. I knew he would relocate somewhere far away from me as soon as his residency was done. He had a propensity for burning bridges.

We had pizza and beer and wine. We laughed and rejoiced that my next birthday party was only nine months away.

I made plans to visit John so I could empty the contents from the safe deposit box. I planned to pay off the balance of Terry's mortgage so Howie could use the Social Security income he and Joey received for living expenses.

I intended to make an anonymous donation to Trish Burke, motivated more by guilt than generosity. I hadn't yet figured out how to do it. Maybe I'd check that index card my mother had left instructions on. The rest of the money, I planned on using to support Brady. I'd already hired Karen Blake, the best adoption lawyer in Boston, to help me adopt Brady now that it had been determined there was no next of kin available or interested in raising him. There was a good chance I might have a job with Karen's firm as an advocate for domestic abuse victims after graduation.

Ryan hung around to help me clean up after everyone had left the party. He'd been attentive and supportive ever since I'd been shot, but a little distant. I figured he and Costa were giving it another go, but didn't ask.

'Do you still have feelings for Daniel?' he surprised me by asking as he put the empty beer bottles into their cardboard containers.

I looked up from the dishwasher, which I had been loading.

'The Daniel I married doesn't exist, Ryan. I can't feel anything for him. Why do you ask?'

'I don't know. I just wondered if maybe when you're ready, not that I'm rushing you, but that you might like to, well you know, go out,' Ryan said, still gazing intently at the pile of empty bottles and cans.

'Like on a date? Aren't you and Costa trying again?' I asked.

'Shoot me, Olivia. No, never again,' he said, looking up and laughing.

'Well then, sure. Maybe we could go skating again. I've never skated at Frog Pond,' I said.

'Boston Common, here we come,' Ryan said, grinning.

I heard the doorbell and found a FEDEX guy standing there.

'FEDEX on Sunday?' I asked, taking the envelope from him.

'Date-sensitive delivery, Miss. It costs people an arm and leg, but we do it. Have a nice evening.' He was gone as quickly as he had arrived.

I walked in to find Ryan sitting at the kitchen island where Daniel had once reigned over me. He was sipping a Sam Adams, the empties all piled next to the door, ready for the recycle bin.

'What's that?' he asked, as I tore open the envelope that had the return address of the legal firm my mother had used for years.

'It's from my mother. I know it's from my mother,' I said, walking into the conservatory, sitting next to the wicker chair she so loved. The large jade plant that had accompanied my mother and me the day we left Boston sat next to its new tiny companion on the table before me. I reached into the envelope, certain I was reaching back into time.

A cover letter from Attorney Mark Lescoe explained that one of my mother's wishes had been for me to receive this letter on my thirtieth birthday. 'In accordance with your mother's instructions, please find enclosed . . .' I couldn't breathe.

In the same beautiful penmanship I had admired, I found an elegant envelope addressed to me. I ripped it open.

Dear Olivia,

By now you either know this story because I have told it to you on your thirtieth birthday, or you are reading it because I am no longer with you. In either event, I promised myself that you would learn the truth when you turned thirty and I was certain you were finally safe.

I hope you will believe that your father and I never intended to hurt you, or really anyone. We were young and convinced things would work themselves out. Your father adored you, Olivia, although he knew you as Ashley.

The letter went on to tell me what I had already learned, but with such tenderness, I could hear my mother's voice.

By the time we realized the danger you and I were in from the people your father was involved with, it was too late. There was nothing for us to do but flee. Your father chose to sacrifice everything so we would have that option.

I read to the end, longing for my mother to be here, telling me what happened, but grateful she had known I needed to hear the truth. She finished with some final motherly advice.

I am sorry for the frustration and agony you have suffered by not knowing your original identity and who your family is. But even now that you do know, nothing has really changed. You are still my Olivia Rose. My strong, smart, sensitive, and sometimes funny daughter. You have grown into a beautiful woman. Don't let looking back blind you from all that you are and all that you have. Don't let my past deprive you of your future.

Live well and love well. As much as I worshiped your father, I'd be less than honest if I didn't share that it was John who taught me the kindness and tenderness a loving relationship brings. Settle for nothing less, Liv.

Ryan stood in the door to the conservatory, close enough to watch me, but giving me the space I needed.

I gestured for him to come sit next to me in the wicker chair my mother normally sat in. The one Daniel would never sit in. Ryan joined me without hesitation. I reached for his hand.

I told him about the large jade plant, which had to be as old as me, and all it had survived since my mother absconded with it and fled to Vermont. The younger jade next to it was all that I would ever have from my half-sister. I read Ryan the letter from my mother.

I looked up at Ryan. 'This is my legacy. Two jade plants and a letter. I spent all that time chasing my family history to find my identity. It turns out I already knew who I was.'

9 781448 311736